PRAISE FOR
THE SEAN McPHERSO

T0013720

PRAISE FOR *IMPERVIOUS*

BOOK THREE

"A propulsive plot with engaging characters . . . "
—*Kirkus Reviews*

"Readers beware—the immediacy of the violent act just as Mick and Emma's wedding ends is jolting—but signals the dangers ahead. The contrast of the cozy writer's retreat with it's mouth-watering meals to comfort all who abide there with the reality of a revenge plot against Mick and others yet to be thwarted kept me glued to the book. Now that the characters are as familiar as family to me, the stakes are high; can't wait to see what's in the next book!"
—**Maren Cooper**, author of *Finding Grace*

"Don't miss this engaging story filled with an intricate plot, realistic characters, and mesmerizing suspense!"
—**Debbie Herbert**, *USA Today* bestselling author

"Buchanan is an up-and-coming star of crime/thriller series. And book three is the best yet. As I read the ongoing adventures of Sean McPherson and his family, friends, and foes, I think to myself this really would be excellent for a television series. Wouldn't be surprised if it's not on Netflix's radar!"
—**Sherry Briscoe**, author of *The Man in Number 7*

"Buchanan has a fresh, very different and fast-paced style. And somehow makes a chef's meal integral to the thrilling suspense. I go from salivating to shocked, chapter by chapter."
—**Christine Desmet**, novelist and screenwriter

"Another winner from Laurie Buchanan. The focus of this story is less on the guest authors who are staying at Pines & Quill than it was in the first two books. It's more on the bad guys working for Gambino, including current police officers who are doing his bidding and trying to permanently silence Mick, Emma, and anyone else who gets in Gambino's way. Buchanan uses lush prose to describe the setting, the food, and the relationships. She takes us deep into the thoughts of all the major characters by frequently switching POVs. Consequently, you know who the bad guys are and what they are trying to do, but you're still riveted to the plot and committed to discovering what happens because Buchanan keeps you turning pages until the end."
—CHRIS NORBURY, author of the Matt Lanier
mystery-thriller series

"At Pines & Quill, the deadliest writers retreat in the Northwest, Buchanan delivers one knockout punch after another, leaving the reader reeling."
—SHEILA LOWE, author of the Beyond the Veil
paranormal suspense series

"*Impervious* is my favorite of the three-book series so far. I love the combination of a type of 'cozy' mystery with the incredible writer's retreat—Pines & Quill; the romance between different couples, all who live individually with some damage, physical or emotional; and the goofy large and lovable dog. But that's the background to not-cozy murders and evil underpinnings that threaten the safety of the characters, and the sanctity of love and living. Death enters, and it's not pretty. Readers are glued to each page that offers suspense interwoven with cozy; page-turning action; and thrills and chills and of course, lots of 'hooks.' I'm hooked on Buchanan's Sean McPherson novels!"
—PAMELA WIGHT, author of *The Right Wrong Man*

"*Impervious* delivers. From the first tragic explosion during a wedding to the last flying bullets in the woods, I was riveted to book three in the Sean McPherson series. Hitchcockian suspense and tension reign in this page turner. I found myself worrying about 'the good guys' throughout the story, given the author's ability to create likable, strong, yet vulnerable characters. The successful overlay of terror and joy jerked me around to provide a heart-pounding, satisfying read."
— SHERRILL JOSEPH, author of The Botanic Hill
Detectives Mysteries

"Who doesn't love to hate a black-hearted villain? *Impervious*, the third in the Sean McPherson series, makes you live every pulse-racing moment, as you follow the ruthless killer, praying there will be no more victims. Buchanan's writing tantalizes all your emotions: there are sweet moments to savor and descriptions for all the senses. But, lurking in the shadows, the dark mind of a devious killer drives the plot, threatening every character you've come to call your friend."
— JOY RIBAR, author of the Deep Lakes
Cozy Mystery series

"Gambino believes he and his minions are 'Impervious' to the good guys, but author Laurie Buchanan persuades her readers to think otherwise. Witness the unfolding of more mystery, murder, and mayhem in a New Orleans bayou setting along with the familiar, and beloved, Pines and Quill Writers' Retreat, nestled in the Pacific Northwest. Happily, amidst a high body count and blood-curdling suspense, the author gives a hopeful hint: the promise of a Blessed Event in her fourth book, *Iniquity*."
— MARIAN BEAMAN, author of
My Checkered Life

"Definitely the high-octane offering of the Sean McPherson series! Readers will hold their breath until the last page, hoping that the hero makes it. For fans of suspense and action, this is the perfect tale!"

—InD'tale Magazine

PRAISE FOR *ICONOCLAST*

BOOK TWO

"An involving thriller with compelling characters. This propulsive novel ably expands Buchanan's entertaining series, which is built primarily on engaging characterization."

—*Kirkus Reviews*

"Buchanan shows a sure hand as an action writer. . . . A smooth, ultra-professional read."

—*Booklist*

"An absolute page-turner . . . Not the one to be missed. With its atmospheric setting, page-turning suspense, and luminous insights into trauma, resilience, recovery, and friendship, this thriller will hook readers and keep them hooked."

—*The Prairies Book Review*

"I devoured every page of *Iconoclast*, turning the pages viciously because I couldn't wait to find out what would happen next."

—*Online Book Club*

"Another deftly crafted and riveting crime novel by Laurie Buchanan, *Iconoclast* is a compulsive page turner of a read from beginning to end."

—*Midwest Book Review*

"Buchanan has knocked it out of the park with this one. The descriptions pull the reader right into the middle of the action. Plan to stay up late!"
—InD'tale Magazine

PRAISE FOR *INDELIBLE*

BOOK ONE

"Buchanan's narrative is well-paced, flying right along. . . . the author has delivered an exciting beginning to an intriguing series."
—*Kirkus Reviews*

"The author of this impressive novel has poured elements from radically different genres into the blender and set it on high spin . . . The last page promises further surprises in a sequel, which Buchanan better deliver soon."
—*Booklist*

"Hard to put down, this page-turner is worthy of praise!"
—InD'tale Magazine

INIQUITY

INIQUITY

A SEAN McPHERSON NOVEL
BOOK FOUR

LAURIE BUCHANAN

This book is dedicated to authors,
their creative muses, and the craft of writing.

Copyright © 2024 Laurie Buchanan

All rights reserved. No part of this publication may be reproduced, distributed, or transmitted in any form or by any means, including photocopying, recording, digital scanning, or other electronic or mechanical methods, without the prior written permission of the publisher, except in the case of brief quotations embodied in critical reviews and certain other noncommercial uses permitted by copyright law. For permission requests, please address SparkPress.

Published by SparkPress, a BookSparks imprint,
A division of SparkPoint Studio, LLC
Phoenix, Arizona, USA, 85007
www.gosparkpress.com

Published 2024
Printed in the United States of America
Print ISBN: 978-1-68463-238-1
E-ISBN: 978-1-68463-239-8
Library of Congress Control Number: 2023915495

Interior Design by Tabitha Lahr

All company and/or product names may be trade names, logos, trademarks, and/or registered trademarks and are the property of their respective owners.

This is a work of fiction. Names, characters, places, and incidents either are the product of the author's imagination or are used fictitiously. Any resemblance to actual persons, living or dead, is entirely coincidental.

NO AI TRAINING: Without in any way limiting the author's [and publisher's] exclusive rights under copyright, any use of this publication to "train" generative artificial intelligence (AI) technologies to generate text is expressly prohibited. The author reserves all rights to license uses of this work for generative AI training and development of machine learning language models.

Names and identifying characteristics have been changed to protect the privacy of certain individuals.

AUTHOR'S NOTE

And while historic Fairhaven Village and
Bellingham are actual locations in Washington state,
I've added fictitious touches to further the story.

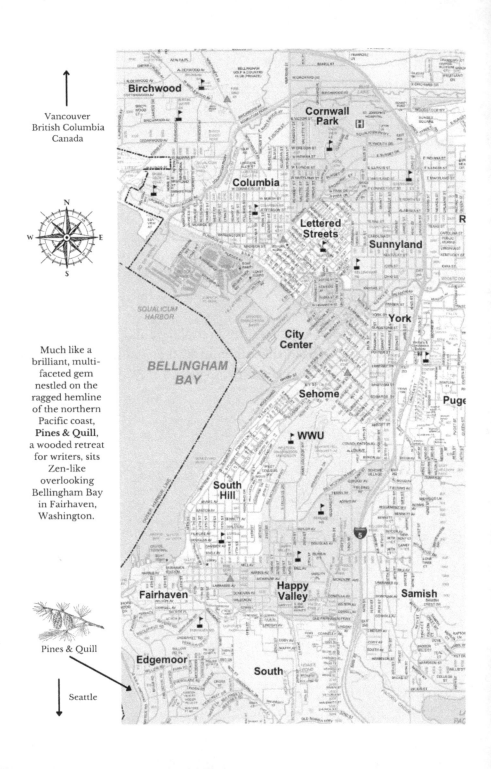

Vancouver
British Columbia
Canada

Much like a
brilliant, multi-
faceted gem
nestled on the
ragged hemline
of the northern
Pacific coast,
Pines & Quill,
a wooded retreat
for writers, sits
Zen-like
overlooking
Bellingham Bay
in Fairhaven,
Washington.

Pines & Quill

Seattle

Bluff, Cliffs, &
Bellingham Bay

Dickens Cottage

Bellingham &
Fairhaven Historic District

Garage & Workshop

Back View of Main House
& Mudroom Door

Austen Cottage

Entrance Gate

PINES & QUILL

Niall's Garden

Brontë Cottage

Tai Chi Pavilion
& Event Center

McPherson Cabin

Bellingham Bay
National Park & Reserve

Thoreau Cottage

N
W   E
S

"Three may keep a secret, if two of them are dead."

—BENJAMIN FRANKLIN

PROLOGUE

"Start with a question. Then try to answer it."
—Mary Lee Settle

Gambino draws a blade across the tip of his left index finger, then presses his thumb into the flesh below the cut. A line of blood beads across his mutilated pad. *I still don't feel any pain.*

He lost most of the feeling in the tips of his fingers decades ago when he tried burning his prints off with cigarettes. When that didn't work, he used hydrochloric acid. *It hurt like a son-of-a-bitch, and I couldn't use my hands for days.* And though it was somewhat successful, the ridges of his prints are still faintly visible.

I'm too smart ever to have been caught, and I've never done time, so my fingerprints aren't on file. But one can never be too careful. That's why I have an army of people in Seattle, New Orleans, and San Francisco who do my bidding for me— most of whom are expendable.

In the privacy of his Seattle penthouse, Gambino wipes blood from the blade, staining what had been a pristine white handkerchief. He folds the knife into its handle and turns off the table-side lamp. In the darkness of the elegant room, he sucks the blood from his wounded finger. The metallic taste doesn't faze him as he relishes the surrounding luxury that satisfies his every whim.

Though off tonight, built-in lights usually add focal accents to the predominantly neutral interior. Each area has its own artwork or an entire array of sculptures. Gambino enjoys the most extensive private collection of Richard Stainthorp's wire sculptures—naturally, he makes his acquisitions under an assumed name. Stainthorp's a UK-based artist whose specialty is sculpting humans so lifelike they look like they may come alive at any second. As Stainthorp's representative told Gambino, "Wire is a perfect medium for re-creating the look of the human body. Its many strands can be used to mimic its muscles and curves, and the finished result is beautiful." Gambino's most treasured Stainthorp piece is a man in free fall—*He looks to have just been pushed from atop a high-rise building.*

Even more so than his wire sculpture collection, Gambino's favorite focal point is the backlit three-hundred-gallon aquarium with red-bellied piranha swimming back and forth looking for prey. *They've proven effective in eliminating evidence of people who've crossed me.* When fully grown, red-bellied piranha get a reddish tinge on their belly. Each piranha can weigh up to eight-and-a-half pounds and reach twenty inches in length.

Gambino lifts the aquarium lid with his left hand and swiftly skims his right index finger across the water's surface, leaving a trail of blood. He quickly pulls his hand out and shuts the lid as the piranha frenzy. He feels a stirring in his groin. *Their bloodthirsty passion never fails to excite me.*

With four en suite bedrooms in addition to the master bedroom with its massive skylight above the bed, his residence also boasts an indoor swimming pool clad in sparkling blue Italian mosaic tiles. Another distinct feature of Gambino's penthouse is the dizzying, suspended Lucite staircase. And there is, of course, a terrace with a teakwood seating area overlooking Seattle.

But tonight, he's settled back in his leather chair in the living room with the piranha nearby. He shifts his gaze out the floor-to-ceiling penthouse windows—one of the many perks of being "King of the Hill." *Aah, the city—close to it, but above it all.* His glass-enclosed top floor boasts a three-hundred-and-sixty-degree panoramic view of Seattle: Downtown and Mount Rainier to the south. Puget Sound and the Olympic Mountains to the west. Mount Baker and Lake Union to the north. And Bellevue and the Cascade Mountains to the east.

During the day, a flood of natural light, horizons of mountains, and water are there for his viewing pleasure. In the evening, he views the city dressed in lights. The Space Needle, one of the most recognizable landmarks in the world, presents an imposing figure at any time of day. Up-lit against an evening backdrop, it's awe-inspiring. *It makes me think of a flying saucer.*

Built for the 1962 World's Fair—the Century 21 Exposition's theme was "The Age of Space"—the Space Needle's futuristic design was inspired by the idea that the fair needed a structure to symbolize humanity's space-age aspirations.

Anger stirs in Gambino's chest. For him, it serves as a motivator. He clenches his fists and lets it build into rage. *And though the triumvirate of Mick, Rafferty, and Bingham didn't kill Toni Bianco, I hold the three of them responsible for me having my daughter killed. I couldn't take the chance that she would turn state's evidence against me. Her death—that sin—is on their heads, not mine. She was a rising star, one of the most lethal people in the ranks who work for me. And she didn't even know she was my kid. Toni didn't need grooming; it came to her naturally.* He rubs the cut on his finger. *It must be in the blood.*

It's taken me two months to devise a plan to bring McPherson, Rafferty, and Bingham to their knees, one that will pit them against each other, that will make them wish they were dead. Gambino presses his thumb under the cut on his left index finger, causing it to bleed again. He walks over to his favorite Stainthorp piece—the man in free fall—flips on the spotlight, and wipes his finger on the sculpture, smearing it with blood.

What's that saying? "God visits the iniquity of the fathers upon their children." He presses his cut finger against his pursed lips. *Well, what's good enough for God is good enough for me. So be it.*

CHAPTER 1

"Write about the emotions you fear the most."
—LAURIE HALSE ANDERSON

The master bedroom in Mick's and Emma's cabin on the southeast corner of the Pines & Quill property line is quiet except for the soft snores coming from Hemingway, their Irish wolfhound, asleep on the floor at the foot of their bed.

Mick's head rests on his pillow. The digital clock on the nightstand displays 6:27 a.m. From this angle, Mick has an unobstructed view through the window. The first light of morning—a wintry orange hue dapples the sky—appears high and far in the distance above Bellingham Bay—a beautiful way to usher in September.

He turns his head and studies the face of his sleeping wife. He loves the impudent freckles that march across the bridge of Emma's nose. *I would do anything to protect her and our unborn child. Gambino hasn't shown his hand in weeks, and that worries me. At least when he's active, I've got an idea of where he's at. It's not knowing that scares me.*

Slow and sure, Mick makes his way down the soft pistachio-green sheets in his and Emma's large bed. When his head is level with Emma's waist, he buries his face in the folds of her pajamas and inhales. *Fresh and citrusy like lime, with a hint of vanilla. But there's another scent.* He inhales again. *Maybe ginger. Whatever the combination, it's wreaking havoc with my senses, making me heady.*

He lifts the hem of her pajama top and speaks to her belly button. "Good morning, Baby McPherson. It's September. The first day of my favorite month, and you're barely a tiny bump in your mommy's tummy. You're almost eleven weeks, and according to the baby books that your mommy and I are devouring, you're about two inches long. So, we've got twenty-nine weeks to wait until we meet you face-to-face. That puts your due date at March twenty-sixth. I'm so excited. I can't stand it!"

Emma laughs and pats her tummy. "I am too. We don't know yet if you're a boy or girl, but we're working on names either way. We won't find out at my doctor's appointment this week, but Dr. Freeman said she'll most likely do an ultrasound at our eighteen-week appointment. Then we can find out your gender if we want."

Mick's heart clenches when an all-consuming fear washes over him—fear of what he's capable of doing as a husband, as a parent. *I know beyond a shadow of a doubt that I will kill anyone who tries to hurt Emma or our child.* He presses his lips to the tender skin below Emma's navel and whispers. "I would do anything to protect you and your mother."

Emma ruffles Mick's hair. "And your daddy's desperate to find out if you're a boy or a girl."

"That's right," Mick says. "But the time will go by fast. August flew by with another wonderful group of writers in residence. Your cousin Ian and his bride Fiona got married here at Pines & Quill. And though you never met him, we had a beautiful memorial service for your Grandpa Connor, my dad." Mick stops for a moment to swallow the lump in his throat.

Reaching up, Mick runs his fingers through Emma's shoulder-length, auburn hair. "I'm so glad you got to meet my dad before he was killed. He'd be so excited about having a baby in the family. He and Mom only have one grandchild, Ian, and he's all grown up now."

Mick returns to his one-sided conversation with Baby McPherson. "Your Grandma Maeve—my mom—gave Ian and Fiona her home and land in San Francisco to set up a veterinary practice, and she moved to Bellingham to be closer to us." He blows a raspberry on Emma's belly. "Correction. Your grandma moved to Bellingham to be closer to *you*." He looks at Emma and laughs. "Your parents are nothing but chopped liver."

Not one to miss out on the fun, Hemingway shoves his muzzle into the fray at the sound of Mick's raspberry and their laughter. His wet nose grazes Mick's hand. "You big lummox." Hemingway's shaggy gray coat is rough and wiry. Because of the long fur over his eyes and under his chin, Connor, Mick's dad, used to say, "He looks like a wise old man."

The decided difference between Hemingway's tall and lanky one-hundred-and-fifty-pound frame and Emma's delicate-looking frame isn't lost on Mick. *But they're both fierce—they've each fought off Gambino's thugs.*

The Irish wolfhound's long wiry tail goes into propeller mode, and he licks Mick's and Emma's hands one last time before bounding into the bed.

"Oh, no, you don't," Mick says in mocking indignation. "Get your huge hairy self back onto the floor, Mister."

Much like a toddler, reluctance turns Hemingway's bones into gelatin. He slides off the bed like a liquid Slinky, pouring himself onto the floor into a puddle of dejection.

Mick reaches over and tousles the Irish wolfhound's head. "You're a good boy. You can have some bacon when we make breakfast."

Hemingway's tail thumps a merry beat on the hardwood floor at the promise of bacon.

"Hey, sis?" "Hey, sis?" "Hey, sis!" three deep voices call out, one after the other, from down the hallway. "You decent?" the final one adds.

No longer a puddle, Hemingway bolts through the doorway toward his friends, who often carry treats in their pockets.

At age thirty-five, Emma's the baby of the four siblings. She answers in the order they'd called out. "Yes, Ellery, Ethan, and Eric. We're decent."

Her three older brothers pop their heads around the doorway.

Eric, age forty-one, is the oldest. *With dark red hair and freckles, he looks the most like Emma, and they both talk with their hands. Maureen, my mother-in-law, told me, "If either of them had to sit on their hands, they wouldn't be able to speak." I've learned that Eric's creative and nurturing, with a strong sense of personal integrity and a drive to help others realize their potential. He also has a talent for helping others with their challenges, like rounding up the men in their family to help ours with the addition over the workshop.*

Ethan, age thirty-nine, falls in the middle. His skin is tan and smooth; his brown hair is close-cropped, and he has a strong jaw like their father. *Emma describes Ethan as the proverbial "class clown." She said, "I'm brokenhearted that after ten years of marriage and two children, his wife, Karen, divorced him." Karen told Emma, "He just won't grow up." But, he also has a big heart. So big, he'll give you the shirt off his back or the last dollar in his wallet. Unfortunately, giving money to his friends, even when they couldn't afford it, didn't help his marriage.*

Ellery, age thirty-seven, is the youngest. Carrot-topped and fair, his skin tends to burn, especially his prominent cheekbones. The depth in his green eyes can't hide the twinkle when he laughs. *And though he's the youngest of the three boys, a year younger than me, he seems wise beyond his years. And not just book smarts, though that too. He has a deep understanding, keen discernment, and a bottomless capacity for sound judgment. Fascinated by logical analysis, systems, and design, he has a knack for seeing possibilities for improvement. That's why his nickname is "The Fixer."*

"We've got to get on the road soon," Ellery says, proffering two steaming mugs of coffee. "We let ourselves in your back door and followed our noses to the brew."

Mick looks at Hemingway. "Some kind of watchdog you are."

Hemingway's tail thrashes back and forth.

"Thanks, guys," Mick says. "We set up the coffeemaker before we went to bed."

Beneath the covers, Mick places a protective hand on Emma's tummy. He feels Emma cup the back of his hand with a warm palm. *The last time all of Emma's brothers were here was for our wedding. After the ceremony, when we'd started dancing, our Jeep blew up, killing Kevin Pierce, one of the two young men we hired to bartend and valet for the event. The car bomb was meant for Emma and me.*

Ethan jockeys for a position between his two brothers. "We heard a rumor you're making us a send-off breakfast."

Eric brings up the rear and playfully cuffs his brothers' shoulders. "Knock it off, you two knuckleheads. But we *are* starving, Em." He winks at his sister. "Working on the addition over the garage and workshop takes a lot out of a guy."

"Yeah," the other two chime in. "We need to refuel."

Emma swings her legs over the side of the bed and accepts her mug. "All right, all ready."

"Coffee and juice all around?" Mick asks, welcoming his mug too.

"Yes, please. All around," Eric confirms.

After taking a sip, Mick raises his mug. "I never had brothers before, and now I've got you guys—'The Three Es.' There's no doubt about it. Emma's the best thing that's ever happened in my life."

———————

Apron-clad, Emma peers through the pass-through between the kitchen and dining areas—a recent remodel Mick did that allows them to be part of the gathering in the dining room while cooking in the kitchen.

"Are Mom and Dad joining us for breakfast?" she asks Ethan, who is sneaking tidbits to Hemingway under the large rectangular red oak dining table that Mick handcrafted. "You know I can see that, right? And even if I couldn't, the way he's whacking his tail against the chairs is a dead giveaway."

"Aw, come on. Let Hemingway think he's getting away with something. And to answer your question, no, Dad drove Mom in the motorhome to Maeve's place in town. Your mother-in-law invited her to stay there. I heard them clucking like excited hens. Apparently, while the addition wraps up, you gals are going to turn your guest room into a nursery. Then when that's done, you're going to paint and furnish the two Jack and Jill bedroom suites above the workshop."

"I'm looking forward to that," Emma says over her shoulder as she continues with the breakfast preparations.

Mick, Eric, and Ellery enter the dining area. The two brothers join Ethan at the table as Mick joins Emma in the kitchen.

"Why are they called Jack and Jill bedrooms?" Ellery calls out. "And what's that delicious smell?" He rubs the palms of his hands together. "Bacon or sausage?"

Spatula in hand, Emma pops her head through the pass-through. "Both. I've got three brothers, one husband, and a giant dog, and I want to make you all happy."

"There's a reason Mom and Dad let us keep you," Eric teases.

Pointedly, Emma ignores him. "'Jack and Jill' denotes two bedrooms joined by a bathroom with two side-by-side sinks at the counter and two lockable doors—one from each bedroom. As part of the construction crew, you know we've now got a total of four bedrooms over the garage and workshop. Two bedrooms on one side of the hall are joined by a Jack and Jill bathroom, a matching set on the other side of the hall, and a small kitchen and spacious gathering area overlooking the entrance lane and roundabout of the main house."

Eric raises his eyebrows in mock surprise. "Do you plan on having *that* many children?"

Emma turns and slides a mischievous glance to Mick. "Not that I'm aware of. Mr. McPherson?"

"Well, I wouldn't be averse to it," Mick says, grinning. "But let's start with one and see how that goes." He slips an arm around Emma's waist while deftly turning sizzling bacon with the other. *I love being part of two close knit families—the one I grew up with and the one I married into.*

"The real reason we added the area over the workshop," Mick continues, "is that in addition to the monthly writers in residence who each occupy a cottage, we host many events. It's convenient for family and friends who've traveled to be able to stay over. I'm hoping for a very interesting guest from Montana to join our Labor Day festivities."

"Oh, yeah," Eric says. "Who's that?"

Emma's heart starts racing. *I heard the change in Mick's tone to one of excitement. I know where this is going.*

"One of the September writers in residence is an award-winning crime fiction novelist. It's been said that her extensive knowledge of guns and police and medical examiners' procedures, which make her books alarmingly authentic, is drawn from her husband's real-life experience as a US Marshal. He's been invited to join our Labor Day picnic."

"I've heard of the US Marshals," Eric says, "but I don't really know what they do."

Oh, Eric, why did you have to encourage him? Mick has no fear. Utterly none. And I already saw the US Marshal page on his open laptop. I'm afraid he's researching it to apply.

In his excitement, Mick leans the upper half of his body into the pass-through as he warms to his topic.

"The United States Marshals Service is the oldest federal law enforcement agency in the United States. They provide security to the federal judiciary and manage the witness security program." He takes a sip of orange juice, then continues. "They manage and sell seized or forfeited assets of criminals, are responsible for the confinement and transportation of federal prisoners who've not been turned over to the Bureau of Prisons, and are the primary federal agency responsible for fugitive investigations."

"That's cool," Eric says.

I need to make them stop talking about this. Emma clears her throat. "Two things, gentlemen. First, breakfast is almost ready. And second, Mick, you were explaining why we added the area over the workshop."

"That's right," Mick says, backing out of the pass-through. "Here, Emma, let me help you with that." Then without skipping a beat, he picks up the explanation about the add-on over the workshop right where he left off. "In the main house, Libby and Niall only have one guest room, and ours is going to be a nursery." He pulls Emma into his arms and kisses the top of her head.

A shiver of delight races up her spine as she leans into his warmth.

"With four additional bedrooms, we can easily accommodate up to four couples. In just a few days, we'll hold our annual Labor Day picnic, and though it's still rather rustic, those who want to test-drive the addition and stay there camp-style this year can."

Emma snags a hot mitt from the counter. "Rafferty, Ivy, and Maggie said they're game. They're driving in from Seattle. And Joe, Marci, and the girls—Carly and Brianna—said they're up for it too. They plan to spend Friday and Saturday nights here and leave on Sunday morning after breakfast. Ivy has classes to teach in Seattle, and the girls have classes to attend in Bellingham."

As Emma and Mick start passing platters, the dining area fills with the enticing aroma of fresh-off-the-griddle pancakes, crisp bacon, smoked sausage, and a hint of warm maple syrup.

Hemingway scoots out from under the dining room table, licks his whiskers in anticipation, and raises his awning-sized eyebrows as if to say, *You promised I could have some bacon.*

"I've got some treats for you here," Mick says from the kitchen as he cuts sausage links and breaks bacon into Hemingway's oversized bowl in the kitchen. Then Mick opens the back kitchen door and sets the bowl on the patio. "Have at it, big fella."

Never needing a second invitation, Hemingway's through the doorway with his nose in the bowl as Mick closes the door and joins the others at the table.

Their heads lift in unison when someone knocks on the front door, followed by, "Good morning."

"Dad, we just started breakfast," Emma says. "Care to join us?"

"I'd love to," Phillip Benton says, pulling out a chair next to Ethan.

Mick gets another place setting from the kitchen. "Please help yourself, and there's fresh-squeezed orange juice in the pitcher. Can I get you some coffee?"

"That would be great. We've got a long drive ahead of us, and coffee wouldn't be amiss." He turns to Emma. "Your mom's in heaven at Maeve's new place in Bellingham. And let me tell you," he says, shaking his head, "those two women have *plans.*" He sets his silverware down and spreads his hands apart. "*Big* plans for decorating the baby's nursery and the addition over the workshop.

"I remember when your mom and I found out we were going to have a girl." He looks at each of his sons in turn and chuckles. "Let me tell you, it was a welcome relief."

"Gee, thanks, Dad," Eric says.

Phillip points his fork at his oldest son. "Don't deny it. You boys were excited too."

Ellery rubs his beard-stubbled jaw. "Well, I suppose she turned out okay."

"It took a while, but eventually . . ." Ethan adds.

Emma smiles at her brothers' good-humored teasing. "Well, then I'm glad I only spit once in each of your cups."

Mick, drinking his orange juice, nearly chokes with laughter.

Once again, there's a knock on the front door, followed by, "What's all the laughing about?"

Libby and Niall—Mick's sister and brother-in-law and owners of Pines & Quill—step into the dining area escorted by Hemingway.

"We would have invited you for breakfast," Emma says, "but you two never get to sleep in. Please join us."

"How did Hemingway come to be with you?" Mick asks. "Not five minutes ago, he was having a bacon and sausage-laced breakfast on the back patio."

Mick gets two more place settings from the kitchen as Libby and Niall take empty chairs at the dining table.

Niall gives Hemingway the side-eye. "He came to the main house complaining that he was *starving*." He turns to the Irish wolfhound. "Didn't you, Bacon Breath?" Niall rumples the wiry hair on the big dog's head. "So we thought we'd walk over to see what's going on."

"We're fueling up before we head back to San Diego," Phillip says. "We always love coming to Pines & Quill, but it's time to go home."

"Where's your beautiful wife, Maureen?" Libby asks.

"I just dropped her off at your mom's place in town. Those two women are plotting and scheming over the decoration of the nursery and the addition over the workshop once the local construction crew wraps up."

Libby rubs her hands together with excitement. "I want to help with the decorating too."

"I'm so glad you're my sister-in-law," Emma says. "The more, the merrier."

Libby turns to her brother, Mick. "I'll have the name-boards ready this afternoon before you head to the airport to pick up this month's writers in residence."

"I wish we were still going to be here to meet them," Phillip says. "You always have the most interesting guests."

Hidden from view, Emma places her hand lightly on her tummy. *We do, indeed. Sometimes they're even killers.*

"What are nameboards?" Ethan asks.

"They're signs I hold up in the arrival area. Each one has a person's first initial and last name. When they see me with the sign, they know I'm their ride to Pines & Quill."

Ethan nods. "I've seen people holding those signs. So that's what they're called."

Libby leans in like a conspirator and raises her eyebrows. "I can tell you a little bit about our new guests if you'd like."

"Do tell," Phillip says.

"Our first writer in residence is Sarah Porter, a well-known crime fiction writer. She's flying in from Billings, Montana. My understanding is she gets some of her material, then fictionalizes it, from her husband, Jake, who's a US Marshal."

"Mick started telling us about that," Ellery says.

Oh, not again.

"Did you know that the US Marshals lead the way in nationwide efforts to rescue and recover missing and exploited children and, by default, aid in the prevention of human trafficking?" Mick takes another sip of juice. "During the pandemic, the US Marshals Service was tasked with making sure no one messed with the world's most sought-after asset, the COVID-19 vaccine."

Phillip's eyes are wide with interest. "How on earth did they do that?"

Under the table, Emma clenches her hands into fists. *Dad!*

"The Deputy Marshals worked hand-in-hand with Operation Warp Speed personnel to provide security to the vaccines from the facilities where they were manufactured to the distribution sites," Mick says. "Deputies were stationed at several points in the distribution process to protect storage stockpiles, manufacturers, transports, and receiving facilities."

Phillip nods. "That's impressive."

"And that, in part," Libby says, "is why Sarah's crime fiction books are so popular. They scream of authenticity."

I've got to steer this conversation in a different direction. "Who else is coming?" Emma asks.

"Our next guest is Sakura Nishiwaka," Libby says. "She's flying in from San Francisco to complete a memoir about her grandmother who was a pearl diver in Japan."

"I remember seeing pearl divers when we went to Sea-World as kids," Ellery says.

"That's right," the other two brothers agree.

"But this writer's grandmother dove for pearls in the ocean—with sharks."

Phillip nods. "Now *that's* dangerous. And not even close to the controlled environment at SeaWorld," Phillip tells his sons.

Libby scoots her chair back a little bit. "You may have

heard about our wheelchair guest on the news. Todd Jones is flying in from Colorado Springs. He got stranded on Pike's Peak during a climb, and due to complications from frostbite, his legs had to be amputated. He's writing a book about his experience."

It wasn't that long ago when I was confined to a wheelchair with transverse myelitis. Emma shivers at the memory of one day being able to walk but paralyzed from the waist down the next. *I'm so grateful I can walk again.*

"I remember that story on the news," Mick says.

Libby nods. "That's right. He was one of the few survivors. The rest of the people in the expedition died."

Ethan shivers. "That had to have been a horrifying experience."

"I can't even begin to imagine," Libby says. "Our fourth and final guest is Dale Brewer. He's flying in from Houston. He just retired. He was a maritime pilot who captained cruise ships around the globe."

"You mean like Carnival, Royal Caribbean, and Holland America?"

Libby nods. "Yes, exactly like that."

"Can you imagine piloting a boat that size?" Phillip asks.

Libby shakes her head. "Not even close. When we spoke on the phone, Dale said the average cruise ship passenger capacity is about three thousand guests. And that one of the world's largest cruise ships, *The Symphony of the Seas*, has a capacity of nearly nine thousand passengers and crew."

Eric lets out a long low whistle. "That's a heck of a lot of people crammed together. I don't know if I could handle that."

"Give me the wide-open spaces of Pines & Quill any day." Emma places a hand on her stomach. "Just the thought of being on a rocking ship makes me queasy."

Mick starts to stand. "Honey, you do look a little green around the gills."

Emma looks at Mick wide-eyed as she gets up from her chair. "The books aren't always right, Mr. McPherson. They say that morning sickness typically lasts from week six through twelve, with the peak between eight and ten weeks. I'm at eleven, and—"

Emma claps a hand over her mouth and bolts from the room, certain she hears her father's "Oh, dear," following her down the hall.

In the privacy of their bathroom, Emma empties the contents of her stomach into the toilet bowl.

Through the bathroom door, Emma hears Mick's concerned voice. "Are you okay?"

"I feel better now. I just need a moment before I come back to the dining room." After resting a minute, she stands, rinses her mouth, and wipes her face before looking at herself in the mirror. She sees fear reflected in her eyes.

I heard the excitement in Mick's voice and saw the way his eyes lit up when he talked about the US Marshals. The man acts like he's bulletproof and barrels headlong into danger. And we're about to become parents. Just because we haven't heard from Gambino for a while doesn't mean we're off his radar. The last message he sent to Mick, Joe, and Rafferty was, "When you least expect it, expect it."

CHAPTER 2

"You have to get to a very quiet place inside yourself. And that doesn't mean that you can't have noise outside. I know some people who put jazz on, loudly, to write.
    I think each writer has her or his secret path to the muse."
              —MAYA ANGELOU

E mma's hands are slick with wet clay, so she can't smooth the raised hackles on Hemingway's back. "It's not polite to growl," she whispers as she, too, warily watches the man in work clothes ascend the interior stairs to the workshop's addition. "No worries, Hemingway. He's just bringing a tool he forgot in his truck." *I wonder how he got that jagged scar running from his temple to his jawline?* Emma shakes her head. *It's none of my business—and he's on Hank's crew, so he's been vetted. I'm worrying for nothing, right?*

    With the workshop's double doors open wide, natural light fills her workspace. Emma points a clay-covered finger to a sunny spot on the floor. "You can lie down now, Hemingway. We're okay."

Hemingway circles a sun-pooled spot on the concrete floor several times before lying down, stretching out all four of his long gray legs and then conforming himself into a tight crescent shape. An *oomph* escapes his whiskered mouth as his eyes close, and he settles in.

To release tension, Emma inhales deeply. As her chest expands, she lifts her chin and relishes the feel of the late-afternoon sun warming her face, bare arms, and the ankles of her legs splayed on either side of her potter's wheel. Emma inhales again. This time she appreciates the scent of pine shavings from the cradle that Mick's making for their baby. She turns her head and looks at his work area in their shared creative space— *A place for everything and everything in its place.*

In Emma's immediate area, there's a wad of excess clay, a small sponge, a wooden modeling tool, a wooden rib, a loop tool, a needle tool, a metal scraper, and a wire clay cutter, all arranged in a tidy manner. *As Mom said, "You and Mick were cut from the same bolt of cloth. You're both neat as pins."*

Emma wets her hands again in the bucket at her side and gets back to work. She hums along to an upbeat tune by Ed Sheeran playing through the speakers from the playlist she created for throwing clay. *He's one of my favorite singers, so I was thrilled when Mick chose the song "Perfect" for when I walked down the aisle.*

A shadow falls across her hands as they work the piece spinning on her wheel.

Hemingway thumps his tail against the concrete.

Emma looks up to see Mick standing there smiling.

With the devilish hike of an eyebrow, he taps the newspaper tucked under his arm. "I bet you can't guess what I have here."

Emma quirks an eyebrow back at him. "Well, Mr. McPherson, unless I'm terribly mistaken, it appears to be a newspaper."

Mick laughs. "You made the paper, Mrs. McPherson." He pulls the *Bellingham Herald* from beneath his arm. "But it's not just *any* newspaper. It's the one that has an article about *you* in it. I'd hand it to you to read for yourself, but," he shifts his gaze from her face and looks at her hands, "you're quite literally up to your wrists in wet clay."

"I was wondering if anything would come from that interview," Emma says. "Do you have time to read it to me before you head to the airport to pick up this month's writers in residence?"

Careful not to disturb Hemingway's beauty rest, Mick pulls a stool over and sits next to Emma but not before planting a kiss on her cheek. "I always have time for you." He opens the paper, shakes out the folds dramatically, and then clears his throat.

"'Emma McPherson is a potter who creates conceptual but functional ceramics and tableware. She is the recipient of the American Ceramic Society's 2023 award for *Heritage*, a collection of handcrafted stoneware with graphic elements made from old family correspondence and ephemera used in her decorative process. The ephemera is scanned and laser-cut in newsprint and then applied to the stoneware objects when they are still *leather-hard*—a term used to describe clay before it's completely dried out and before it is put in a kiln while it still has moisture in it.

"'McPherson uses underglazes to adhere the ephemera to the clay, which she says have some clay content in them so they attach to the clay—it acts as a glue to stick the paper to the clay. She says she likes the depth of surface that is created with the treatment. 'Some of the ephemera that I've scanned comes from old family recipes from the women in my family and in my husband's family, and also baby book entries, just sort of those quiet, domestic labors of women that often go unnoticed.'"

Mick stops reading and gazes at Emma. "It goes on to talk about your love of polychromy. Let me see here." He pauses to find the spot where he left off. "They describe polychromy as 'the art of painting in several colors, especially as applied to ancient pottery, sculpture, and architecture.' They say, and I quote, 'McPherson's use of vivid polychromy is what makes her sculptures so unique.'" Mick taps the paper for emphasis. "How about that?"

Emma laughs. "Well, let's not quit our day jobs just yet, Mr. McPherson." She looks down at her tummy. "We've got a college fund to start saving for."

"That we do. Speaking of which, one of my jobs is to get to the airport and pick up our guests. I'd invite you along, but you've got your hands full."

Emma lifts her clay-slicked hands as she tips her head back. "But I can still have a kiss."

Mick snakes a hand behind her neck and into her thick auburn hair. He presses his mouth against hers and gives her a long, slow, and deliberate kiss—one she won't forget anytime soon.

I love this man more than anyone on earth.

Their breaths mingle between them as they pull apart.

Mick winks at Emma. "A little something to remember me by."

"As if I could forget," she says, a little breathless.

Wanting some of the attention, Hemingway stands and nudges himself between them.

"I'm going to run upstairs really quick," Mick says, "and check on the construction crew to see the progress they've made."

"Hank said it's just a skeleton crew today," Emma says.

"It's amazing what a few people can accomplish when they put their minds to it." Mick turns to the big dog. "You want to come with me?"

Hemingway thrashes his tail back and forth—an obvious yes.

Her insides still aquiver, Emma watches Mick's denim-clad backside appreciatively as he and Hemingway bound up the interior stairs. *And the doctors thought Mick would never walk again after a sniper killed his partner and their squad car crashed head on into a bridge embankment.* Rehabilitation was a long haul, but Mick's physical injuries finally healed, and eventually, he learned to walk again. The part that hasn't healed is his emotions. He still suffers from survivor's guilt. *Mick told me, "Sam and I drew straws that Friday morning as we'd always done. It was our last day as police officers. On Monday, we were to start our new roles together as homicide detectives. But Friday, Sam got to be the driver and, unknowingly, the sniper's target. Sam was a husband and a father. I regret that I pulled the passenger straw."*

Emma shakes her head to clear the nightmare image. *And though Mick's limp is more evident when he's on stairs, nothing slows that man down. He can outrun the best of them, including two of my three brothers.*

Emma looks down at her belly. "You're going to love that daddy of yours. And you've already got every child's dream—Hemingway's practically the size of a pony."

Mick looks down at Hemingway when they reach the top of the stairs. A ridge of raised hackles runs the length of the big dog's spine. Mick learned a long time ago to trust Hemingway's instinct. "What is it, boy?" Mick reaches for the gun at the small of his back. *Nothing but air because I'm heading to the airport to pick up guests.*

With Hemingway at his side, Mick walks the length of the hallway, head swiveling into each open doorway, alert to danger. He sees Hank, the foreman, and three other guys in one of the recently framed and Sheetrocked bedrooms. He recognizes two of them: *Bill's an electrician, and Damian's a plumber. But I don't know the construction worker. He looks like a weightlifter—formidable, like he could demolish anything with just his bare hands.*

The four men are studying a blueprint spread out on a makeshift table with two sawhorses for legs.

Hemingway's eyes lock on the man Mick doesn't recognize. A growl comes from deep within his chest.

Mick's left leg is against Hemingway. He feels more than hears the rumble. He smooths the hair along the big dog's back. "It's okay, Hemingway. Go see Hank."

Hemingway walks over to the foreman and bumps his hip with his nose.

Hank turns. "Hey, Hemingway. Are you looking for a treat?"

"Always," Mick says. He walks over and shakes Hank's hand. "How's it going?"

"It's coming along. Because of your in-laws, we're ahead of schedule. Those four guys really know their stuff."

"That's great." Mick turns to each guy and extends his hand. "Bill. Damian." When he gets to the third man, he holds out his hand. "I don't think we've met. I'm Sean McPherson, but everyone calls me Mick."

The guy nods and takes Mick's hand in a tight grip. Any firmer, and it would have been aggressive. "My name's Giovanni Adolorata. It's a mouthful, so everyone just calls me Tank."

Mick notes the jagged temple-to-jawline scar on the left side of Tank's face. *He's about six foot four with his work boots on, has black eyes, bushy eyebrows, collar-length black hair, and an unshaven face. And I'll bet that nose has been broken more than once.*

Mick nods and releases his grip. "Are you new to the area?"

"I just relocated."

"This is a nice place to live. Where are you from?"

"Most recently from Prudhoe Bay, Alaska." He lifts his chin toward the northeast. "I worked on an oil rig."

"Well, welcome," Mick says, then they both turn their attention to the blueprints along with the rest of the men.

In his peripheral vision, Mick observes Tank watching him, assessing him. *It's not the man's size or his don't-fuck-with-me vibe that I don't like. There's something else.*

"Well, I'll leave you to it," Mick says, looking around the space. "It looks great." He pats his thigh. "Come on, Hemingway."

As he descends the stairs, Mick furrows his brows in thought. Then, Emma's profile comes into view. *She's pregnant. The last thing she and the baby need is worry.* He places a smile on his face and calls out, "It shouldn't be long before you, Mom, and Libby can have at it and decorate the addition to your hearts' content."

"I think it's going to be fun," Emma says.

Mick turns to Hemingway and scratches his bearded chin. "You stay with Emma." *I can't imagine Hank would hire anyone Emma needs protection from, but Hemingway would do anything to protect her.*

He shifts his gaze back to Emma. "I'm going to swing by the main house and get the nameboards from Libby, then head out to the airport." He bends and gives her another memorable kiss. "I'll see you when I get back."

Walking toward the main house, Mick studies the trucks parked in the roundabout driveway. *Hank's is the red Ford F-150, Bill drives the dark-blue Toyota Tundra, and Damian's is the white Chevy Silverado. That means the all-black Dodge Ram 1500 without a bit of chrome, including the rims, belongs to Tank.* Mick makes a mental note of the plate number. *Call Joe on the way to the airport and have him run the plates. I've got a bad feeling about this guy—a very bad feeling.*

———————

Libby sees her brother, Mick, walking up the lane toward the main house. A light breeze carries the scent of pine as it billows the sheets. Other than birdsong from the year-round resident black-capped chickadees and the distant sound of a nail gun over the workshop, the area is soundless.

She cups a hand over her eyebrows to block the sun. *Mick's hands are shoved in his front jean pockets, his shoulders are hunched up around his ears, and his brows are furrowed. His body language is screaming that he's upset about something.*

Libby pulls the remaining laundry from the clothesline next to her flower garden in the side yard—*I love the smell and feel of air-dried laundry*—and folds it over her arm, laying it in the wicker laundry basket. *I wonder what happened?*

"Hey, Mick," Libby calls out. "I'm just heading in. Are you here for the nameboards?"

"Yes. But I'd like to ask you a favor."

"Sure. What is it?"

"Emma's working on a piece in the shop. Hemingway's with her, but one of the guys on the construction crew triggered my gut." Mick shakes his head. "I can't explain it, I just don't feel good about him. I'm going to have Joe run his plate and see if anything pops. In the meantime, if you haven't got the cottages ready for the guests yet, will you ask Emma to help you?"

"I put the finishing touches on the cottages this morning. But your gut has a great track record, and I trust your instinct. I'll head over to the workshop and talk with Emma about decorating the baby's nursery. If she's close to finishing her project, I'll suggest we go to your cabin so we can take measurements and talk colors. She'll love that, and so will I."

"Thank you, that's great. Where's Niall?"

"He's in the kitchen dotting his i's and crossing his t's to make sure nothing goes awry with this evening's dinner,"

Libby says. "You know that the first meal for the writers in residence at Pines & Quill sets the tone for the next three weeks, and Niall's a perfectionist when it comes to all things cooking and wine pairing."

Mick transfers the laundry basket from his sister's hip to his own.

Libby smiles. "You're just like Dad. Always the gentleman."

Mick tips his head back and looks at the sky. "I think about him every day."

Libby touches her brother's forearm. "I miss him too."

"Last month, two of the guests had dietary restrictions," Mick says.

Libby knows her brother changed the subject back on purpose. *Talking about Dad—our loss—could turn into a crying fest for both of us. It's happened before.*

"If I remember right," Mick continues, "one is a vegan, and the other is gluten intolerant. But it didn't slow Niall down in the least, even with the limitations. Every meal and dessert that came out of his kitchen was still Michelin-star worthy."

"This month, September," Libby says, "not a single guest made a mark or notation in the dietary restriction portion of their residency application."

"Oh, good. Then maybe I can talk Niall into serving one of his best menus: steak with garlic mustard sauce, twice-baked potatoes drowned in butter, sour cream, chives, and Parmesan broccoli. And no one makes crème brûlée better than Niall. No one."

"I think I gained a pound just *listening* to you."

Mick laughs and nods toward the door. "After you," he says as they enter the main house through the mudroom.

A cross between a utility room and a large walk-in closet, the mudroom is separated from the spacious, open-plan kitchen and dining area by a Dutch door. Divided horizontally into two half doors, it allows either half to be left open or closed. The mudroom is where the MacCulloughs stow outerwear, boots, and anything else they might need when venturing outside, including items for Hemingway. It also houses his food and water bowls, leash, and bed.

Most people prefer not to have a curious, tail-wagging, pony-sized dog in their midst while eating, so the MacCulloughs close the bottom, leaving the top portion of the Dutch door open during meals. This allows Hemingway to pop his head over—with his awning eyebrows and mop-like beard—and still be part of the gatherings without being in their midst.

Entering the dining area, the delicious aroma of sage wafts in the air, teasing Libby's and Mick's nostrils.

"I better get those nameboards and leave while I still can," Mick says. "Otherwise, I'm going to go into the kitchen and eat everything in sight."

Niall steps around the corner, wiping his hands on a dish towel. "I thought I heard you two."

"You're killing me, Niall," Mick says. "My stomach's all jacked up on this delicious smell, and I can't do anything about it because I've got to go pick up the guests."

Niall laughs. "It's not ready yet anyway. But it'll be perfect shortly after you get back."

"You might as well put me out of my misery," Mick says. "What are we having?"

"The appetizer is figs with a blue cheese and balsamic reduction."

"*Ohhh*, man," Mick moans.

"The main course is pork tenderloin stuffed with butternut squash, goat cheese, and sage."

Libby snaps her head up. "Where on earth did you get butternut squash at this time of year?"

Niall smiles and wags a finger back and forth. "A chef never reveals his sources. But I can tell you this." He leans in conspiratorially. "The pan drippings from the tenderloin make an incredibly flavorful gravy. I'm serving it with brown butter risotto that'll soak up the gravy beautifully."

Libby raises her eyebrows. "And for the wine?"

"Pork tenderloin tends to be the most delicate, least 'porky' portion of the pig, so I want a wine that's not going to drown out the more subtle flavors of this cut of meat. That's why I'm going the red route and serving a juicy old vine Zin from our friend Byron Rivers at Zendeavor Cellars in Napa Valley."

"The guy you're writing a cookbook with, right?" Mick asks.

"That's right," Niall says. "*Zins of the Father: Guide to Zinfandel Wines & Food Pairings.*"

"You might as well just shoot me now and tell me what's for dessert," Mick says.

Niall rubs his palms back and forth. "One of your favorites—brown butter rum cannoli."

"You're killing me, man."

"Would you like one for the road?"

"You know it." Mick places an arm around his brother-in-law's shoulder. "Lead the way."

Libby's heart fills with worry as she watches two of her three favorite men—her husband and brother—step around the corner into Niall's sanctuary—the kitchen. *It used to be four: Dad, Mick, Niall, and Ian, our son. I almost can't bear that Dad's dead, murdered by one of Gambino's henchmen. I'm afraid that a cannoli's only a temporary reprieve for Mick's worry. There's no way Gambino's through with our family. There've been at least a dozen deaths since May, including Niall's brother, Paddy. And a couple of failed attempts on Mick's and Emma's lives. Gambino's not going to stop until one or both of them are dead—unless we can stop him first.*

CHAPTER 3

"The best way is always to stop when you are going good and when you know what will happen next. If you do that every day . . . you will never be stuck."
—ERNEST HEMINGWAY

Mick's hands grip the steering wheel as the Pines & Quill retreat van approaches an overpass on the route to Bellingham International Airport. It triggers a grim memory of the night a sniper killed his partner, Sam. Mick watched helplessly as Sam slumped forward in the driver's seat, the shoulder belt preventing his weight from hitting the steering wheel but not from gunning the accelerator. Their squad car surged onto the right shoulder, and Mick braced himself for the inevitable impact of metal against the concrete abutment.

He remembers the horrific crash, the smell of fuel, and red and blue flashing lights, but not being life-flighted to the hospital. They told him afterward that he almost died during transport. The surgery that saved his life is a total blank. It left him with a limp and survivor's guilt.

Mick shakes his head to clear the memory and refocuses on the deep, confident voice coming through the speakers on the dashboard. When it finishes relaying the information, Mick says goodbye and presses the button on the steering wheel, ending the call with one of his best friends, homicide detective Joe Bingham.

He confirmed that the plates on the black Dodge Ram parked in the roundabout at Pines & Quill belong to Giovanni Adolorata—Tank—one of the new guys on the construction crew working on the addition over the workshop. Joe also checked with the DMV and said that Tank's driver's license photo matches the description I gave him. Interestingly, he did two short stints in a New Orleans jail for being drunk and disorderly, so his prints are on file, but nothing pops with them. Shortly after cooling his heels behind bars the second time, Tank relocated to Prudhoe Bay, Alaska, where he worked on an oil rig prior to his recent relocation to Bellingham, Washington. He didn't do any jail time in Alaska.

Mick drums his fingers on the top of the steering wheel. *New Orleans is one of Gambino's three headquarters; it was the first, San Francisco second. And now he's set up shop in the greater Seattle area, including Bellingham. With Seattle to the south, the Canadian border a stone's throw to the north, and Bellingham Bay—a gateway to the Pacific Ocean—immediately to the west, Bellingham is the ideal location for the Gambino crime family to traffic drugs, weapons, and humans.*

I need to talk with Hank, the construction foreman, and determine how Tank came to be on the crew. If he's one of Gambino's men posing as a construction worker, he's there for one purpose only—to kill Emma and me.

Mick's hands tighten on the steering wheel. To relax, he gazes out the driver's window of the retreat's van. Even though the sun won't set for a few more hours, it's beginning to wane. Thin rose-colored clouds stretch through the sky, and shadows along the roadside lengthen in the westerly light. The sun is easing toward the Pacific Ocean, and the beginnings of a rose glow promise a spectacular sunset. *It would be nice to watch the sunset with Emma tonight.*

In the side mirror, Mick sees that the white panel van he'd noticed a while ago is still two cars back. The vehicles between them block its plates. At the very last moment, Mick takes the next exit ramp. The white panel van—no rear or side windows—continues in the direction it had been traveling. *This whole business with Gambino is making me paranoid.*

Mick stays on the unplanned route to the airport. After parking the van, he gathers the nameboards from the front passenger seat and heads toward arrivals. A female pedestrian is walking toward him in the crosswalk. As they're about to pass, a white panel van roars around the bend and makes a beeline straight for them.

Mick drops the signs, grabs the woman, and lurches out of the way as the van screams by, missing them by a hair's breadth.

Mick shakes his head to clear it. "Are you okay?" he asks the trembling woman as they both get to their feet.

"Oh, my gosh. Did that van just try to hit us?"

A crowd begins to gather. "I just called 911." "I witnessed what just happened." "Me too."

A man in the crowd picks up the nameboards and hands them to Mick. The same man juts his chin toward the woman Mick shoved out of the way. "I saw you drop these when you saved her."

Embarrassed at the word "saved," Mick busies himself, brushing down his jeans with his free hand. *What I did was almost get an innocent woman killed. That driver was after me. She would have been collateral damage.*

As realization dawns on the woman, she turns to Mick. "You *saved* my life. Thank—"

Airport security arrives—one male, one female—on the scene. "Okay, folks. Traffic's backing up," the man says. "Let's get out of the middle of the street."

Careful not to seem to take charge, Mick leads the security officers and the woman to a shaded area behind one of the portico's support poles covered in rough-hewn brick-sized stones. *A good size for cover and concealment.* After taking their statements, the security officers return inside the airport, the woman walks toward the parking area, and Mick heads into the baggage area. Mick's adrenaline spikes as he replays the near-miss in his mind. *It was the same white van that had been tailing me.* He runs a shaky hand through his hair. *Emma—pregnant Emma—would have been with me if she wasn't working on a project.* The thought nearly guts him.

Passing an arrival and departure board, he sees that he has ten minutes before Sarah Porter's flight is due to land, so he fishes his cell phone out of his back pocket, calls Joe, and explains what just happened.

"Did you get the plate number?" Joe asks.

"It's a Washington plate. Probably stolen." Mick rattles off the first two letters. "That's all I got before diving out of the way. And the windshield and front side windows were tinted, so I couldn't see any faces."

"A white panel van, Washington plates, and tinted windows. It's a start," Joe says. "And they can't have gotten far. I'll put out an APB within a hundred-mile radius of the airport. In the meantime, watch your back." He disconnects the call.

Mick's thoughts return to his surroundings. *Once a cop, always a cop*—his gaze sweeps the space. *Who among you is a killer?* He mentally notes people's hair color, facial expressions, body language, tattoos, jewelry, clothing, footwear, and baggage details. *And with gang activity steadily on the rise in Whatcom County, I always keep my eyes open for gang-specific clothing, tattoos, and hand signs associated with specific groups. The Sureños, for example, are identified with nearly all shades of blue, but it's royal blue bandanas that they're best known for. And as brutal as the Sureños are, they're child's play compared to organized crime boss Georgio "The Bull" Gambino—the man who most likely ordered today's failed hit.* Mick shakes his head. *I'd hate to be the driver of that van. They've probably already been executed as an example of what failure leads to.*

I need to be careful about announcing myself to the arriving guests. Holding a nameboard over my head in an arrival terminal is equivalent to placing a target on my chest.

Sarah Porter places a hand on her chest, not because of the flight turbulence but because she hasn't heard from Jake, her husband, in two weeks. *As part of the Special Operations Group in the US Marshals Service, he's on call twenty-four hours a day for SOG missions, and I hate it. But he loves it. The specially trained deputy marshals provide security and law enforcement assistance to the Department of Defense and the US Air Force when Minuteman and cruise missiles are moved between military facilities. And it's all hush-hush. Jake couldn't even tell me where he was going. I don't like it, not one little bit. He lives for the adrenaline rush, the thrill of it. At least at Pines & Quill writing retreat, I can use my time to be productive and finish my current manuscript instead of sitting at home and worrying.*

With a layover in Seattle, Sarah's flight from Billings, Montana, to Bellingham, Washington, is just over four hours.

"Ladies and gentlemen, we've started our descent into Sea-Tac, the Seattle-Tacoma International Airport. Please make sure your seatbacks and tray tables—"

Yeah, I know the drill. I don't like being crammed in the confines of what amounts to a flying soup can hurtling through the sky with a hundred other people. I'm used to the wide-open spaces of Big Sky Country, so it'll be nice to get off the plane and stretch my legs for a few minutes before I catch my connecting flight to Bellingham.

Sarah extracts a compact and lipstick tube from her purse under the seat in front of her. When she opens the mirror, she scrutinizes herself. Emily, Jake's best friend's wife, recently suggested that she might consider coloring her hair. *"You know,"* she said, *"to keep the competition at bay."*

After applying a touch of Framboise Moi, a rich raspberry pink lipstick, Sarah adjusts the mirror to see her hair and touches a silver strand. *Did Emily's husband say something to her about Jake?* Sarah's heart constricts with worry. *Was Emily insinuating that Jake isn't satisfied with my appearance? Does he want someone younger?*

The usually confident Sarah puts her lipstick and compact back in her purse and then replaces it under the seat in front of her as the plane touches down. *Oh, God. What if Jake's having an affair?*

While walking to the gate of her connecting flight, Sarah passes an Elliott Bay Book Company. Through the window, she sees a rack of slick magazines. On one of the covers is a knockout photo of a Hollywood actress. *Her hair is short, hip, and dark brown—not a hint of gray.* Sarah checks her watch. *It's four o'clock Pacific time. I can do this if I hurry.* She makes a beeline for the magazine, pays the cashier, and rushes to her gate that's now boarding.

Jake promised that he'd fly to Bellingham to be with me over the Labor Day weekend when Pines & Quill celebrates with family and friends. She clutches the magazine to her chest. *And in twenty-five years of marriage, Jake's never broken a promise. Including the one to be faithful. That, and to always come back home alive.*

Sarah looks at the cover of the magazine again and mentally compares herself to the actress.

Todd Jones can't help but wince at the discomfort on the flight attendant's face as she's pulled into a discussion about the "delights of extra legroom when you're seated behind the bulkhead." *Apparently, the ass sitting next to me hasn't noticed that I don't have legs.*

Todd's nonstop flight from Colorado Springs to Bellingham, Washington, is two hours and fourteen minutes. *The flight from hell.* He pinches his nostrils shut and swallows, trying to pop his ears. It doesn't work. He sticks his nose back in his book and reminds himself, *Do not engage.* His new mantra. He turns to the flight attendant and points at the beverage cart. "I'd like a glass of wine after all. Red, please."

Todd sets his book on his lap. The cover, pictured with an open book of matches, says, *Anger Management Workbook for Men: Take Control of Your Anger and Master Your Emotions.* He's been working on anger management issues with his therapist. He reminds himself of what that's all about. *Anger management is the process of learning to recognize signs that you're becoming angry and taking action to calm down and deal with the situation in a productive way.*

Todd sips the red wine. *Anger management doesn't try to keep you from feeling anger or encourage you to hold it in. Anger is a normal, healthy emotion when you know how to express it appropriately—anger management is about learning how to do this.*

Todd looks at his glassless hand—the one with the white-knuckled stranglehold on the armrest between him and the ass. *I'm the one that got stranded on Pike's Peak, got severe frostbite, and had to have my legs amputated. It is what it is, so there's no point in lashing out. Spewing anger isn't going to change anything.* He takes another sip of wine. *But if I'm going to point blame, it should be at the only person responsible—myself.*

He looks at his watch, calculates the time difference between Colorado Springs and Bellingham, and determines they have about a half-hour before landing. He leans into the aisle and looks both ways. *That had to have been the last beverage cart pass they're going to make. Dammit!* He slugs back the remaining wine. *I can do this.*

Once the plane lands at Bellingham International and comes to a stop, most passengers, except Todd, stand. Wheelchair passengers deplane last for the same reason they board first—they need more time to get on and off the plane. That, and Todd doesn't have his wheelchair. It was stowed when an attendant boarded him with a slender aisle chair designed for aircraft.

The ass steps across him into the aisle. *No "excuse me," nothing.* Todd watches him reach into the overhead compartment, extract a bag, and face forward with the rest of the passengers jostling for position. *Do not engage.*

When the plane's empty, an attendant brings him an aisle wheelchair. Not needing assistance, Todd transfers himself. Once they've deplaned and are inside the terminal, Todd shifts himself again, this time to his own wheelchair. As he tips the assistant, he asks where the baggage carousels are. On the way, he stops at the restroom, where he transfers himself again. *I may not have any fucking legs, but I've got the arms of Atlas. With all of the workouts my arms and back get, I could hold the world's weight on my shoulders. And most days, it feels like I do.*

Dale Brewer never tossed his cookies aboard a ship, not even in the middle of the ocean where the sea can be rough. *Right now, I could run to the head and puke my guts up.* Instead, he checks the seat pocket in front of him to ensure there's a barf bag. *Thank God.* He wipes the sweat from his brow with the back of a hand.

On this beautiful September first afternoon, Dale's non-stop flight from Houston, Texas, to Bellingham, Washington, is ahead of schedule. Instead of taking four hours and twenty-three minutes, they ran into less headwind than normal and knocked twenty minutes off the flight. He checks his watch. *It's only four-thirty Pacific time. I gained two hours traveling from the Central Time Zone to the Pacific Time Zone.*

Dale looks around him at the other passengers. *Not a single person is green around the gills like me. Well, I guess that comes from thirty years of calling the shots, of piloting a cruise ship, of not being at someone else's mercy—a passenger.*

It must have been like this when Heidi shouted at me while hanging onto the oh-shit bar and stomping imaginary brakes right through the floor mats. "Dale, honey, slow down. I'm telling you, if you're not careful, we'll go over the cliff!"

I assured her repeatedly that we were fine. "It only feels that way because you're not the driver."

"No, darlin'," she'd say. "You drive too fast. You're always in a hurry."

Heidi. I can't believe my dear sweet wife's been dead for nearly two years. When I retired, the doctors told me that I was a candidate for a heart attack. I needed to work on lowering my blood pressure. I needed to lose some weight. No one ever said a word of caution to rail-thin, health-conscious Heidi. She helped me lower my blood pressure and lose weight. Then she dropped dead from a heart attack.

Overwhelmed with sadness, Dale covers his face with his hands to hide his grief.

When I first retired and was at a loss for something to do, Heidi said, "You should write a book. For goodness' sake, Dale, you were a maritime pilot for thirty years. Just think of the stories you can tell!" So she signed me up for a writing class at the local community college—even came with me the first few times to make sure I went—and then cheered me on once I began.

Dale tilts his gray-circled tonsure against the headrest, then wipes the palms of his hands on the tops of his thighs. *I'm keeping my promise, honey. My creative writing teacher at Lone Star Community College said, "You have a striking talent with the written word. You need to start sending query letters."*

"What's a query letter?" I asked.

My instructor explained, "A query letter is a way to introduce your writing to editors, literary agents, or publishers. Writers use these letters to pitch their ideas. In a single page, the writer aims to get the editor, agent, or publisher interested in reading the entire manuscript for potential publication."

That's when I contacted Libby MacCullough at the Pines & Quill writing retreat in Fairview, Washington. I'm heading there right now for a three-week writing residency. Libby is going to read it, critique it, and possibly even point me in the direction of a publisher.

I have to tell you, Heidi, I'm both excited and scared.

Sakura Nishiwaka nods her head graciously as she accepts a hot wet towel from the end of silver tongs that a flight attendant is extending toward her. It's a service only offered to first-class passengers. She feels a little bit guilty. Not because she's flying first class. *I work hard for every penny I make. For the past two decades, I've worked for one of the twenty largest and premier companies in San Francisco— Wells Fargo.*

The guilt is because of the business article she'd recently read. It said that in-flight hot towel service might become a thing of the past because airlines are reinventing their offerings to be more sustainable. It detailed the push to force airlines to become greener—to take measures to reduce weight and waste. They used Scandinavian Airlines Systems as an example, stating, "This week, SAS announced it was ditching hot towels on its short-haul business-class flights as part of its new sustainability efforts."

Many airlines use hot towels that are never washed or reused, simply thrown out with the rest of the cabin rubbish, and are often non-biodegradable, so I agree with SAS's logic in eliminating them. Sakura checks her watch. *We must be nearing the end of the flight.*

She uses the hot towel to wipe her hands, wrists, and forearms. Then after examining her hands, she uses it again, this time more vigorously on her fingertips that picked up red ink when she was writing in her journal. Satisfied, she wads the towel and places it on the tray table in front of her, then opens her journal and flips through the pages, noting the sharp slant of her script. *I was angry when I wrote this.*

In writing her grandmother's memoir about being a pearl diver in Japan, Sakura has been studying her genealogy. That research has taken her on a paper journey to many Japanese prisoner of war camps.

Sakura is ethnic Japanese, but as a *nisei*—a person born in the United States or Canada whose parents immigrated from Japan—she was born in America and identifies fully as an American.

In school, we learned about internment camps in Europe, but the teachers never taught us about our camps in the United States. Her investigation led her to a paper written by Arnold Krammer, a professor of history at Texas A&M University. He writes, "Few Americans today recall that the nation maintained 425,000 enemy during the Second World War in prisoner-of-war camps from New York to California. The majority of these captives were Germans, followed by Italians and Japanese."

Sakura discovered that Washington State was home to

six base camps, ten branch camps, three hospitals, one federal prison, three internment locations, and three cemeteries. She slams her journal shut and tucks it, along with a red ink pen, into her tote.

While at Pines & Quill, I intend to visit the places where many of my ancestors died.

———

Libby opens her eyes wide in surprise when she enters the guest room—soon-to-be baby nursery—in Mick and Emma's cabin. All of the furniture is in the center, covered with drop cloths.

She turns to Emma. "You've been busy."

"*Mick's* been busy," Emma says. "He won't let me lift a finger in my 'condition.'" She makes air quotes when she says "condition."

Libby laughs. "Niall was the same way when I was pregnant with Ian. He wouldn't let me do a thing. I remember wishing for the gestation period of an elephant. Can you imagine two straight years of pampering?"

Emma shakes her head and smiles. "No. I think it would get old."

"Not to me," Libby says. Then she points to a corner with several small paint containers and brushes sitting on newspaper on the hardwood floor. "What on earth is this?"

"I went to the hardware store and picked up a few samples."

Libby raises her eyebrows in question. "A *few?* There's at least a dozen here."

"Well, after talking with *my* mom and *your* mom, there were so many opinions that I couldn't make up my mind."

Libby squats on her heels, picks up the sample cans one at a time, and reads each label aloud. "Balboa Mist. Bird's Egg Blue. Soft Fern. Baby Chick. Powderpuff Pink. Peach Parfait, Gentle Butterfly, and Sparrow Gray." She turns to Emma. "Which one is Mick's favorite?"

"Without seeing the colors on the wall first, we both like the idea of the combination of Gentle Butterfly, a light teal, and Sparrow Gray—the advantage being that it's gender neutral."

"Have you thought about painting a rainbow on one wall using *all* the colors?"

"No," Emma says. "But I like the idea."

"Well, there's no time like the present," Libby says. "Let's pop them open and paint a test swatch of each one on the wall."

Emma stifles a yawn.

"Am I keeping you awake?"

Emma laughs. "You reading the relaxing paint names made me sleepy."

At the sound of Emma's laughter, Hemingway enters the nursery, walks to an unoccupied corner, circles a few times, and then with a *harrumph,* lies down and closes his eyes.

"It looks like it made him tired too," Libby says.

"Let's test a few colors?" Emma says.

"Okay, but don't we need to stir the cans first?"

"No, they were just poured yesterday," Emma says. "And the woman in the paint department said that the samples are small enough to just shake vigorously."

Libby and Emma shake and open each can. Then taking a can and brush each, they approach the wall with the most daylight hitting it from the adjacent window. They talk as they work.

"We can be as messy as we want," Emma says. "It's washable, one-coat paint. So, once we decide on a color or two, we'll just paint over the whole thing."

At first, Libby dabs her brush against the wall. Then she makes a large swath. She steps back to get a better look at the color—Peach Parfait.

"I wish I'd made more progress on my pottery piece today," Emma says, "but I was a bit distracted."

"How so?" Libby prompts as both women continue to dip, dab, and swathe.

"When one of the guys working on the upstairs addition walked through the workshop, Hemingway growled."

Libby turns to Emma. "That's not like him. Not at all."

"I know, right?" Emma dabs her color, Balboa Mist, next to Libby's Peach Parfait, then steps back to scrutinize the combination. "But Hemingway's an excellent judge of character, so I can't seem to let it go."

At the sound of his name, the big, wiry-coated dog stands and stretches behind them. Then, his curiosity piqued, he walks over to the corner and noses an open can of paint, accidentally knocking it over. Hemingway sniffs the liquid, wags his tail, then lowers himself onto the floor and rolls in the colorful paint, tipping over the other cans as his shoulders move back and forth and his paws bicycle the air.

The women turn simultaneously at the volley of thunks. Stretching out their arms, they cry, "*No!*" as Hemingway stands and shakes his wet coat, flinging drops of color in every direction, including the ceiling.

The women turn to each other, horrified, then begin to laugh as they see colorful splats of paint on each other's faces, in their hair, and on their clothes.

"Shut the door!" Libby shouts. "We can at least limit the damage to this room."

In the comedy of the situation, Libby decides, *I'm not going to tell Emma that Mick asked me to get her out of the workshop because he has the same feelings about the construction guy that she has. And based on multiple failed murder attempts on Mick's and Emma's lives, I do too.*

Libby glances at her watch, then thumbs a dollop of paint off its face to see the time. "Let's clean up this mess."

She turns and gives a mock glare at Hemingway.

The multicolored dog thumps his tail on the floor.

"Emma, I swear he's smiling at us."

"It sure looks like it."

Libby points at Hemingway. "Then we'll hose this guy off." She puts her hands on her hips. "Look who's smiling now," she says, giving him a toothy grin.

Hemingway whacks the wall behind him with his tail, leaving strokes of Powderpuff Pink.

Libby shakes her head. "After that, we'll head to the main house. Mick will be here soon with this month's guests. And you know from experience that it's fun to have a welcoming committee. Better yet, a colorful one." *As long as none of the guests is a killer.*

CHAPTER 4

"The beginning is not where your story starts,
but where your story starts to get interesting."
—Jenna Kernan

Mick's nostrils catch the smell of jet exhaust, fast food, and the heady mixture of perfumes and colognes that hang like an invisible cloud over the crowd of bustling people in the Arrivals Terminal at Bellingham International Airport. Standing by the luggage trolley he secured for their guests' baggage, he raises the first nameboard so it can be seen from a distance. *I'm as good as a target.*

The first three flights arrive almost simultaneously, bearing Todd Jones from Colorado Springs, Sakura Nishiwaka from San Francisco, and Dale Brewer from Houston. After introductions, they gather baggage from the conveyor belts. Mick loads it onto the luggage trolley and then holds up the last nameboard—S. Porter.

The four of them turn at the sound of heels thudding toward them.

The approaching woman looks like she just stepped off the rodeo circuit with her bootcut jeans, blue paisley snap Western shirt, brown leather belt with a large turquoise buckle, a matching leather and turquoise bracelet, and brown leather cowboy boots that add an inch or so to her height.

The only thing missing is a cowboy hat.

She points to the nameboard and then extends her hand to Mick. "I'm Sarah Porter."

After Mick introduces himself and the others, he says, "Let's get your luggage."

As the two of them jockey for position by the baggage-laden conveyor belt, Sarah points first to one, then another piece of luggage. "That one's mine. That one too."

Mick hefts them off the belt. "Is this everything?"

Sarah shakes her head. "No. There's one more piece, but I don't see it yet."

They make small talk as the conveyor belt parades luggage past the newly arrived Montana passengers.

Sarah's eyes light up, and she points. "There it is!"

Mick turns and raises his eyebrows. "Is that what I think it is?"

Sarah smiles. "It depends on what you think it is. But I bet you can guess."

Mick grabs the large, hard-sided case from the baggage carousel. "I'd say it's a compound bow."

"You got it," she says. "And it stores a dozen arrows."

Walking back toward the others, Sarah says, "Compound bows use a levering system of cables and pulleys to bend the limbs, giving the user a mechanical advantage. They're widely used for hunting because the higher rigidity and higher technological construction improve their accuracy, making them deadly weapons."

Mick nods. "I'm familiar with compound bows. What I don't understand is why you brought one to a *writing* retreat?"

Sarah tucks a strand of chin-length brown hair behind an ear. "I guess it seems strange, doesn't it? Unless, of course, you're writing about a serial killer who's an archer."

Mick is aware that the look on his face screams bafflement.

"My books are bestsellers because they're authentic. And they're authentic because they're well-researched. I began practicing with it on our ranch when I started writing my current book."

"Where do you plan to use it while you're here?" Mick asks. *Compound bows are extremely dangerous. Someone could get killed. It could even be made to look like an accident when it might not be.*

"On the Pines & Quill website, I saw a massive bluff overlooking Bellingham Bay. I thought we could set up a bale of hay, and I'd use that as my target."

Todd looks up as Mick and Sarah approach. "Target?" Then, as his gaze takes in the compound bow case, he raises his eyebrows.

Would a killer flaunt their weapon under their intended victim's nose? Mick wonders. *To throw them off track, they most certainly would.*

Mick leads the group to the parking area. When they reach the van, he presses a button on his key fob, and both side panels slide open for the waiting guests.

The MacCulloughs had the body of their vehicle modified to offer three entry points and a rear lift gate for wheelchair users. Guests using a motorized wheelchair that doesn't fold have different needs than those who can transfer themselves into a vehicle and collapse their chair.

After stowing the luggage in the back, Mick watches the guests enter the van and situate themselves. *Over the years, I've learned that observing this simple exercise can reveal a lot about personalities. For example, people who sit in front tend to be outgoing, those who choose the back are more reserved, and those in the middle can go either way.*

Todd's toned muscles make his transfer into the van easy. Once seated behind the driver's seat, he collapses his wheelchair, stowing it in the space to his right.

Dale gets into the far back. He sits in the middle of the bench seat in front of the stowed luggage.

Sarah takes the seat behind the shotgun position, opens her purse, extracts a compact, and inspects her makeup. She turns her head from side to side. Then, after touching up her lipstick, she replaces the items in her purse.

In her stylish executive attire, Sakura slips into the front passenger seat and pulls the visor down to check her appearance in the mirror.

She's using the opportunity to look at the people behind her. Mick starts the engine and turns to Sakura. "I grew up in San Francisco just across the Golden Gate Bridge from Marin County. What part do you live in?"

"I live in Presidio Heights."

Looking over his left shoulder, Mick merges into traffic. *I wonder what the heck she does for Wells Fargo? The average price for a home in that coveted neighborhood is about five million dollars. Then again, being a high-powered executive would make an excellent cover for a hitwoman.* Mick rubs his jawline. *And San Francisco is one of the three gems in crime boss Georgio "The Bull" Gambino's crown. It's where he had my father shot and killed while Dad was following a lead that could have nailed him.*

Mick looks in the rearview mirror and narrows his eyes. *Why is Dale draped over the back of his seat?* He continues to watch. "Dale, would you put your seatbelt back on, please?"

At the sound of his name, Dale whirls around. His gaze locks momentarily with Mick's in the mirror before, redfaced, he lifts a small bottle. "I get motion sick."

A maritime pilot who suffers from motion sickness? I find that hard to believe. And what did he slip into his pocket with his other hand?

During the short drive, the group begins to chat among themselves. "Where are you from?" "How was your flight?" "How did you find out about the writing retreat?"

Dale leans forward. "Todd, I noticed your Denver Broncos T-shirt. You must be a fan."

In the rearview mirror, Mick sees Todd smile. "I am." Then Todd purses his lips and lowers his brows. "Dale, don't tell me you're a Kansas City Chiefs fan, or I'll have to take you out."

Dale shakes his head and holds up his hands in mock surrender. "No, not me."

I know Todd was kidding, but man, for a moment there, the look in his eyes was deadly.

To smooth the momentary discomfort, Mick says to the group, "If you wear a watch, you won't need it. The pace at Pines & Quill is tranquil and slow." *Except for the recent rash of murders and a car bomb.* He glances at each person. *I hope none of you is on Gambino's payroll.*

The van rounds a bend and stops at a massive wrought-iron entry gate. Its overhead sign silhouetted against a cobalt blue sky beckons, WELCOME TO PINES & QUILL.

Mick presses a button on the remote attached to the visor over the driver's seat. The huge gate swings open and trips a buzzer in the main house. *Niall and Libby know that we're here.*

Although Mick is well-traveled, this tranquil location is his favorite place on the globe. It's separated from the rest of the town by a long road and acres of trees.

When he hears the passengers' appreciation of the forested surroundings, he uses the automatic controls to lower the windows. The scent of pine fills the van. His nostrils flare, taking it in. *Home—this is what home smells like to me.* Then,

Mick continues the lengthy drive to the main house, slowing so they can drink in the beauty.

———

Set on twenty forested acres, the Pines & Quill writers' refuge provides respite from the distractions of everyday life so writers can focus on what they do best—write. An environment that offers peace, quiet, and inspiration, it boasts four secluded cottages—Dickens, Brontë, Austen, and Thoreau—each cottage handcrafted by a long-dead Amish man whose skill and devotion to his trade are still evident in his work. When the structures were modernized, meticulous care was taken to create the same excellence in craftsmanship.

Libby enjoys free rein expressing her natural flair for style and interior design in the main house and the four cottages. And while the original Amish builder saw that each cottage was similar in size and design and surrounded by its own type of tree, she ensures that they each have unique personalities: color scheme, furnishings, and hand-selected artwork created by local artisans.

In addition to electricity and internet access, each cottage has air-conditioning, a wood-burning stove, and a bathroom with a shower. They're also equipped with an efficiency kitchen that includes a mini-fridge, microwave, toaster oven, coffeemaker, and a fat-bellied tea kettle—ideal for a long day of writing.

Each spacious work desk has a phone. Retro in design, they're bulky and square from an era before cell phones—even before cordless. Their sole purpose is to connect with the main house. A guest needs only to lift the receiver and dial zero to ring through to the MacCullough's kitchen.

The main house, large and rustic, is inviting in a down-home sort of way. Built for comfort not grandeur, it sits at the center of Pines & Quill. And while each writer has the option to have breakfast and lunch delivered from the main house to their cottage door, they gather for dinner each evening at the enormous pine table Libby acquired at an auction in Seattle. Said to have seated a dozen threshers at mealtime in the early 1900s, it now serves the writers who've come to escape the distractions of life—who've come to this nurturing place for the sole purpose of writing.

The cookery and the herb and vegetable gardens at Pines & Quill are Mick's brother-in-law's cathedrals. Niall believes the casual atmosphere of sharing a meal in the spacious open-plan kitchen and dining area of the main house is conducive to *esprit de corps*—camaraderie. Every scratch and divot, a history of purpose and bustling activity, reads like braille on the wide, buttery pine boards of the floor in his sanctuary.

With the arrival of each group of writers in residence, Libby and Niall nod to each other under copper-bottomed pots that hang from the ceiling. In over thirty years of marriage, they've built an extensive repertoire of facial expressions that only they're privy to the meaning of.

Each month, they settle back like satisfied cats washing their whiskers. They smile as they watch a small community form, bonds deepening through conversation, as their guests share stories, histories, breakthroughs, and roadblocks, offering advice and feedback and challenging each other to take risks.

With its bevy of comfortable, overstuffed chairs, the living room is the after-dinner gathering place for guests to continue visiting over dessert while enjoying drinks from the small but well-stocked main house bar, the Ink Well. The floor-to-ceiling bookshelves and massive fieldstone fireplace serve as an ideal focal point. The large mirror above the mantel gathers the entire room in its reflection.

The retreat's journal is housed in this community space, a journal in which each guest is invited to make notations during their stay. With entries dating from its inception in 1980, the

Pines & Quill journal is a living legacy, a way for writers to connect with those who've come before and those who'll come after. And on more than one occasion, it has served as a guide, yielding clues that helped solve mysterious occurrences at the writers haven over the years.

Between nonfiction and fiction, every possible genre of literature has been penned here. Dedicated writers come to Pines & Quill to gift themselves with time and space, to let go and connect with nature's muse, to find their creative rhythm, and to write about the many intersections of human activity and motivation—both good and evil.

Seated on the periphery of Bellingham, a spot where urban civilization adjoins agriculture and wooded wilderness, this writing refuge consists of fog-kissed bluffs, great horned owls and red-tailed hawks, winding paths, solitude, and the blissful absence of noise, demands, and chores. It's an ideal place for contemplating many things.

In addition to Niall's gourmet meals and wine pairings, another popular feature at Pines & Quill is Libby's movement meditation offering. She provides misty morning tai chi sessions that many guests avail themselves of to prepare for a productive writing day.

———

Mick pulls the van to a stop where the casual yet elegant roundabout drive widens at the main house's front door. He activates the sliding side doors of the van. Once open, Niall, Libby, Emma, and Hemingway step forward to greet the new arrivals.

Mick widens his eyes in surprise as he looks at the welcoming committee. *What on earth? Hemingway's soaked. Did he just have a bath? And my wife and sister both need one. It looks like they were on the losing end of a paintball war.*

Libby steps forward, one hand holding Hemingway's collar, the other extended in greeting as Sakura exits the van.

"It looks like we missed out on all the fun," Sakura says, taking Libby's hand in one of hers and petting the top of Hemingway's wet head with the other.

Emma steps forward as Mick, Sarah, and Dale exit the van. "We'll tell you all about it over dinner."

"Speaking of dinner," Niall says. "You've got about forty-five minutes before it's ready."

"What are we having?" Dale asks.

Todd uses the opportunity to transfer himself from the van to his wheelchair.

Niall rubs the palms of his hands together. "I'll tell you the 'bookends'—the beginning and end. The appetizer is figs with a blue cheese and balsamic reduction. And let's just say that there's a *killer* dessert."

"You had me at 'balsamic reduction,'" Sarah says.

While Libby and Emma speak with the guests, Mick and Niall shift the luggage from the back of the van to the back of an ATV.

"You might want to use the time to check out your cottages and freshen up," Libby says. "I know I'm going to, and I bet that Emma is too."

Emma nods. "A hot shower is foremost on my mind."

Libby points the guests toward their cottages. "For those of you who'd like a ride, Mick will give you a lift in the ATV when he takes your luggage to the cottages, or you can join Emma and me on the pathways."

Without exception, all of September's guests want to make their own way to their homes away from home for the next three weeks.

As Mick drops off the luggage at each cottage, he decides not to tell Emma about the close call with the van. *She's pregnant and doesn't need any extra stress. But I'm going to keep a close eye on this month's writers. Gambino has used guests before to try to kill Emma and me. I intend to keep her and our baby safe at all costs.*

Libby looks up from putting the finishing touches on the dining table as Emma and Mick enter. "You look much better," she and Emma say at the same time, pointing at each other.

"Jinx, you owe me," they say again at the same time, then burst into laughter.

Mick shakes his head. "You two could be sisters."

"We're sisters-*in-law*," they say in unison and continue to laugh.

Hemingway sticks his almost-dry wiry head over the top of the Dutch door, already relegated to the mudroom for the duration of dinner.

There's a knock on the front door.

"I'll get it," Mick says.

He returns shortly with Todd, Sakura, Sarah, and Dale.

"Oh, me. Oh, my!" Sarah says, holding a hand with chunky turquoise rings to her chest. "What on earth smells so divine?"

Apron-clad, Niall steps out of the kitchen with a hot mitt and a wooden spoon. "Come in. Come in. Welcome."

"Niall," Libby says, "Sarah was just asking what smells so good."

Delighted at the opportunity, Niall shares the rest of this evening's menu. "You already know what the appetizer is. The main course is pork tenderloin stuffed with butternut squash, goat cheese, and sage."

Sarah moans, "*Ohh*, man."

"Just wait," Emma says. "It gets even better."

Niall continues. "There's also a brown butter risotto made with the pan drippings from the tenderloin. All paired with an old vine Zinfandel."

Dale pats his stomach. "And I didn't pack my jogging clothes."

"What's for dessert?" Mick prompts, knowing full well it's one of his favorites.

"Brown butter rum cannoli. We'll have that in the Ink Well after dinner."

As the guests take their seats, Libby notices Sakura extracting a leather-bound journal from her tote. She puts it on the table to the right of her place setting and then places a pen on top of it.

I just saw that pen in the Levenger catalog; it's a clear Montblanc filled with red ink. She swallows as she remembers the price. *It retails for just under eight hundred dollars.*

Around the table, with strains of Carole King singing softly in the background, the formalities begin to slip away. Rims meet and clink. The skittle and clack of cutlery are drowned out by robust conversation as the writers in residence get to know each other.

"This Zinfandel is excellent," Todd says, holding up an empty glass.

Libby refills it, checking the other guests' glasses while she's up.

The conversation expands and contracts, voices rise and fall, and faces flush with the exhilaration of the discussion and the wine. Then, as Libby and Emma share why they'd been covered in pastel-colored paint when their guests arrived, everyone laughs.

Niall, the epitome of efficiency, interjects, "Okay, everyone, it's time to adjourn to the Ink Well. I'll join you soon."

As the writers make themselves comfortable, Dale asks, "Didn't I read something online about a special journal?"

"Yes, you did." Libby walks to a thick book on an oak stand. She rests her hand on the cover and continues. "We encourage guests to make entries during their stay. We have entries dating from 1980 when Pines & Quill opened its doors."

From a deep leather chair, Sarah asks, "And if memory serves me well, didn't it also say that on more than one occasion, the journal has provided clues that were helpful in solving mysteries that occurred here?"

"That's right," Libby says, smiling at Sarah. She opens the book to the most recent entry and squints, realizing that she doesn't have her glasses on. Libby reaches for a pair of readers from the fireplace mantle. Silently, she reads the most recent entry. Her stomach grips, and her heart first flutters and then pounds as her brain takes in the message's implications written in a blistering red slant:

I warned you. My people can infiltrate even the most inaccessible places to do my bidding. When you least expect it, expect it—The Bull.

CHAPTER 5

"The worst enemy to creativity is self-doubt."
—SYLVIA PLATH

As Niall and Hemingway approach the Ink Well, Niall, carrying a dessert-laden tray, sees a stricken look on Libby's face. *Oh my God, what's happened?*

She glances at him, and the expression on her face says it all—*Distract our guests.*

His gut twists with worry. *I can do this.* With that goal, he steps into the room and bows dramatically. "Ladies and gentlemen, dessert is served." As he proffers the tray, all eyes except his lock onto the brown butter rum cannoli.

The room fills with the sound of *oohs* and *aahs* at the sight of the tube-shaped shells of fried dough brimming with sweet and creamy filling.

Hemingway's long tail whips the air. Well-muscled, lean, and strong, his appearance is commanding. An ancient breed, wolfhounds were bred to hunt with their masters, fight beside them in battle, and guard their castles. He possesses the ability of a fierce warrior, but he's gentle with family and guests, a magnificent combination of power and grace.

Sarah, the crime fiction novelist, points. "And they're drizzled with chocolate and dusted with powdered sugar."

Niall watches Libby sweep the Pines & Quill journal off the stand, tuck it under her right arm, and exit behind the loveseat where Mick and Emma are sitting.

───────

Something's wrong, terribly wrong. Adrenaline crashes through Mick as he watches the unspoken exchange between his sister and brother-in-law. Then he sees Libby, her face pale, tuck the journal under her arm and bolt through the door behind him.

Leaning into Emma, he says, "I need to speak with Libby for a minute. Would you mind starting our guests on the card drawing part of the evening?"

"Sure, I'd be happy to."

As the writers in residence enjoy the cannoli, Emma lifts a small box off the coffee table and says, "This is one of my favorite parts of the after-dinner portion of the evening. It's called *The Observation Deck: A Toolkit for Writers* by Naomi Epel. She designed it to help writers get traction and gain momentum."

Dale licks powdered sugar from one of his fingers, garnering Hemingway's attention. "How does it work?"

As Mick makes his way to the door behind the loveseat, he hears Emma. "At Pines & Quill, each guest draws a single card from the box. Each one contains a word or phrase that will be their focus for the next day's writing." Handing the box to Dale, she continues, "Why don't you select the first card to get us started?"

Mick nods at Niall over the guests' heads. Niall takes his

leave the way he came while Mick, with Hemingway on his heels, exits through the other door.

I know my sister, and there's only one word for the look on her face—fear.

———

Panic surges through Libby as she looks at the journal in her trembling hands. *A mob boss invaded my home!* She looks up when Niall, Mick, and Hemingway find her in the Pines & Quill office behind the dining area.

Niall puts an arm around Libby's shoulders. "What's happened, love?"

With trembling hands, Libby opens the journal on the desk in front of her and points to the most recent entry.

Niall and Mick bend over the page and read.

I warned you. My people can infiltrate even the most inaccessible places to do my bidding. When you least expect it, expect it—The Bull.

Her brother, Mick, balls his hands into fists at his sides. "What the hell?"

"When did Gambino get into our home?" Niall asks. "And *how?* Hemingway would rip him to shreds."

Libby strokes the top of Hemingway's head. "Unless he was lured away with raw steak." She studies the big dog's face and sees intelligent brown eyes between awning-sized gray eyebrows and a matching mop-like beard. *I love this dog.* She scratches him behind one of his ears, the only unassuming thing about him.

Quaking inside, she continues. "Gambino's minions are like cockroaches; they infiltrate even the most inaccessible places to do his bidding. For goodness sakes, he had at least three dirty cops in the Bellingham precinct—Toni Bianco, Emilio Acardi, and Adrian Padula."

Niall picks up the journal and rereads the entry. "And look what happened to them. They're all dead. Gambino's goons are disposable."

"But he doesn't just use cops," Mick says. "There's not an echelon of society where Gambino doesn't have a toehold—law enforcement, government, military, medical, academic. For all we know, he has religious leaders in his pocket, too. They come and go as they please, and no one's the wiser."

Libby holds up an index finger. "But the one thing they all have in common is a 'Family First' tattoo on the small of their backs."

"That's true," Niall says. "But we can't go around lifting people's shirts."

Mick flat palms the desk. "At least Chief Simms at the Bellingham Precinct initiated a surprise inspection overseen by Human Resources of all personnel, including himself. And they didn't find any more 'Family First' tattoos. So hopefully, the station's clean."

Niall shakes his head. "I wouldn't count on it. Gambino's at the top of the food chain because he's smart. I'm sure he's well aware of the inspection and has probably instigated a different type of 'brand' on the people he owns."

Libby taps the closed journal with a fingertip. "The latest entry, Gambino's, is written in red. Did either of you notice at dinner that Sakura was taking notes in her journal?"

Niall shakes his head.

"I saw her write every now and then," Mick says. "Why?"

Libby opens the journal and points to the entry. "*Red* ink. And Sakura was writing with a clear Montblanc pen filled with *red* ink."

"Well, we can't inspect her for a tattoo," Mick says.

"And we just determined that may no longer be Gambino's brand," Niall says. "So, what's the plan?"

"We're going back into the Ink Well before anyone gets suspicious, and we're going to act as if nothing has happened," Mick says.

Niall raises his eyebrows. "And if they ask about the journal?"

Libby glances at the big dog. "I'm sorry, Hemingway, but I'm going to place the blame on you."

At the mention of his name, the Irish wolfhound slices the air with his tail.

Libby continues. "I'll say that Hemingway tried to make a chew toy of the journal, ruined a page in the process, and I had to tear it out."

Niall rubs Hemingway's wiry crown. "It's a solid plan."

"I agree," Mick says. "And on Friday, Joe and Rafferty are joining us for a weekend of Labor Day festivities. That's only two days from now. It won't hurt to have a homicide detective and an FBI agent help us to keep tabs on our guests. In the meantime, it's up to us to monitor them."

"There've already been enough deaths at Pines & Quill." *How am I going to sleep again knowing that Gambino was inside our home?* Libby wonders. "Let's hope the September group of writers in residence isn't harboring a killer."

⸺⸺

Hemingway trots ahead of Mick, Libby, and Niall into the Ink Well. As Mick scans each face in the room, he roughs the top of Hemingway's wiry head. The big dog thumps his tail against the floor. *There'll be hell to pay if one of you is on Gambino's payroll.*

"We're on the third card pull," Emma says. "Dale and Sakura have already drawn. It's Todd's turn."

Todd selects a card from the deck and reads. "The title is 'Zoom In and Out.' It says, 'Try using your mind as a camera. If you are writing about a group of people, zoom in for a close-up of one person's face or hands. Or focus on some object that lies between them.'"

Mick zooms in on Todd. *There's a lightweight blanket draped over his thighs. Perfect for concealing a weapon.*

Todd continues, "'Pull back from the scene as if you had a camera mounted on a helicopter: see the place where the characters have gathered in a broader perspective.'"

As Todd reads, Mick takes in the gathering as a whole. *If one of you is a killer, which one?* He moves his gaze from Todd to Dale, who's reaching for another cannoli. *I find it odd that a maritime pilot suffers from motion sickness. And just what was it from the luggage area that he slipped into his pocket?*

Sakura Nishiwaka leans forward to scratch the wiry gray hair on Hemingway's back.

Is she the one who wrote Gambino's cryptic message in red ink in the Pines & Quill journal? Is she a hitwoman he sent to kill us?

"It's Sarah's turn to draw a card," Emma says.

Sarah Porter selects a card from the box. "It says, 'Ask a Question.' The *San Francisco Chronicle* columnist, Jon Carrol, wrote five columns a week. When asked how he did it, he recited these lines from Rudyard Kipling's *The Elephant's Child*: 'I have six humble serving men, they taught me all I knew. Their names are What and Where and When and Why and How and Who.'"

Did you bring a compound bow to a writing retreat to authentically write about a serial killer archer? Or is it you who's going to place an arrow on your bow when one of us is walking in the surrounding forest?

After Sarah finishes reading, Libby addresses the group. "I'm sure you saw on our website that I offer morning tai chi sessions. Many guests avail themselves of the opportunity to prepare for a productive writing day." She glances at her watch. "It starts at six, so we should call it a night."

"In the *morning*?" Dale croaks.

Libby chuckles. "Yes, six in the morning. How many of you will be joining me?"

Except for Todd, everyone raises their hand.

"You're not going to join us?" Libby asks.

Todd looks down at his thighs, then back at her pointedly.

"Don't be hesitant to participate because you're in a wheelchair," Mick says. "When I was in a wheelchair, I did tai chi every day." Then he turns to his sister. "Libby *made* me."

"And when I was in a wheelchair," Emma says, "I did tai chi every day." She turns to her husband. "Mick *made* me."

Mick shifts his gaze to the lightweight blanket covering Todd's thighs. *Don't discount anyone's motives or abilities. I know from experience that people in wheelchairs are more capable than many people give them credit for. Not only physically but in every other way—including the ability to kill.*

"Wait a minute," Sarah says, looking at Mick and Emma. "You both were in wheelchairs, and now you're not. What on earth?"

"It's a long story," Mick says.

"For a different night," Libby adds.

Todd lifts his eyebrows. "But how do you do tai chi in a wheelchair?"

"From the waist up," Mick, Libby, and Emma say in unison.

"Well," Todd says. "If it's doable, I'm game." He looks at the clock on the wall. "But it's been a long time since I was presentable at six in the morning." He grins. "I'm going to head to my cottage now so I get plenty of beauty rest."

"Me, too," the others chime in.

Once their guests leave, it's just the five of them—Mick, Emma, Niall, Libby, and Hemingway. As they clean up the aftermath, Libby says, "I wonder if one of them's on Gambino's payroll?"

Emma snaps her head up. "Why would you ask that?"

Mick closes his eyes in resignation. *I forgot to tell Libby and Niall not to say anything to Emma. With her being pregnant, I don't want her to have anything to worry about.*

———————

Sakura, Todd, Dale, and Sarah pause on the front steps of the main house before heading to their cottages.

Sakura checks her cell phone. *It's already nine o'clock. I need to get to my cottage and plan a visit to where my ancestors were held captive.*

Evening had arrived full-on while they'd been in the main house. The trio descends the steps. Sakura peers into the darkness, where deep purple shadows cling to the trees. She flares her nostrils in the light breeze. *The air smells of saltwater and pine.*

"That was fun, wasn't it?" Sarah asks.

Dale pats his well-fed stomach. "It was delicious!"

"Yes, it was," Sarah agrees. "On both counts—fun and delicious."

As they walk along the path, Dale inhales deeply. "The pine trees sure smell wonderful, don't they?"

Sakura nods. "According to one Japanese study, a pine scent can decrease anxiety and lower depression and stress levels."

"I wish I'd known that after my wife, Heidi, died," Dale says.

"I'm sorry for your loss," both women say.

Sakura continues. "The research discovered that participants who went on a walk through a pine forest reported significant feelings of relaxation."

Dale tucks his hands in the front pockets of his slacks. "I'll definitely take advantage of that while I'm here."

"Well, goodnight," Sakura says before turning on the path to Brontë Cottage. "I'll see you at the tai chi pavilion in the morning." She points. "It's that way."

"Impressive," Dale says. "It's like you have a built-in compass. How'd you do that?"

Sakura laughs. "I enjoy the dark. I'm good with it."

Each of them makes their separate way to their cottages.

When Sakura opens the door to Brontë, she flips the switch on the wall to her left. Golden light bathes the welcoming space. Earlier in the day, she climbed the wrought-iron spiral staircase that leads to a sleeping loft. *It strikes the ideal balance between Parisian chic and relaxed bohemian romance.*

Now, though, she gravitates to the kitchen to once again enjoy the scent in the glass diffuser she discovered on the countertop with the handwritten note saying:

Designed to enhance clarity, the top notes are Sicilian mandarin and Italian bergamot, the middle note is night-blooming jasmine, and the base note is Tahitian vanilla. Enjoy!

Sakura adjusts the tote strap on her shoulder and walks to the cozy window seat, which has a thick, inviting, jewel-toned cushion and matching throw pillows of emerald, ruby, and sapphire. Her gaze takes in the gem-toned palette as she admires the surrounding space before she removes her journal from her tote. She smiles as she remembers what her mother said. "We have two ears and only one mouth for a reason, Sakura. Listen twice as much as you speak."

I got to where I am because of Mom's advice. By listening and taking notes, I learned things that others missed. People think I'm shy, but I'm not. I'm smart.

Sakura opens her journal and reads the notes she took at dinner:

SARAH PORTER: *Montana. Best-selling author of crime fiction novels. Working on* Optical Delusion. *A suspense thriller about an ophthalmologist/archery buff by day, serial killer by night.*

TODD JONES: *Colorado. Working on* Colder than Hell. *His memoir of being stranded on Pike's Peak and getting frostbite that resulted in the amputation of both legs.*

DALE BREWER: *Texas. Working on* Making Waves. *A memoir about his thirty years as a cruise ship captain. Note: his hands trembled until shortly after he swallowed something from a prescription-type bottle he slipped from his pocket.*

NIALL AND LIBBY MACCULLOUGH: *Owners of Pines & Quill. Niall is coauthoring* Zins of the Father: A Guide to Zinfandel Wines & Food Pairings *with Byron Rivers, a vineyard owner in Napa Valley. Libby is tight-lipped about what she's working on.*

MICK AND EMMA MCPHERSON: *Newlyweds. Mick is Libby's brother and groundskeeper. He's also a private investigator who often works with Rafferty, an FBI agent from Seattle, and Joe, a local homicide detective, to help solve crimes. Emma is a potter. Note: With the way she kept palming her stomach, I think she's pregnant.*

HEMINGWAY: A massive five-year-old Irish wolf-hound who's helped solve crimes. He seems friendly, but I can well imagine the damage he could do.

Sakura closes her journal and looks again at her sur-roundings. On the east side of the cottage is a work-worn desk that hugs the wall beneath a massive window. On the Pines & Quill website, she learned that Libby MacCullough supports local artisans. Beneath a photo of one of Libby's favorite pieces—one that's showcased to catch exterior light on the wide windowsill in Brontë Cottage—it explained that a native glassblower created it.

Sakura approaches the work of art to get a better feel for it. About five feet wide and three feet tall, it consumes the entire width of the window. The multi-length cast iron hooks holding the bottles are twisted, giving them texture. Peering closer, she notes the pins attached to the slender nine-inch tall gem-toned glass bottles—carnelian, ruby, citrine, peridot, and turquoise—are curlicued at the ends. She touches the ruby-colored bottle. It catches the interior light as it rocks back and forth.

Sakura peers through the window into the darkness. She smiles, knowing that she'll rise at daybreak for the next three weeks to watch the sun's fingers grip the horizon and pull itself into the morning sky. *Its mandala of inspiration is sure to stir my creative juices and lift the heaviness of heart I feel, knowing that so many of my ancestors were held captive and died in internment camps near here.* Her fingers drum the top of her leather journal. *And justice was never exacted for those crimes.*

Mick and Emma walk to their cabin beneath a diamond-studded black silk throw of sky with their arms around each other's waists. *I don't feel like we're being watched, but I know that darkness can camouflage many things—including people who don't want to be seen*, thinks Mick.

Ahead of them on the path, an orchestra of startled crickets becomes instantly silent at Hemingway's approach. He diligently marks the fern leaf buckthorn as if to warn intruders: "No trespassing—this is my property." Then, happy with his stamp of ownership, he wags his tail.

Emma looks up at the stars pricking the black sky. "Do you think that one of this month's guests is on Gambino's payroll?"

Mick pulls Emma into his side. "He's done it before. So, yes, I think it's possible. That's why we have to keep our eyes and ears open. And that's why that big galoot"—he points to Hemingway—"is coming home with us tonight."

"But what about Libby and Niall?"

"Neither of them is pregnant."

Emma chuckles. "So Hemingway's my bodyguard now?"

Branches snap. Mick and Emma turn to see Hemingway frolicking after an evening moth.

"Just because he's acting like a knucklehead right now doesn't mean he wouldn't protect you with his life." *And so would I.*

After Mick opens the front door of their cabin, he turns and slaps a hand on his thigh. "Come on, Hemingway. Time for bed."

Hemingway bounds past them into the living room, then turns and pokes his wet nose into Mick's hand.

"*You're* looking for a treat? *You*, who singlehandedly redecorated the baby's nursery?"

Hemingway thrashes his long tail back and forth as if to say, "Yes, me. I'm the one!"

After Hemingway wolfs down a biscuit and Mick and Emma brush their teeth and change, the big dog digs at the rug on Emma's side of the bed, circles around, then nestles on top of the mess. Finally, he lets out a sigh of satisfaction and closes his eyes.

Mick and Emma slip under the covers of their bed. He curves his body along the back of hers and places a hand on her belly. "Good night, Baby McPherson." Then he nuzzles Emma's neck. "Good night, Mrs. McPherson."

Mick feels Emma's hand flutter to the mahogany pendant at her throat—a *honu*, a Hawaiian green sea turtle.

"Mick, I've never taken this pendant off since you gave it to me. I love it."

"I'm glad you love it, Emma. I enjoyed every minute of carving it for you."

"Do you remember what you said when you gave it to me?" Emma asks.

Mick nods, then speaks into the back of Emma's warm neck. "Yes, it symbolizes good fortune, endurance, and long life. When lost, turtles are excellent navigators and often find their way home—in your case, I hope it's always to me."

Please, God, don't let there ever be a reason for Emma not to come home.

CHAPTER 6

*"No one can write decently who is distrustful
of the reader's intelligence or whose attitude
is patronizing."*
— E. B. WHITE

Libby's exhausted from lack of sleep. Her mind continues
to play an endless loop of questions since her discovery
of the red-inked threat in the retreat's journal: *Did Gambino
himself enter our home? Or did one of his henchmen? Is one
of this month's writers in residence on his payroll? Is it a coincidence that Sakura uses a red ink pen? If she works for Gambino,
why would she tip her hand? Wouldn't she want to maintain a
low profile? I don't know the answers, but I intend to find out.*

Cries of red-winged blackbirds tear through the morning air. Libby glances at her cell phone and sees the time. *It's
five fifty-five, and sunrise is in half an hour. I wonder how
many guests will show up for this morning's session. I wonder
if Sakura will come.*

Malibu lights glow along the still-dark, mist-covered pathway as Libby walks toward the tai chi pavilion. A large, raised, open-sided building, it has a pagoda-style copper roof, patinated with age, and corners that flare out over Chinese-red supports.

Arriving at the structure, she slips her shoes off, ascends the few stairs, and activates the tiny white fairy lights artfully wrapped around the rafters. *It looks magical in the lifting mist.* Then she begins to limber up her body.

Sarah arrives next. She, too, removes her shoes. "How long have you been doing tai chi?" she asks, joining Libby's stretches.

"Niall would tell you, 'Since the day after dirt,'" Libby teases. "But the truth is I've been practicing tai chi for about thirty years. I started in my early twenties and fell in love with it. It's become a way of life."

Sarah fingers the top button of her spruce-green and dove-gray flannel shirt. "Well, I can understand why. I've only done it once and enjoyed it. My schedule didn't permit me to continue at the time. But I'm looking forward to it now."

Libby nods while stretching her hands toward the overhead beams. *My muscles are still vibrating with fear at Gambino's entry into our home.* "It has a way of dissolving blocks—energetic and otherwise. It also provides a complete workout, deep relaxation, a clear mind, and inner peace, and it leaves a person feeling both rested and invigorated." *Except it's not working this morning. My body's clogged with dread while we wait for Gambino's next move.*

Sarah mimics Libby's stretches. "By the way, do you mind if I take one of the bicycles into town this morning? I scheduled a cut and color at Tangles Salon. Thank you for the referral."

"You're welcome. And yes, feel free to use one of the bicycles. There's a map of Fairhaven inside each of the covered saddle baskets."

Over Sarah's shoulder, Libby sees Sakura moving toward the pavilion with graceful purpose. *She doesn't look like a killer. But, then again, what killer does?*

Sakura slips out of her shoes and joins them in the pavilion. "I'm ready."

Dale walks briskly alongside Todd's wheelchair. As Dale toes off his shoes next to the steps, Todd rolls up the parallel ramp with ease.

Rafferty, Ivy, Maggie—Ivy's guide dog—and Joe will arrive this morning. Even though school has just started, the private school in Seattle where Ivy teaches special ed took the day off, giving their teachers a four-day holiday. Unfortunately, the school district in Bellingham didn't take the extra day. So, Joe's wife Marci, and their daughters, Carly, age thirteen, and Brianna, age eleven, will arrive after school lets out this afternoon.

Mick, Emma, and Hemingway come into view on the pathway. *Emma's practically walking on air. Last night she told me she has a prenatal appointment with her doctor today—the last one before she and Mick find out the baby's gender.*

Libby presses her palms together and takes a deep breath. *Everyone's here except for Niall. He's at the main house preparing breakfast for delivery to the cottages and a sit-down meal for the other guests. But after last night's discovery, I'm scared for him being alone.*

Positioning herself in front of the group, Libby begins the first form, transitioning smoothly from one move to the next. The steps—done in a rolling motion, placing her bare feet with balanced weight one in front of the other—are usually soothing. This morning, her every nerve tingles with residual fear. *Gambino, or someone who works for him, was in our home.* Libby's heart constricts. *They wrote a threat in the Pines & Quill journal in red ink.* She looks at Sakura, the guest who writes with red ink.

Sakura returns Libby's gaze with a smile.

Libby offers a faint smile before shifting her eyes to take in the entire group. Even though it's chilly, she feels perspiration film her skin with fear. She watches the group move in harmony as they follow her lead. Libby's grateful when Mick steps in periodically from the back to help refine body mechanics when needed.

I'm so tense. I limbered up before we started, but my muscles are contracted like they're preparing for a fight-or-flight response. Libby looks out the side of the pavilion at the surrounding woods. In the shadows, she imagines deer. *I feel exposed, "like a deer in headlights." But, it's more than that. I feel violated. Our home is no longer safe.*

Normally, when I do tai chi, tension drains from my body, leaving an imaginary pool of stress at my feet. But now it's red ink. And instead of pooling at my feet, I feel like I'm drowning in it.

Sean Rafferty—"Rafferty" to keep him sorted from Sean "Mick" McPherson—drives by rote from Seattle to Fairhaven as he considers the call he received from Mick last night. *Gambino's upped his game by entering, or having one of his goons enter, the main house at Pines & Quill. That was a considerable risk. And why is he resurfacing now after laying low for a month? You can run, Gambino, but you can only hide for so long. We're going to catch you.*

Rafferty looks first in the side and then rearview mirrors before changing lanes. Two almost-black eyes stare back at him in the rearview mirror. That's followed by swishing noises as Maggie's short tail whisks the leather upholstery. Her long pink tongue lolls out the side of her mouth. *I swear she's smiling at me.*

In the front passenger seat, Ivy laughs. "Yes, Maggie," she says to her guide dog, a standard-sized, black-and-white Parti poodle, "You'll get to see Hemingway soon."

Rafferty smiles when he recalls how Sister Margaret Mary McCracken—"Maggie" for short—got her name. Ivy told him that when Maggie's trainers described her two-toned coloring to Ivy—black with a white wimple, similar to a traditional nun's habit—she couldn't resist giving the dog a nun's name. That, along with the fact that Ivy grew up in a convent. Shortly after Ivy was born and her parents learned she was blind, they left her at a convent in upstate New York. She, along with dozens of other children, was raised and educated by progressive nuns who didn't teach them *what* to think but *how* to think.

"Rafferty, why are we moving so slow?"

"We're stuck in a gridlock of cars."

"But I thought if we left early enough for Pines & Quill, we'd miss the rush-hour traffic."

Rafferty taps the steering wheel with an index finger. "Yes, but it's the Friday before Labor Day, and it looks like we *all* had the same idea." He glances out a side window. "There's an orangish light in the eastern skyline." The digital clock on the car's dash informs him that it's six twenty. "The sun will be up in about ten minutes."

Rafferty rotates his head and shoulders to work out the early-morning kinks. The bullet wound from when he was shot in the upper left side of his chest during the Fourth of July fireworks display barely registers pain anymore. *Probably because Stewart Crenshaw—my commander in the Seattle office—made me take off the month of August. I'm stoked that Mick, Joe, and I can dive back into the Gambino investigation. I always feel more alive when I'm working on a case. And with this latest development, it appears it's none too soon.*

Ivy touches Rafferty's shirt sleeve. "You promised that you'd tell me about your son's death." Her voice is gentle. "Perhaps now would be a good time."

Rafferty's gut clenches as he grips the steering wheel. *I*

keep promising Ivy that I'll tell her, but I haven't yet. She has said, "It feels like you're shutting me out." If I were Ivy, I'd want to know too. And I don't want to screw this up—I don't want to lose her. He squeezes his eyes shut momentarily. Then, finally, with nowhere to go and nothing else to do, he clears his throat and starts talking.

"Almost three years ago, my son, Drew, was killed in a car accident just before his sixteenth birthday. He was a passenger in his best friend's car. The friend, Jack, had just turned sixteen and gotten his driver's license. They were just two young guys—radio on, seat belts on, no one was drinking, and no drugs were involved. Drew was in the front passenger seat, and somehow, without any reason the authorities were able to discover, Jack lost control of the car. It flipped over and smashed into a tree. Drew was killed on impact. His friend, Jack, committed suicide six months later. The survivor's guilt he felt became too heavy for him to carry, to live with."

Ivy bites down on her bottom lip and shakes her head. "That's awful. I'm so sorry."

Rafferty swallows. "Thank you. It *is* awful." He blinks back tears. "Pamela, my ex-wife, and I took an emotional beating. We couldn't get past it. Our counselor said that the death of a child usually polarizes the existing factors found in a marriage. That's why some marriages get worse, others get better, some just maintain, and others end in divorce. Ours ended in divorce."

"Are you still friends?" Ivy asks.

"It was amicable, if that's what you're asking," Rafferty says. "She's remarried now, and they moved out of state."

Ivy squeezes Rafferty's forearm. "Thank you for telling me."

Rafferty nods before remembering that she can't see the gesture. "You're welcome. I'm relieved it's finally out there."

They drive in silence, each of them in private contemplation without the need for pointless words.

I still wonder why the crime scene investigation team couldn't determine why Jack lost control of the car. When the police questioned him, he sobbed, "I don't know. When we got to the bend in the road, everything quit working. No brakes. No steering. Nothing."

───

Niall bakes when he's upset, and in the kitchen of the main house, he's at it with gusto. *Gambino made an entry in the journal right under our noses!* Niall feels a pounding sensation in his neck and realizes that his blood pressure is rising. Heeding his doctor's advice, he intentionally shifts gears and hums a Scottish tune that his grandmother sang. Then, with exaggerated aplomb, he puts the finishing touches on the sheet tray of pancakes with peaches and strawberries before popping them into the oven. *Think of something pleasant.*

He smiles when he remembers Emma begging for the recipe. "*Please*, Niall. Mick loves it."

He wrote it on a recipe card and handed it to her. "They're pancakes that don't need to be flipped. Just whisk the batter, pour it into a sheet tray, and stick it in the oven. Then put your feet up and read the newspaper until breakfast is ready. You're welcome."

Niall couldn't decide on sweet or savory for this morning's meal, so he's also making chilaquiles—a traditional Mexican breakfast dish consisting of corn tortillas cut into quarters then lightly fried or baked in salsa to soften them up. Niall serves the dish with poached eggs and spicy honey on top. *It delivers both sweet and savory in one fell swoop.*

He got the recipe for chilaquiles from New York City–based chef Jenny Dorsey when he attended her online cooking class. *She takes traditional Mexican chilaquiles, a savory dish by all accounts, and gives it a touch of sweetness, thanks to spicy, Ancho chili-infused orange blossom honey.*

The pancakes and chilaquiles are easy to deliver to the Pines & Quill guest cottages. In 1980, when they opened their doors, they used Chinese takeout boxes for breakfast and lunch deliveries. But they soon discovered that the aroma escaping the cartons was enticing Tolkien, Hemingway's seventh great-grandfather. Since then, Faulkner, Kipling, Huxley, Poe, Wordsworth, Whitman, and now, Hemingway—all Irish wolfhounds, all exceptional animal companions—have been part of the writing retreat.

Back in the day, unbeknownst to Niall and Libby, Tolkien was on their heels, eating the meals as fast as they delivered them. So now they use glass containers with airtight lids that they leave in insulated totes. *Ha! There hasn't been a stolen meal since. Not by Irish wolfhounds, squirrels, raccoons, opossums, or even the occasional skunk that wanders through the property.*

As Niall prepares to set the table for the nonwriter guests, he stops to count the number of place settings needed. Talking out loud to himself, he says, "Let's see now, there's Maeve, Maureen, Rafferty, Ivy, and Joe. Monica, Carly, and Brianna won't arrive until this afternoon after school lets out. Mick, Emma, Libby, and me. That's nine."

He continues humming as he arranges the table for the people he considers family. Then he stops. *Family.* Niall's eyes glisten. *I miss my brother, Paddy. He always loved visiting with family, friends, and writers at Pines & Quill.*

Patrick MacCullough—Paddy—a longtime priest at St. Barnabas Catholic Church and loved by everyone in the parish, was shot to death in June through the partition of the confessional. It's still an open case that Mick, Joe, and Rafferty are investigating. So far, Paddy's death appears to be related to the other killings ordered by Georgio "The Bull" Gambino.

Normally calm and collected—a gentle soul—Niall's knuckles turn white as he tightens his grip on the flatware. *If I ever meet Gambino . . .*

Maeve clears two blue-and-yellow pottery mugs from the living room of her new condominium in Bellingham — chunky mugs that her daughter-in-law, Emma, made for her.

Returning from the kitchen, Maeve observes her house-guest from beneath her eyelashes. *If Maureen questions the locked door in the hallway, I'll explain, "It's where I store Connor's things." But I'm sure she won't press a newly widowed woman. That would be tactless, and she's the epitome of diplomacy.*

Emma's mother, Maureen, is staying with Mick's mother, Maeve, until the new addition over the Pines & Quill work-shop and the baby's nursery in Mick and Emma's cabin are completed. The two grandmothers want a hand — or two, or seven — in the preparations. And with the influx of out-of-town guests, this arrangement makes things easier.

Maeve sweeps her silver hair up into a loose chignon and skewers it with a hair stick that Mick carved for her. "I'm look-ing forward to seeing Libby and Mick at Pines & Quill this weekend. You'd think I'd see my kids more often now that we're practically neighbors, but we all lead such busy lives."

Maureen twists her lipstick tube, then colors and blots her lips. "I'm looking forward to seeing everyone too. Espe-cially Emma. I wonder if she's got a baby bump yet?"

Both women are primed and ready.

"We'll know soon." Maeve zips her tote shut and gives it a tap. "It's going to be fun giving Carly and Brianna something a bit old school. It'll be like time travel — transporting them back to 'the olden days' when Connor and I were in the FBI."

Maeve had enjoyed a long and distinguished career as a criminal psychologist (CP). She worked with the FBI to help solve crimes by developing profiles of murderers, kidnappers, rapists, and other violent criminals. And she still helps Mick, Joe, and Rafferty. Her expertise is the *why* behind criminal activity—the motivation—particularly for violent crimes. When law enforcement agencies try to figure out who a criminal is—for instance, a serial killer—they often bring in a CP. The CP uses a mix of psychology, pattern recognition, and inductive reasoning to predict a suspect's age, background personality, and other identifying characteristics to create a profile. Then, law enforcement uses the profile to narrow down their pool of suspects quickly.

She smiles as she thinks about Libby and Niall's son, Ian, her grandson. He calls her a "psychological sleuth." Because it was perfect for Ian and Fiona's newly established veterinary practice, Maeve recently gave her home and land in Marin County to the newlyweds. She knew it would be too much to maintain by herself after her husband, Connor, was murdered in July by one of Gambino's thugs while he was helping "the boys"—Mick, Joe, and Rafferty—with a case.

On the record, Maeve is retired. But off the record, she has clearance from Jim Beckman (FBI special agent in charge of the main office in San Francisco, the man who took over Connor McPherson's position when he retired) and Stewart Crenshaw (Rafferty's commander in the Seattle office) to continue working with the trio. And with that authorization comes access to the FBI databases she's accustomed to.

Maeve and Connor met at Quantico during training. However, his area of focus was different. He was there for NAT—New Agent Training with the FBI. He worked his way up through the rank and file, and by the time he retired, he was the FBI's special agent in charge of the Marin, Napa, and San Mateo County offices, in addition to the main office in San Francisco.

Maureen raises her eyebrows. "What's the 'old school' thing you're giving Carly and Brianna?"

"A pair of encrypted walkie-talkies. *No* cell towers, *no* way to track a signal. Mick said that we're going to play Spy over Labor Day weekend and split into teams like we did last year. The goal is to outwit each other. All locations on the twenty acres of Pines & Quill are fair game. Last year, the team the girls were on won because they hacked into an opposite team member's cell phone and geolocated them."

"Impressive," Maureen says. "But isn't that cheating?"

"Nope. All's fair in the world of espionage." Mauve unzips her tote, pulls out one of the walkie-talkies, and hands it to Maureen. She fishes in her bag again and, this time, extracts a small black pouch. She dumps the contents into her other palm.

Maureen steps closer. "They look like AirPods."

Maeve nods. "Similar. They're wireless earpieces that connect to the belt-mounted radios." She points to the one in Maureen's hand. "The range is significantly more than enough for this weekend's purposes, but with much less risk of being tracked than a cell phone."

Maureen looks at Maeve. "Wow, you're retired, yet you take this game very seriously. I wouldn't want to have been a bad guy when you were still in the FBI."

Maeve replaces the items in her tote. *If Maureen only knew what's inside the locked door in the hallway: passports, cash, a small arsenal, night-vision equipment, two go-bags, two backup generators, a satellite hotspot, laptops—hers and Connor's—and their encrypted burners that communicate with only two others—Mick's and Libby's.*

She'd relocated the secure site from their Marin County home set up at the insistence of Connor—Mick and Libby's father. Only the four of them—three, now—know about it in the event of the unthinkable.

CHAPTER 7

*"Trust your reader. Not everything needs to be
explained. If you really know something, and
breathe life into it, they'll know it too."*
— ESTHER FREUDE

Emma and Mick, wrapped in damp bath towels, jockey for position in front of the steamy master bathroom mirror in their cabin.

Mick places a hand on Emma's belly. "Have I told you lately that you're beautiful?"

"Yes, Mick," Emma says. "But you still haven't answered my question. Gambino, or one of his thugs, wrote a threat in the retreat journal, and I'm worried." Her hand joins Mick's on her belly bump. "Are we safe?"

"We have to be cautious until we catch him and put him away."

"I understand that, Mick. But are we *safe*?"

"We're as safe here as we would be anywhere else," he says. "I won't lie to you. Gambino's latest move wasn't only unexpected, but it proves that he can access places we thought were outside of his reach."

"So, what are we going to do about it?" Emma says.

"*We* aren't going to do anything. I don't want you involved with whatever could potentially hurt the baby. This weekend, Mom, Joe, Rafferty, and I are going to devise a plan that Gambino can't possibly escape." Mick pulls Emma in for a hug. "But let's not talk about that right now," he says into her hair. "It's upsetting. And worry isn't good for a pregnant woman or the baby."

"Okay, then," Emma says. "I trust you and the others to come up with a plan to put Gambino behind bars." She looks up at Mick. "But there's something else that I'd like to talk about."

"Fire away."

"You built this cabin when you were still single, right?"

"That's definitely a change of subject," Mick says. "Yes, I did. Why?"

"Well, I vote that while we're in the construction mode, we at least put in a double-sink vanity." She points to the farthest wall. "And then we could—" Her towel slips to the floor.

Mick waggles his eyebrows and smiles. "*Now* we're talking, Mrs. McPherson."

Emma scoops her towel up from the floor, but before she can rewrap it, Mick places his outstretched hands on her shoulders. His eyes smolder as he gazes at her naked figure.

"Pregnancy suits you, Emma."

"Oh, no you don't, Mr. McPherson." Emma wraps and tucks the towel. "You just enjoyed a romp in the shower."

Mick's nostrils flare. "As did you, Mrs. McPherson."

"Be that as it may," Emma says, "not only are we due at the main house for breakfast, both of our *mothers* will be there. And," she places her hands on her hips, "I've got an appointment with my obstetrician, Dr. Freeman, today, and she'll know."

Mick bursts into laughter. "Emma, our mothers are going to be *grandmothers*. They're aware that we have sex. In fact, *they* had sex, or we wouldn't be here."

He picks up her wide-toothed comb from the counter, turns her toward the almost steam-free mirror, and slowly works it through her wet hair. "And because Dr. Freeman is seeing you for an eleven-week *pregnancy* visit"—his eyes meet hers in the mirror—"I'm pretty sure *she* knows that we have sex."

Mick turns Emma to face him and touches his forehead to hers. "I'd love to come to the appointment with you."

Emma cups Mick's jaw with a hand. "I know you would. But I *also* know that you, Joe, Rafferty, and Maeve need to strategize about Gambino before the Labor Day festivities begin."

She stands on tiptoe and kisses Mick. "The appointment that's *imperative* you be at is at eighteen weeks—the one when we find out the baby's gender."

Mick swoops Emma up into his arms. Then, as he carries her to their bed, he says, "I wouldn't miss it for the world."

Emma circles her arms around Mick's neck. *And I wouldn't have you miss making a plan to take Gambino out of commission before he kills another friend or family member.*

Joe Bingham replays his phone conversation with Mick about Gambino and the ensuing implications. *If this were a military situation, Gambino's breach of Pines & Quill would escalate the THREATCON level from Bravo to Charlie. But if he'd touched one of our family or friends, it would have gone straight to Delta—the highest level of threat. I'm glad that Rafferty and Maeve will be here, too, so we can make a plan to catch that homicidal maniac and put him away. Or die trying.*

He glances through the open driver's window as he pulls up to the entry gates at Pines & Quill. Inhaling the crisp pine-scented air, he sees the brightening eastern sky cast an orangish-pink glow. The *cree-cree* chatter of red-winged blackbirds pierces the morning's hush. When his fists tighten around the steering wheel, his cuff hikes up, exposing his watch—*seven o'clock.*

I promised Marci and the girls that I wouldn't work the weekend. That we're here to enjoy ourselves and have fun, but that was before Gambino reared his ugly head again. Because Mick, Rafferty, and Maeve will be here, it's the ideal time to strategize how to catch Gambino and put him away. How am I going to explain this to my gals?

Joe fishes in his pocket for an antacid tablet. *That and the fact that Gambino's ability to get on the property undetected means Pines & Quill is no longer safe. Not for any of us.* He takes a deep inhalation to calm himself. His warm breath forms a white cloud in the cold air when he exhales. He purposely lowers his shoulders and takes this moment to appreciate his alone time. Being a homicide detective and living with three women—his wife, Marci, and their two daughters, Carly and Brianna—the only time to himself is when he works on his "baby"—a 1980 Chevrolet Camaro Z28—in the garage.

The females in our home aren't at all interested in the car. Well, except for Carly. At thirteen, she calls my car a "stud magnet" because all the boys gather around and drool on our daddy-daughter date nights when we pull into Boomer's Drive-In. Pop the hood, and they go slack-jawed at the beautifully polished components.

Joe opens the car door, walks to the entry gate, and inputs the code. When he turns back to his car, he smiles. *I do love Carousel Red. And when you finish it off with seriously wide rubber on iconic Cragar SS wheels, it's a total power package that looks right and handles like a mean machine should.*

Driving toward the main house along the winding lane, Joe maneuvers the first bend, but the car keeps moving in the direction of the turn. He has to overcorrect the steering to stay on the road. "Well, crap! I've got a flat tire." He pulls to the side, cuts the engine, and gets out of the car. Opening the trunk, he's astounded that the spare and the jack are missing.

"What the hell?"

———————

Maeve and her passenger, Maureen, drive up the winding lane to Pines & Quill in companionable silence. Maeve fixes her gaze over the steering wheel out of the windshield. *That's strange. I wonder why Joe's muscle car is on the side of the road.* She pulls to a stop behind his car and turns to Maureen.

"I'll be right back."

After exiting her vehicle, she walks around Joe's Chevy. She doesn't see him inside but notes the flat tire. When she gets back in her car, she says, "Joe's got a flat. He must have walked the rest of the way to the main house."

"I wonder why he didn't change it?"

"He probably didn't want to get all dirty before breakfast."

Maeve starts her car, then, like a pendulum, her mind swings back to the problem at hand—*How do we flush Georgio "The Bull" Gambino out of hiding?*

No one knows what he looks like; he could be among us, and we wouldn't be any the wiser. The last known photograph of him is decades old. And the last time I saw his face was over thirty years ago when I was formally profiling cases for the FBI. But since then, he's probably had plastic surgery and most certainly conducts his legitimate business dealings under an assumed name. That he, or one of his lieutenants, entered the main house is like a chess threat. We were taught to think about tactical moves like chess in FBI training. The instructors drilled it into our heads: "It's fundamental in chess to be able to detect the opposing threat before thinking of your own attacking possibilities. Since you know the value of the pieces, you're probably looking at opportunities to capture your opponent's pieces. But then again, so is your opponent."

Maeve tightens her grip on the steering wheel as she remembers the instructor's example. *"Let's imagine you capture the opposing bishop, thus taking a three-point advantage, and your opponent captures your queen on the next move. He'll get a huge six-point advantage on the material balance—because your queen is worth nine points—and we've already seen that a six-point advantage is usually enough to win the game. So, in this case, spotting an incoming threat is more important than finding the opportunity."*

Fear constricts Maeve's throat as she transfers the chess threat scenario to real life. *Is Gambino about to take a hostage? If that's the case, how can we stop him?*

Deep in thought, she taps her fingers on the steering wheel. *Georgio and his assumed identity can't ever be in the same room at the same time. Now, that's an interesting prospect. How we can leverage it to checkmate "The Bull"?*

Rafferty slips back into the car after inputting the code on the massive entry gate at Pines & Quill. *I wonder how everyone's doing after last night's discovery? With Gambino upping the ante, we have to act fast. But I don't want to scare Ivy.*

Rafferty pats his belly. "My stomach's growling in anticipation of Niall's cooking."

"I'm hungry, too," Ivy says. Maggie emits little yips of joy throughout a nonstop full-body wag in the backseat.

Ivy taps the red-tipped white cane folded on her lap. "It's a good thing Maggie's off duty when she's here. I bet she already smells Hemingway's scent. And I'm pretty sure she's going to bolt from the car the minute you open the door, so I'm glad I already took her harness off."

"Speak of the devil," Rafferty says.

"What is it?"

"Hemingway's barreling down the lane. Even though he knows my car, I'm sure he's already picked up Maggie's scent." Rafferty brings the car to a stop and gets out. "Hey, big fella."

When Hemingway screeches to a stop, he stands on his hind legs, gives Rafferty a cursory lick up the side of his face, then maneuvers to see into the open rear passenger window. Delirious with joy, his long, slightly curved tail whips back and forth—dangerous if Rafferty hadn't moved.

"All right already," Rafferty says, careful to stand clear as he opens the back door.

Maggie's lithe body bursts from the car, and, like a streak of white with black lightning, she sprints up the lane.

Fast on her heels, Hemingway kicks it into breakneck speed and passes her.

She stays on him like white on rice.

Rounding the bend, they're soon out of sight. But Rafferty and Ivy hear them barking ecstatically, as if the world's just been dunked in gravy.

Before slipping back into the car, Rafferty looks around for danger. *The tall, thick foliage between the tree trunks is perfect camouflage for someone who wants to hide.* He also gazes up into the thick-leafed limbs.

"I think Maggie's smitten with Hemingway," Ivy says.

Rafferty takes Ivy's hand and squeezes it. "I think it's a two-way street." From the smile on her face, he knows she caught his double meaning.

Gambino's breach of the main house at Pines & Quill was a taunt. That madman believes he's untouchable, so he continues to traffic drugs, weapons, and humans. But it's not the first time a kingpin's been under the wrong impression. Everyone has a weak link. And we're going to find his, then nail him to the wall.

As Niall and Libby return from delivering breakfast to the writers in residents' cottages, he squeezes Libby's hand. "One breakfast down. One to go."

"I'm looking forward to sharing a meal with our *other* guests and catching up. I wonder if any of them are here yet?" Libby says.

Just then, two dogs whip past them.

Niall grabs his hair like he's hanging onto it. "They went by so fast it was hard to tell, but I think that was Hemingway and Maggie."

Libby laughs. "They're probably out on the bluff by now."

When they enter the main house through the mudroom, Niall sees that all but two of the nine place settings are occupied. He lets his gaze go around the table: Maeve, Maureen, Rafferty, Ivy, Joe, Mick, and Emma. The remaining two place settings are for him and Libby.

Niall bustles toward the kitchen area. Over his shoulder, he says, "Why are your plates empty? You should have dug in."

Libby joins him, and they don striped bistro aprons and oven mitts. As they carry hot platters to the table, a combination of decadent scents, both sweet and savory, fills the air—sweet, from the peach and strawberry sheet tray pancakes, and savory, from the Mexican chilaquiles.

Niall says, "Joe, would you pour the coffee, please? And Mick, will you pour the juice?"

"On it," the men say in unison as they scoot back their chairs.

The hum of conversation around the table rises and falls as they eat, catch up, and exclaim over the meal.

"I've lived in San Diego for decades," Maureen says. "It's just across the border from Tijuana. And I guarantee you that I've never tasted chilaquiles this good. These are exceptional."

Niall beams. "Thank you."

"And I've never had sheet tray pancakes with or without peaches and strawberries," Ivy says. "I'd love to have this recipe."

"I'd be happy to share it with you," Niall says.

Barking sounds outside the mudroom door interrupt the conversation.

"That's Hemingway and Maggie," Mick says. "I'll let them in."

"Please close the bottom half of the Dutch door, Mick," Maeve says. "As much as I love dogs, I don't want to share my meal with them."

After Mick closes the Dutch door behind him, walks past the washer and dryer, and opens the exterior mudroom door, he quickly slams it shut. "Oh, my God!"

Niall grabs his chest. "What is it?"

"One or both of them got sprayed by a skunk."

"Oh, Lord," Niall moans, scraping back his chair. He looks at each man in turn—Joe, Rafferty, and Mick. "This isn't the first time this has happened."

Mick turns around in the mudroom and opens a cupboard. "I know where the skunk kit is."

"What's a skunk kit?" Maureen asks.

"It's a box loaded with everything we need," Niall says. "The first time it happened was to Kipling, Hemingway's third great-grandfather. We called Dr. Sutton. He's still our vet out at Fairhaven Veterinary Hospital. Anyway, he gave us the de-skunk recipe, and it's never failed. Of course, we double it because of Hemingway's size, but basically you mix together a quart of three percent hydrogen peroxide, a quarter cup of baking soda, and a teaspoon of dishwashing soap. And we need to hurry. Guys, we've got to put on rubber gloves and wash the dogs—"

"Outside with a hose," Libby interjects.

"Right," Niall nods. "We're going to rub the mixture into their coats, careful to avoid their eyes. Then we wait about twenty minutes before rinsing their fur. After that, we'll bathe them with dog shampoo and rinse them again."

"And we'll repeat the process as many times as necessary," Mick says.

Niall's in his element. *There's nothing like family, friends that are family, and our dogs.*

Libby clasps her hands in front of her chest as she looks at the women seated around the table. "Ladies, while the guys are otherwise occupied—" She pinches her nostrils together with a thumb and forefinger. "What would you think about helping me decorate the pavilion for the Labor Day festivities?"

Emma stands from the table. "I would love to help, but I've got an eleven-week appointment with Dr. Freeman, so I need to get going."

"Watch out," Maureen, her mother, says. "If you smile any wider, your face is going to split."

Emma laughs. "I'll see you when I get back. If there's anything left to do, I'll be happy to jump in and help." And with that, she heads down the hall and out the front door.

"I swear that girl is walking on air," Maeve says.

Libby clears her throat. "Getting back to business, ladies, do I have any volunteers?"

Ivy's hand shoots into the air. "Count me in," she says. "I'll supervise."

Everyone's quiet until Ivy slaps the top of her thighs and laughs. "Seriously, though, I want to come along. You can tell me what you're doing as you work."

"That's brilliant," Libby says. "And *you* can help me carry the ladder. If I take the front end and you take the back, I can lead the way. Sort of like Maggie, but without the stink."

"Well," Ivy says tentatively, "it's worth a shot."

Maeve turns to her daughter. "Libby, where are the decorations, hammers, nails, and the rest of the supplies?"

Libby gestures toward the sliding glass doors. "They're in covered plastic totes on the patio."

"All right, then," Maeve says, standing from the table. "Once we gather everything, we'll take your cane, Ivy, so you'll have it with you at the pavilion."

Much boisterous laughter later, the women finally arrive at the structure and get serious. First, Libby opens a folding chair for Ivy and places it in the center of the floor. Then she and Maureen open the ladder by one of the large corner supports.

"Libby, are you good with heights?" Maureen asks.

"Yes, I sure am."

"Oh, good, because I'm not." Maureen turns to Maeve. "How about if the two of us bring Libby what she asks for?"

"That works for me," Maeve says.

After ensuring the spreaders are locked into place, Libby climbs the ladder to the third rung from the top—well below the safety warning. She turns, peers up into a dark corner, and makes an exaggerated shiver. "I sure hope there aren't any spiders up there."

Removing the cell phone from her back pocket, she activates the flashlight feature and then aims it into the dark recess. What she sees is much more frightening than any spider. Libby is staring into the fishbowl lens of a surveillance camera.

———

Joe—up to his elbows in soap suds and wet dog fur—says, "Hey, guys, the cell phone in my butt pocket's going crazy. I need to check it."

He steps away from the water spray, peels off the bright yellow rubber gloves, and extracts the phone. *Oh, crap. Marci's been texting, calling, and trying to reach me.*

Joe speed dials Marci.

When she picks up, he starts to explain why he was preoccupied but is cut off by Marci's frantic, rapid-fire words.

After fifteen years of marriage, Joe can tell that she's barely holding it together. So, he lets her talk without interruption.

As Marci's words register, fear wraps its icy fingers around his throat and squeezes.

———————

Emma can't help the face-splitting grin she wears as she walks from the doctor's office to her car under the blue dome of the early September sky. The medical center is busy today, so she parked across the street in the outer lot. *No problem. A good brisk walk is good for the baby and me.*

As she walks, she thinks about what Dr. Freeman said. "At eleven weeks, you're still in the first trimester, which, as you know, is conception through week fourteen. Your baby's no longer an embryo. This week is the beginning of the fetal period. All vital organs are in place, and many of them have already started functioning. By the end of this week, your baby's external genitals will begin developing, and in a few weeks, you'll be able to see on an ultrasound whether you're having a girl or a boy.

"At this stage, your baby's just over one and a half inches long from head to bottom; it's about the size of a fig. He or she weighs about a quarter of an ounce and is almost fully formed. Their hands will soon open and close into fists, tiny tooth buds are beginning to appear under their gums, and some of their bones are beginning to harden."

Emma pauses at the street and places a hand on her belly. She hears the *tic tic tic* of the crosswalk timer. *I can hardly wait to get home and tell Mick.*

As she steps off the curb, a white panel van screeches to a halt in front of her. The side panel bursts open, and two men jump out to grab her. Their heads are covered with black hoods like balaclava face masks but with black mesh over the eye areas. Her scream is stifled by a meaty hand as she tries to jerk free. One of them hauls her off her feet and throws her into the van. She hits her head as she lands on her back. Before she can move, another hooded man with a roll of duct tape straddles her.

The panel door slams closed, and the van drives away.

As the man straddling her belly duct tapes Emma's mouth shut, she bucks up from beneath him, wrenching out of the other man's hold. Aiming for his face with the heel of her hand, she makes contact. His hands fly to his hooded face. He tumbles off her, howling.

Emma rises to a sitting position, rearing her elbow back and connecting it hard with the other man.

He whirls her around and slaps her across the face. "You fucking bitch!"

The driver yells over his shoulder. "The boss said don't hurt the merchandise."

"Then someone stick her with the goddamn syringe."

Ice-cold tentacles of fear wind their way through every nerve in Emma's body.

The guy she'd hit in the face grabs a syringe from a duffle and removes the cap. When he gets within range, she shoots out the heel of her foot and slams it into his groin.

CHAPTER 8

*"One of the few things I know about writing
is this: spend it all, shoot it, play it, lose it, all,
right away, every time. Do not hoard what
seems good for a later place ... something more
will arise for later, something better."*
—ANNIE DILLARD

M ick knows Joe all too well. While on the phone, Joe's posture changes from carefree to ramrod straight. Distress lines etch his face.

No longer the focal point, Hemingway and Maggie take the opportunity to slink away from the men who minutes ago were elbows deep in suds, hell-bent on bathing them.

Mick watches the blood drain from Joe's face. *It's gone from healthy and robust to ghostly since he called Marci.* When the call ends, Joe croaks, "I need to borrow your Jeep."

Mick pulls off the yellow rubber gloves, digs in his front jean's pocket, then tosses his keys to Joe. "What's wrong? Are Marci and the girls okay?"

One-handed, Joe catches the keys. "She said the girls—"

Just then, Mick's, Joe's, and Rafferty's phones ring simultaneously.

Mick feels a foreboding twist in his gut.

Joe's phone is still in his hand.

Mick and Rafferty retrieve cell phones from their pockets.

Mick sees a FaceTime call from "Unknown" on his screen. He looks at Joe and Rafferty, raising his eyebrows in question.

"FaceTime. Unknown," they both say.

"Answer on the count of three," Mick says. "One. Two. Three." He nods and they each press accept.

A hooded man is visible on their displays. He sits in front of a plain white background. "Hello, gentlemen." He chuckles. "You've got to love technology."

"Who are you?" Mick asks.

"If you have to ask, then you're not as intelligent as I gave you credit for."

"You're Georgio Gambino," Mick says as he realizes who's on the other end. Wet from washing the dogs, Mick's already chilled, but Gambino's call ups the ante, sending icy sparks shooting up his spine.

The hooded figure nods. "Yes, that's correct." He then raises a black-gloved hand and points to the camera. "I know what you're thinking, and you can forget about it. Regardless of how long *I* keep you on the phone, this call is not traceable. And yes, you heard me correctly. *I'm* in charge of this call." He points to his chest. "*I'm* the one who's calling the shots."

Mick rubs the thigh of his damaged leg as he paces in the yard. "What do you want?" He studies the hooded figure on the phone. *Why is he wearing gloves?*

"I think Mr. Bingham already knows, isn't that right, Joe?"

"I just spoke with my wife. She said that our daughters didn't make it home from school."

Mouths agape, Mick, Niall, and Rafferty turn their wide-eyed attention to Joe.

"That's right," Gambino says. "Marci—" He pauses and tilts his head to one side. "You don't mind if I call her *Marci*, do you?"

Mick sees Joe ball his free hand into a fist as his anger mounts with each of Gambino's words.

"I've got Carly and Brianna," Georgio says. "But that's not all."

Mick's throat constricts with fear as he glances at the time on the cell phone display. *Emma should be home by now.*

"That's right, Mick. Unfortunately, Emma's a bit late from her eleven-week prenatal appointment."

Heart racing, Mick's brain feels like it's spinning out of control. He clenches his free hand; the fingernails bite into his palm. "Where is she?"

"Oh, she's in good company. She's with Carly and Brianna. But let me tell you—" He slaps his thigh. "One of my men may no longer be able to father children after tangling with her. She got him right in the nuts."

Mick's breath is unsteady. He inhales from his diaphragm to calm himself. Sweat from his hairline stings his eyes. He uses his forearm to wipe them. "What will it take to get them back?" He hears the tremble in his voice.

Just then, Libby, Ivy, Maeve, and Maureen rush up. Ivy, guided between Libby and Maeve, stands next to Rafferty.

"What's going on?" Libby asks.

Mick lifts his cell phone. "Gambino FaceTimed us."

Shock washes over the women's faces.

Libby and Maureen step over to Mick so they can see his screen.

Maureen and Niall look at Joe's.

Gambino rubs his gloved hands together. "Welcome. I'm so glad we're *all* here now," he says in a saccharine-coated voice. "Now that I have your attention, I'd like you to look at Maeve and tell me what you see."

When Mick sees the red laser sight dot on his mother's forehead, he dives, taking them both to the ground.

Gambino roars with laughter. "I believe I've made it abundantly clear that you're in my sights both literally and figuratively."

Mick helps his mother to her feet. The red dot's still on her forehead.

Their eyes scan the area, looking for Gambino's sniper.

"You won't find him," Gambino says. "He's a long-distance marksman, like the one Mick and Emma encountered in June on their whale-watching trip to San Juan Island."

"That guy missed," Mick says.

"I can demonstrate that *this* one won't. Would you like me to prove my point?"

"No," Mick says, moving to stand in front of his mother.

"Okay then," Gambino says. "Let's get back to business." He rubs his gloved hands together. "Libby, just a few minutes ago, I watched as you discovered one of my security cameras. The look on your face was priceless."

The men turn to Libby. "A security camera?" Mick asks.

"Not *a* security camera," Gambino corrects. "But one of *many* set up throughout your property."

Mick's mind races as the sinister turn of events washes over him. Like a tidal wave, it nearly knocks him off his feet. *Gambino has my wife, our unborn child, and Joe's daughters. We've got to do something. Fast. But what? Where do we even begin?* Mick inhales deeply as the feeling of helplessness overwhelms him.

Gambino's voice interrupts Mick's thoughts. "Oh, and Joe, before I forget, I saw that you had a flat tire. You'll want to be sure to check that valve stem. And in case you're wondering where your spare tire and jack are, I've got them. It's my way of letting you know that I can infiltrate *any* place, even a homicide detective's home. Just like I did when I had one of my lieutenants write that message in the journal in the Ink Well at the main house."

Joe's face looks stricken; his Adam's apple bobs rapidly.

Mick repeats his unanswered question. "What will it take to get Emma, Carly, and Brianna back?"

With a look of horror on her face, Libby grabs her brother's arms. "He's got them?"

Mick nods.

"Oh, but you *don't* get them back," Gambino says. A scathing tone has replaced the playfulness in his voice. "Toni Bianco was my daughter, and she's dead. I don't get *my* kid back. You don't get *your* kids back."

Unable to contain himself, Mick shouts. "Give them back, you bastard!"

"Don't interrupt me," Gambino says. "She was a cop on the inside of the Bellingham precinct. Do you have *any* idea what that was worth to me?"

Joe, Toni's ex-partner, opens his mouth to say something.

Gambino holds a hand up. "Stop. That was a rhetorical question. I'm a *business* man. I trade and sell drugs and weapons to the highest bidder. And I sell women, girls—and a few boys every now and then—to customers who have . . ." He pauses a moment. ". . . let's call it a *special* taste in entertainment. And with Toni's assistance, much of that went unnoticed."

Mick's mind mounts with terror at every word Gambino utters. He tastes blood from biting the inside of his cheek. "But we didn't kill her. After she shot Rafferty during the fireworks on the Fourth of July, Toni was wounded and went to the hospital. She pulled through surgery and her prognosis was good."

"That's right," Gambino says. "Her prognosis was *too* good. She would have turned state's evidence against me to save her own skin. And though I would have understood it, I couldn't have it. So I resolved the problem."

Oh, my God; he killed his own daughter. He's like a lion who hunts and eats its own young to eliminate rivals.

Gambino aims a thumb at his chest. "Toni paid for the sins of her old man. Now *your* children are going to pay for *your* sins."

"But we haven't done anything," Mick says, buying time as a plan starts to form in the back of his mind.

"You're trying to shut me down. And in doing so, you've cost me time, money, and people. Now I have Joe's kids. And in Emma's case, I got a twofer because she's a necessary incubator for your child."

You're damn right we're going to shut you down, you psychopath. Mick remembers what his psychology professor said. "Narcissists, sociopaths, and psychopaths make great chameleons. They manipulate situations to get what they want. Psychopaths in particular view the world as an instrument to fulfill their desires."

Joe swallows a sob and shakes his head. "We'll find them."

"No, you won't. That's the beauty of my plan," Gambino says.

"What plan?" Rafferty asks.

"I'm going to spell it out for you," Gambino says. "And I'm only going to say it once, so listen carefully."

Like a snake, his voice slithers through their cell phones, coiling around their hearts.

"I am going to dismantle your lives and everything you hold dear.

"*Joe*, if you try to save your daughters, Carly and Brianna, I will kill Mick's wife. And the child she's carrying will die as a result.

"*Mick*, if you try to save Emma and your unborn baby, I will kill Joe's daughters.

"*Rafferty*, I already killed your son, Drew. So, if you try to save Emma, Carly, or Brianna to help your friends, I'll have to kill Ivy. She won't even see it coming." Gambino laughs at his joke. "Get it? Ivy's blind. She won't *see* it coming."

Ivy presses her palms against her stomach as if kicked in the gut.

Mick's anger contracts to a hard point of rage. *Check yourself, Mick. If you lose it, Gambino wins.* Mick intentionally lowers his shoulders. *That's right, do what Dad taught you—leverage your anger to hone your plan.*

Rafferty's face contorts from anger to disbelief back to anger. "You won't lay a hand on her," he says through clenched teeth. "And what do you mean you *killed* my son? He died in a car accident."

Mick hears the choking rage in his friend's voice. Aware that Gambino is watching them, Mick works to maintain calm—at least on the outside. *Don't feed the psychopath's ego.*

Gambino makes a *tsk* sound with his tongue and teeth. "Three years ago you were getting close to nailing a high-stakes case that would have meant the loss of a great deal of money for me. I *had* to do something." He lifts his gloved palms and shrugs. "So, I orchestrated that car accident as a diversionary tactic to derail you. It worked. And once again, a child paid for the sins of their father."

Rafferty bends at the waist and grips his thighs with his hands. His gut-wrenching cry sends riptides of electric fear through Mick.

Rafferty's anguish hits Ivy like a tsunami. She drops to her knees and covers her mouth with a hand to keep from crying out.

"There, there now," Gambino says to Rafferty in mock placation.

Rafferty releases his thighs and stands. Tears course down his cheeks.

Beyond rage, Mick plunges to an emotional depth that makes it hard to breathe. He positions his cell phone close to his face. "Don't you *dare* harm a hair on their heads."

"Says the man with a laser dot on his chest," Gambino taunts.

Mick looks down at the red dot over his heart. *After we get Emma and the girls back, I'm going to kill that bastard.*

"I wouldn't think of harming them," Gambino says. "As long as they remain in pristine condition, they'll fetch an extremely large price. Especially Emma with her deep red hair and pale skin—she's a much sought-after commodity where she's going."

Fear feasts on Mick's mind; his body vibrates with anger. He fists and releases his free hand. He feels the veins in his neck bulge against his collar.

Gambino shakes his head. "No, I wouldn't dream of killing them. Of course, they'll *wish* they were dead, but it won't be by my hand. I give you my word. Now listen up.

"Do *not* contact the police or the FBI. You're to maintain business as usual. No one is to be made aware of Emma's, Carly's, or Brianna's abductions. I'm sure you'll think of a plausible excuse. Come on now," he continues, "it's Labor Day weekend. You're supposed to have fun."

Gambino shifts in his chair, leans forward, and points a gloved index finger. "But remember this. I have eyes and ears *everywhere*. I monitor your emails, landline, cell phone conversations and locations, vehicles, credit card activity, and internet searches . . . *everything*.

"If you find and remove any surveillance equipment or tracking devices—yes, they're on all of your vehicles—I'll start picking your guests off one by one." Gambino shakes his hooded head. "And as a businessman, I guarantee you that it won't be good for Pines & Quill.

"Do. Not. Fuck. With. Me."

After Gambino disconnects the call, everyone starts talking at once.

Mick raises his hand in a silencing motion, then places his cell phone on the ground and gestures for the others to do the same. *Follow me*, he mouths before leading the group out to the bluff overlooking Bellingham Bay.

Emma wakes to vibration and the unmistakable whir of helicopter blades. She tries to open her eyelids, but they're heavy. *The noise is deafening, and my head is pounding.* When she attempts to cover her ears, she sways sideways, and her shoulder comes into contact with some type of barrier. *My hands are restrained behind my back.*

She tests her legs. *I can separate my knees, but my ankles are bound.*

Then, with startling clarity, it all comes rushing back— *The van. The men. The fight. The doctor's appointment.* A rush of adrenaline hits her system. She tries to protect her stomach, but with her hands secured behind her back, it's futile. *Oh, God, please let the baby be okay.* Her cry is muffled by tape across her mouth.

And though she's managed to slit her eyes open now, it's almost dark—*all except for tiny pinpoints of light.* Emma inhales deeply through her nostrils and smells wool. *They must have put one of those hoods they're wearing over my head too. But it doesn't have any mesh where my eyes are. They probably put it on me backward so I can't see anything.*

Emma tips her head back. From beneath the edge of the hood, she sees the back of the pilot's head and shoulder and the same view of another person in the front passenger seat. *They're wearing headsets to communicate over the noise of the helicopter's rudder and blades.*

She shifts herself closer to the vibrating barrier and tips

her head back again. *There's light just below my chin.* When she leans her head back even farther, she sees that she's next to a window. Scooting even closer, she angles her head to see out. In the distance, she sees a mountain. She recognizes its familiar silhouette against the sun. *Mount Baker. We're heading east.*

Sitting back in her seat against her arms, she calculates. *It's just over thirty miles as the crow flies from Bellingham to Mount Baker.* When she slants her head against the window to contemplate this information, the opening of the hood below her chin shifts, and she sees two pairs of legs bound at the ankles by duct tape. She twists her neck for a better view. *There are two hooded people next to me. Who are they, and where are they taking us?*

Emma cocks her head when she hears the noise signature of the helicopter blades change from *thwack thwack thwack* to more of a slap that seems to keep time with the pounding fear of her heart.

As the helicopter descends, the front passenger removes his headphones and slips a black hood over his head. He steps toward the back, leaning past her and the other two passengers. Then he widens his stance and slides what looks like a rescue basket between his legs. Finally, he turns and angles it horizontally on the floor between the front and back seats and gives a thumbs-up to the pilot.

When realization dawns on Emma, she remains limp against her seat, letting the hooded man think that she's still unconscious.

He grabs her shoulders, pulls her forward, and spills her into the metal form, letting gravity do the work. After positioning her body, he secures it with five straps pulled tightly across her sternum, ribs, waist, thighs, and shins.

Wind whips inside the helicopter when the door slides open. Even so, Emma hears what her dad and brothers use

when they go off-roading and a truck gets stuck in the mud—
the whine of a winch system.

Terror stabs Emma's heart when she's launched out the
door and freefalls. Then a sudden jerk of her entire body
informs her that the chain or rope or whatever's holding her
basket midair has reached its initial length and is now descend-
ing mechanically.

Someone whisks the hood off Emma's head when the
basket reaches the ground. She's surrounded by four black-
clad, hooded men in a small forest clearing. Panic surges
through her veins. It's hard to swallow around the fear lodged
in her throat. She closes her eyes. *Oh, Mick, I've never been
this scared in my life. Please find me.*

When she opens her eyes, Emma gazes past the men and
looks more closely at the tree line. *Those are bristlecone pine.*
She remembers what Mick said when they picnicked in the
Snoqualmie National Forest. "Bristlecone pine only live in
mountain regions of six western states. Mount Baker in Washington is one of them."

And though the prop wash from the helicopter hovering overhead scrambles the words, Emma is certain she hears,
"Welcome, Mrs. McPherson, we've been waiting for you."

CHAPTER 9

*"Let the world burn through you. Throw
the prism light, white hot, on paper."*
—RAY BRADBURY

US Marshal Jake Porter brings his rental car to a stop at
a massive wrought-iron entry gate. Its overhead sign
silhouetted against a softly caressing sun beckons, WELCOME
TO PINES & QUILL.

His nostrils catch the scent of pine when he opens the
door and steps out. Goosebumps rough Jake's arms—but not
from the weather. *Someone's watching me.*

He places his Stetson on his head, then takes in the surroundings from under the shade of its brim. He does a full
three-sixty—noting the tall pines and long, winding drive that
disappears after the first bend—but doesn't hear or see anyone.

After pressing the intercom button on the gate's keypad,
he continues to scan the area.

Outwardly, Jake maintains what looks like idle curiosity.
*Anyone watching me will see a regular Joe—a man in a chambray
snap-pocket shirt, bootcut jeans, and Ariat cowboy boots.*

Inwardly, he's actively assessing his tactical exposure—finding points of egress and possible cover—the way he does when entering any enclosed space.

Jake glances at his watch. *It's just after one.* He draws his brows together. *That's odd. I wonder why no one's answering?* He presses the button again. Then, after waiting for a few more beats, he fobs the rental car locked and climbs over the gate. When he lands, he adjusts his hat, then checks the five o'clock position at his waist. *My gun's still secure in the clip holster.*

He was glad when the US Marshals Service SOG—Special Operations Group—that he's part of started using the STI 2011. It's a double-stack 9mm variant of the venerable 1911 pistol—a design that's over one hundred years old.

Jake bends and dusts off his Ariats. His backup—a .38 revolver—is in his left boot. Straightening, he continues to scan the area. *Sarah sure will be surprised; I'm a day earlier than she expects. Let's see now . . .* He scratches the bristle on his jawline. *Sarah showed me the Pines & Quill website after receiving her cottage assignment—Thoreau. It overlooks a national park on the south end of the property.*

With the tall pine trees blocking his view of the sun, he checks the compass on his watch. Bypassing the lane that leads to the main house, Jake heads south. After a bit, he sees what he believes to be Thoreau Cottage. He also sees two large dogs charging toward him through the tree trunks. Teeth bared, the huge gray one barks an ominous warning. The black-and-white one echoes the menacing threat.

Oh, shit! Jake runs, bounds over the porch steps, and sees a sign: THOREAU COTTAGE. *Please let the door be unlocked.* He twists the knob, yanks it open, and jumps inside just as the two wet dogs land on the porch, snarling.

Jake slams the door and leans against it, panting. *Holy Mother of God. What the hell was that?*

Mick leads his family and friends to the windswept bluff above Bellingham Bay. He knows experientially that for him, clarity sharpens in crisis mode. With each step, his mind races with a plan to save Emma and the girls. He scans the area for security cameras. *Just because I don't see any doesn't mean they're not there. And the red laser dot on Mom's forehead and my own chest earlier proves that Gambino's not bluffing.*

After they're well past the tree line, Mick stops at a spot a few yards from the cliff overlooking Bellingham Bay. The clear expanse offers them a breathtaking view. Rolling steel-blue waves shimmer beneath a cloud-flecked sky as they bulge and retreat against the boulder-strewn shore. Their murmur has a hypnotic rhythm. A raft of seabirds lifts off the chop a hundred yards out and then skims over the surface of the waves. Mick closes his eyes and inhales deeply to brace himself. The sweet and pungent scent of ozone—the telling smell of a coming storm—mingles with the tang of brine.

He turns to face his family and friends. "Since Gambino's tracking our cell phones, let him think we're still standing in the side yard next to the main house. Out here"—he gestures with a hand to the expansive bluff—"there's no place to hide surveillance equipment. And the noise from the wind and the waves hitting the shore makes listening impossible.

"Gambino told us to conduct business as usual. So we'll set up a shooting range for target practice on the bluff as part of our Labor Day festivities. If he's been watching us, he knows that's not uncommon. We'll use that task to talk. Outside of that, we'll have to write and pass notes."

Mick looks into the haggard faces of the people he loves—Maeve, Maureen, Rafferty, Ivy, Joe, Niall, and Libby. "Does everyone agree?"

Each of them nods.

Maeve says, "I have something that might help. Because I thought we were going to play Spy this weekend, I brought a pair of encrypted walkie-talkies. They don't use cell towers, and there's no way to track a signal."

Mick nods. "That's excellent, Mom. But if Gambino has placed listening devices throughout Pines & Quill, he might hear us speaking into them. And the range probably isn't much more than the acreage here. We need something to communicate with when we leave Pines & Quill."

"I'm glad to hear you say that," Joe says, "because there's *no* way I'm not going to go find my daughters."

"And there's *no* way I'm not going to go find Emma," Mick says. "I have an idea, but I need to talk with my mom and Libby first. Will you give us a minute?"

After the three of them step away, Mick says, "Mom, Libby and I each have an encrypted burner and you have two, yours and Dad's. They were never supposed to be used outside the family."

"Your father said they're for 'the unthinkable.' This qualifies."

"I agree," Libby says. "Now let's get back to the others so you can share what's on your mind."

When they get back to the others, Mick looks at Joe. "Business as usual includes getting Marci. We also need to get two tires and a jack for your car. Gambino will see the charge on your card, but it falls under his qualification of business as usual."

"Why *two* tires?" Niall asks.

"To replace the flat and the spare that Gambino took." Niall nods.

"We're with you so far," Rafferty says.

"My dad set the four of us—him, Mom, Libby, and me—up with encrypted cell phones in the event 'the unthinkable' happens. Well, it has. The three of us—me, Joe, and Rafferty—will each take one."

"Who gets the fourth?" Niall asks.

"If you all agree, I think we should enlist the help of Sarah Porter's husband, Jake. He's a US Marshal, and he's due to arrive tomorrow."

"I'm good with that," Rafferty says.

"Are all four phones here at Pines & Quill?" Joe asks.

"No. Two are at Mom's condo." He turns to Maeve. "You and Maureen returning to your condo tonight is business as usual. No change there. You were going to do that anyway."

"That's right," Maeve says.

"Do you think it's bugged?" Maureen asks.

Maeve shakes her head. "It's not," she says with confidence.

Maureen raises her eyebrows a fraction of an inch. "How can you be so certain?"

"Being trained by the FBI during the Cold War, Connor and I were in the habit of sweeping our place every day. Even though he's gone, the habit's stayed."

"That mistake's going to cost Gambino," Rafferty says.

"What mistake?" Niall asks.

"He didn't count Maeve as a threat. And you know what they say: 'Never underestimate the power of a woman.'"

Maeve smiles at Rafferty. "And I swept the car too. There's no tracking device on it either."

Rafferty tips an imaginary hat. "I can only hope that one day I'll be half as good as you."

Mick puts an arm around his mom's shoulder. "The weather forecast said that though it's unusual for this time of year, there's going to be a storm tonight. Under cover of darkness, I'm going to walk to your place and get the other phones. When you get home, I need you to do two things."

"Just tell me what they are," Maeve says.

"Bag the phones in a plastic garbage bag and put them in the trashcan just inside your back gate. And then use the secure site and contact Emma's father and brothers. We're going to need them."

"Secure site?" Rafferty and Joe ask in unison.

"Yes," Mick says. "I'll explain later." He turns to Emma's mother. "Maureen, I hope you don't—"

Maureen holds up her hand to stop her son-in-law. "I don't mind at all. They would rather *die* than not help Emma and the girls. But won't Gambino see them on his surveillance equipment when they get here?"

"Yes, he will," Mick says. "But he'll think it's me, Joe, and Rafferty. And we'll need Phillip offsite, monitoring the equipment in the secure site while Mom and Maureen are here being accounted for."

"I don't understand," Libby says. "How will Gambino think that Eric, Ethan, and Ellery are the three of you?"

"We bought two different colored sets of baseball caps for the Spy teams this weekend. They'll pull the bills low. And whichever one we think looks the most like me will need to limp when he walks so it appears as authentic as possible. While Gambino thinks we're here doing business as usual, we'll actually be looking for Emma, Brianna, and Carly."

Rafferty rubs his jawline. "It just might work."

"It *has* to work," Joe says. "Now let's go get Marci. I don't want her to be alone."

"And remember," Mick says. "Once we get back to the main area, *write* anything that Gambino shouldn't hear. And be careful passing notes. It can't be obvious. If he's got surveillance everywhere, then it has to be part of something natural, like passing a casserole, or shaking someone's hand. Gambino warned that if he sees anything that's not business as usual, he'll kill Emma, Brianna, and Carly."

Emma blinks rapidly as one of the hooded men pulls a knife from a sheath and steps toward her. Terror mounts with each of his successive steps.

He bends over her. When he brings the knife down, she squeezes her eyes shut.

"Don't cut the straps," she hears one of the men call out. "We've got two more to bring down."

Relief floods Emma's veins, and she opens her eyes. Instead of cutting, he releases the buckles on the straps that secure her to the rescue basket.

Another man steps forward. They each grab one of her upper arms and yank her to a standing position, where she almost tips over. The man with the knife bends and cuts the duct tape around her ankles. When he stands up, he jerks her arm. "If you try anything, I'll gut you like a fish."

Emma remembers this morning's weather forecast; it predicted an unseasonable storm this evening. And though the temperature hasn't dropped yet, she's chilled to the bone, and her teeth chatter. *I've never been this scared in my life.* In her mind, she screams. *Mick, please help me!*

She knows she may not have time to wait for outside help. *If I'm going to save myself and the baby, I've got to pay attention.* As they walk her to a cabin perched at the edge of the clearing, Emma does a quick assessment. *The two windows I can see are boarded and have window security bars. There's a stone chimney, but no smoke rising from it. I don't see telephone poles, wires, or cables of any kind. And there are three trucks parked on the side of the cabin—one silver, two black—but I can't see the plates.*

Fear claws Emma's gut as they near the cabin. The thought of being trapped in an enclosed space with these men fills her with dread.

One of the hooded figures opens the front door. The other one shoves her into the space where two black-clad men hastily turn away and don black hoods.

I didn't see much; they both have longish dark hair, beards, and mustaches.

"Ya coulda warned us," one of them growls, then leans forward, rests his arms on his thighs, and lets his hands drop loose.

His skin is white.

"Knock it off," the man on her left says. Menace swims under his words, circling like a shark.

He must be the leader.

Emma takes a deep breath to brace herself but immediately regrets it. The stale smell of sweat and week-old pizza assaults her nostrils. *It smells like a frat house.* She scans the room, taking in as much as she can. *There's a card table with four folding chairs around it and two off to the side, an ice chest, several duffels and sleeping bags strewn on the floor, and a stack of porn magazines.* The top one lays limply open at the centerfold.

She continues to scan the room. *An overturned wooden crate next to the folding table holds a lit kerosene lamp, and there are two more, unlit, on the fireplace mantle.* Finally, Emma narrows her field of vision and homes in on a pizza box. The writing on the lid confirms her location—*Mount Baker Pizza. It's one of the last eateries before the long and winding drive up the mountain.*

Like bookends, the two men walk her down a dim hallway. The pounding of Emma's heart nearly drowns out the echo of their footsteps. *Why don't they cover my head?* She wonders as she counts doors—*Three on the right, two on the left.* Panic rises in the back of her throat as realization dawns on her. *They're going to kill me, so it doesn't matter what I see.*

When they reach the second door on the right, they stop. *The door's metal, and the hinges are on the outside.* The man on her left releases three shutter slide bolts—*they're about eight inches long and look like hand-forged iron.*

"Back away," the one on her left shouts, then kicks the door open with a clang.

The foul smell of human waste hits Emma so hard that her eyes sting. She gags behind her taped mouth.

The dim light from the hallway behind them does little to light the interior.

"I'm going to cut your wrists free," the man on her right says. "If you move, I might just *slice* you." All the more sinister, the word "slice" is delivered in a sibilant whisper.

A chill rises from Emma's heart.

"Hang on a sec," the leader says. He leans back out the doorway. "Bring a lamp and hurry it up."

On high alert, all of Emma's senses are heightened. She hears the thump of footsteps in the hallway as they draw near. *What sounds like gravel stuck in a boot tread makes a crunching sound with every other step.*

The man on her left steps back and says, "I'm going to let go of you. If you try anything, my friend here will make sure it's the last thing you ever do." He releases her arm.

From behind, Emma hears the pluck of a match. The hiss of a wick. Through the stench, she catches a whiff of kerosene.

Like a beacon in a storm, flickering light from the oil lamp illuminates the room.

Dread twists Emma's gut as several gaunt and dirty faces with despair-filled eyes stare back at her.

CHAPTER 10

*"Writing isn't about using words to impress. It's
about using simple words in an impressive way."*
—SIERRA BAILEY

Sarah Porter hops off the bicycle and places it back in the rack between the main house and the garden at Pines & Quill. She's thrilled with the hair makeover she received at Tangles Salon in Bellingham. *I'm so glad they were able to work me in. Libby was right; Rebecca's a magician.*

After removing the bicycle helmet, Sarah runs her fingers through her freshly cut and colored hair. *Oh, my gosh, I hope that Jake likes it when he gets here tomorrow.* She fluffs her bangs. *I don't want to have helmet hair if I run into anyone on my way to Thoreau Cottage.*

Just then, Sarah gets an uneasy sensation. *It feels like someone's watching me.* She pulls a compact from her purse and pretends to check her reflection while slowly sweeping the area behind her. *No movement, nothing.* She scans the shadows in the foreground and still doesn't see anything. *That's odd.*

Rather than put the mirror away, Sarah takes the opportunity to examine her new hairstyle and color. Her once chin-length brown hair threaded with silver strands is now pixie-short, sassy, and strawberry blond. She uncaps a tube of lipstick and applies a fresh touch of Framboise Moi—a rich raspberry pink that compliments her medium complexion and goes well with her new hair color. And though Sarah has been applying lipstick without a mirror for decades, she uses it to scan the area again. *Nothing.* Convinced she's mistaken about being watched, she smiles at her reflection. *You look good, Mrs. Porter, even if I say so myself.*

Sarah takes her time as she strolls toward Thoreau Cottage, her home away from home for three weeks. She looks up at the wispy clouds pinned to a crayon blue sky. *I don't see how this morning's weather forecast can be correct. There's no way there's going to be a storm tonight.*

Grass-like evergreen foliage with spikes of lilac-purple flowers whisper-shake in the gentle breeze on either side of the walkway. When Sarah had asked about the lush flowering shrubs, Libby'd said, "It's a bulb-type plant called Big Blue lilyturf. It's a perennial that blooms best in the late summer to fall and does well in both sunny and shady areas."

To her right, Sarah passes a copse of blue elderberry trees. *Beyond that is Austen Cottage, where Dale, the retired mariner pilot, is staying during his September residency.*

As she approaches the south end of the property, Sarah starts to pay even closer attention. *Thoreau Cottage is easy to miss because it blends in so well with the western red cedar trees that surround it.*

About twenty yards away, Sarah watches as two large dogs—*One is Hemingway, and the other one looks like a Standard poodle*—bound from Thoreau's front porch and lope toward her.

Hemingway sits on the ground at her feet. Happy to see her, his tail dusts the walkway.

Sarah, an animal lover, scratches the still-smelly dog underneath his whiskered chin. "Who's your friend?" She nods toward the smaller but equally wet and debris-ridden dog next to Hemingway.

Both dogs pant hard, but no answers are forthcoming.

"I'd love to play," Sarah says, "but I lost some time this morning and need to work on my manuscript." She points in the direction of the main house. "You two better go back home. I bet you can wag your way into a treat there."

At the word "treat," both dogs take off like racers after the bang of a starter's pistol and disappear in the thicket.

Sarah mounts Thoreau's front porch steps, passes the Adirondack chairs, and enters the cottage. As she walks past the bedroom doorway toward the living room and small kitchen area, a man's voice says, "Oh, my goodness. It seems I've made a mistake. I'm in the wrong cottage."

Adrenaline crashes through her before the voice registers. Sarah whirls around, her right arm cocked, and throws a punch.

With hair-trigger reflexes, Jake catches her fist in his mitt-sized right palm.

The surprise on her husband's face is nearly as big as the fright he'd given her.

"I meant to surprise you. Not scare you."

"Jake!" Sarah throws herself into his arms.

"That was quite an impressive reaction," Jake says.

Still hugging him, Sarah speaks into Jake's neck. "I think the combination of not expecting you until tomorrow and having just had the feeling of being watched pushed me over the edge into self-defense mode."

Jake takes Sarah's shoulders in his hands, steps back an arm's length, and looks into her eyes. "It's interesting you should say that because when I pulled the rental car up to the entry gates and got out, I had the feeling that I was being watched, too."

"That's odd. But it's got to be a coincidence. Right?" Sarah says. "We're both a little on edge. I know I'm still getting used to Pines & Quill. And you just came off a top-secret mission." She takes Jake's hands in hers. "Now tell me, when did you get here? Did Libby tell you which cottage is mine? I'm so happy to see—"

Jake interrupts her rapid-fire questions. "Let me get a good look at you." He studies her appearance and twirls her to see every angle. Then waggles his eyebrows and lets out a long low whistle. "You're a sight for sore eyes. You look completely different. I thought I was in the wrong cottage. You nearly gave me a heart attack."

Sarah lifts a hand to her hair. "So, you like it?"

He angles his head to the side. "I don't *like* it. I *love* it. You look great."

Sarah's heart nearly bursts with joy as Jake picks her up bride-style and carries her over the bedroom threshold. In part of her research for one of her books, she learned that during ancient times when women were married by capture, the bride obviously wouldn't go willingly into her husband's home. Thus the tradition of the groom carrying her over the threshold.

Sarah smiles into Jake's neck. *I'm more than willing.*

———

Joe rides shotgun as he, Mick, and Rafferty get into Mick's Jeep. Having worked undercover on a case with the FBI Child Exploitation and Human Trafficking Task Forces, Joe's painfully aware that after twenty-four hours, the odds drop dramatically for a victim's chances of being recovered alive and relatively unscarred. *I've been in a lot of tight places and seen some awful things, but I've never been this scared before in my life.* Succumbing to the feeling of dread, his stomach curls into a fetal position.

He turns his head and looks out the passenger window so Mick and Rafferty can't see the tears welling in his eyes. *I'm worried sick about Marci. She was frantic when she called. She and the girls are my world. On the first night of our honeymoon, I promised Marci that I would always protect her. And then, when we had children, I promised the same thing. I remember when the girls were born. I got to cut the umbilical cord each time. Now at thirteen, Carly wants to be a model. And at eleven, Brianna wants to be a NASCAR driver.* He unclenches his fists and wipes the tears that slide down his face. *Goddamnit! When we find Carly, Brianna, and Emma, I'm going to kill whoever has them.*

Joe mulls over the plan to get Emma's brothers and father to Pines & Quill and have the brothers stand in as lookalikes for him, Mick, and Rafferty so they can leave the property without Gambino's knowledge. *But what if it doesn't work? What then? Mick's as worried about Emma as I am about the girls. Gambino warned that if I try to find the girls, he'll kill Emma. If Mick tries to find Emma, he'll kill the girls. And if Rafferty tries to help either of us, he'll kill Ivy. The bastard's trying to pit us against each other. But I'll see him in hell first.*

Joe's mind shifts gears when they see a car with no driver parked just outside the Pines & Quill entrance gate.

They drive a few moments in silence, and then Mick furrows his brow and says, "Whose car is that?"

Joe points to a reminder note he taped to the dash—

Only say what we don't mind Gambino hearing.

He thinks back to a few months ago when he and Rafferty obtained authorization from Federal Judge Watson to plant listening devices in Toni Bianco's home and workstation at the precinct. That's when he learned that "bugs" can also be planted in vehicles. Easy to come by, they can be purchased over the internet, installed in cars, and then used to listen in on conversations.

The range can vary and the size can be anywhere from a deck of cards to a small matchbox for the general public. But for government, law enforcement, or when the cost is no object—like for Gambino—as the price and range increase, the size decreases to something about the size of a pinhead.

And though we didn't tap Toni's cell phone, I learned how easy it is with today's advanced technology. All you need is a cell phone number and a little technical savvy.

Mick slows as he pulls the Jeep next to the empty vehicle. Joe shakes his head. "Hurry!" he mouths to Mick.

We've got to get to Marci before she does anything. She's like a mother bear protecting her cubs when it comes to our girls. That, combined with her fear, means she's ready to do something. Anything. I don't want Gambino to take her too.

The Jeep's tires scorch the pavement. When they reach the main road, the side mirror informs Joe that a white van has pulled in behind them, three cars back. "Well, Gambino, if you're listening, you're as good as your word. We've got company."

Mick uses the rearview mirror, and Rafferty turns to check their tail out the back window.

"I can't be sure," Mick says, "but it could be the same van that tried to run me down at the airport."

"Count on it," Joe says. "But Marci was coming to Pines & Quill for the weekend anyway, so we're not out of line. Even if they report back to Gambino that we've left the property, what's he going to say? That we picked up Marci, some tires, and a jack? It's business as usual."

His gut twists again. Joe swallows a hot blast of bile climbing the back of his throat, then shouts, "Pull over!"

Before the Jeep comes to a complete stop, Joe opens the passenger door and spews the contents of his stomach on the shoulder of the road. Spent, he flops back onto the seat, reaches into his pocket, then pops a few antacid tablets into his mouth and chews.

Joe uncaps a water bottle from the middle console. He takes a swig to rinse his mouth, spits out the door, then wipes his face with the back of his hand. While replacing the bottle, Joe notices a tiny, barely raised surface that blends in with the cupholder's interior wall. Taking a closer look, he sees that it's a listening device similar to the one he and Rafferty used in Toni's house, only this one's even smaller. *Bingo!*

He gets Mick's and Rafferty's attention, gestures for them to remain quiet, then points to the device to confirm that Gambino's listening.

They give him a thumbs-up and nod in acknowledgment.

Joe feels the tiniest glimmer of hope in the darkness of the situation. *Now that we know for sure Gambino's listening to our conversation, we can use it to manipulate him.*

Blind with fear from not knowing where her daughters are and not hearing back from her husband, Marci enters the walk-in closet in her and Joe's master bedroom where she heads straight for the handgun safe. It has a three-point entry system—biometric, PIN, and key. She uses her fingerprint for faster access and removes her Glock 26 and belly band concealed-carry holster.

Marci makes sure it's loaded before putting it on. She doesn't have to manually engage a safety because, like all Glocks, the Glock 26 has three internal safeties that work seamlessly to prevent accidental discharges and safety hazards. She pulls her shirt back down, concealing the gun and band. *Joe's made sure I know my way around a gun. Being married to a homicide detective for fifteen years has its perks.* Between their monthly date night with Mick and Emma at the shooting range and regular target practice out on the bluff at Pines & Quill, both women are accomplished shooters.

Before closing the safe, Marci removes a box of 9mm ammo. Then, she turns out the closet light and pulls the door closed behind her. On her way out of the bedroom, she snags the roller bag she packed for the Labor Day weekend festivities.

As Marci walks through the kitchen toward the interior garage door, she pictures Carly and Brianna sitting on barstools at the center island, arguing over who gets to read the box of cereal. *I'd give anything to hear them bickering right now.*

She removes her keys and purse from the wall-mounted rack and tucks the ammo box inside the handbag. Entering the garage, she reaches to her right and pushes the button on a panel that opens the two-car automatic garage door. The other button opens the one-car door where Joe parks his "baby" — his 1980 Chevy Camaro. The space is currently empty because he drove it to Pines & Quill.

When Marci raises her key fob to open the locks on her car, Mick pulls his Jeep into the driveway.

As Joe jumps out the front passenger door, Marci runs into his arms and starts to cry. Then, between sobs, she says, "Where have you been? Our daughters are missing!"

Joe pulls her tight against his chest and rocks her back and forth. When she's calmer, he whispers in her ear. "Marci, don't say a word. Not here or in the car. Gambino and his goons are watching us, and he may also be listening."

"Does he have Carly and Brianna?"

Joe nods. "Yes. And he has Emma too. Their safety depends on us doing exactly what he says. I'll fill you in on everything in the car."

Marci feels her entire body quiver with a combination of fear and anger. She lifts her head and tiptoes to look over his shoulder. She turns her mouth against Joe's ear and whispers. "Is it the guy in the white van that just pulled in front of the Pasternak's house?"

Joe doesn't lift his head to look. "A white van's been following us. Do you have a pen and paper in your purse?"

When she nods, he squeezes her again. "Okay. I'll write everything down. And remember, don't say a word."

She nods.

With his arms still tight around her waist, Joe whispers, "You're wearing your gun." It's a statement, not a question. "Where were you when you put it on?"

"In our closet. Why?" Marci says against Joe's neck.

He hugs her to his chest, lifting her off her feet. "Because if Gambino has a surveillance camera in our bedroom, he didn't see you. I doubt he'd install one in a closet."

Marci gasps, and her body tenses involuntarily. She leans back and widens her eyes in shock as she looks at Joe and mouths, "A camera in our bedroom?"

He mouths, "It's possible," before setting her back on her feet and getting her roller bag from the garage.

Rafferty moves into the front passenger seat and says, "This way, you two can sit together."

Next to Joe in the back of Mick's Jeep, Marci gets the pen and grocery tablet from her purse and writes,

Don't leave anything out.

On the way to the Auto and Tire Center in Bellingham, Mick gets glimpses of the silent exchange between Joe and Marci in the rearview mirror as he drives. *Joe bites his upper lip when he writes. Marci's eyes are wide open, and she arches her brows with questions as she reads the words on the tablet. They've been married fifteen years and are still madly in love with each other. I want at least that many years with Emma, hopefully more.* Mick starts to sweat. His gut twists with fear for her safety. *Where is she? What's happening to her?*

After making their purchases, Mick opens the back of the Jeep so they can stow the tires and jack. That's when he sees a note tacked to the cargo area floor. He unpins it and reads:

To make sure you understand I mean business, take a look behind your spare tire. Don't be alarmed. Only I can detonate it. Play by my rules—business as usual—and I won't have to.

An anvil drops in Mick's stomach when he sees the bomb. He returns to the driver's seat.

In the Jeep, everyone sits rigid with fear, barely daring to breathe.

Mick checks the rearview mirror. The white van maintains a fair distance behind them, monitoring their every move. Finally, as Mick pulls off the main road onto the lane that leads to the entrance gate at Pines & Quill, the van eases back until it's lost from view.

As they round the final bend, Mick squints his eyes. *The car that was by the entrance when we left is still there.* The sight of it triggers a memory of a different unknown vehicle outside the Pines & Quill entrance gate. *But that time, it was a black truck. Just a few months ago, on a June night, Hemingway woke me up from a sound sleep because he needed to go outside and relieve himself. A breeze-carried scent caught Hemingway's attention, and he bolted down the lane toward the entrance. The closed gate wasn't a problem for him. Hemingway cleared it in a single bound and kept pounding forward, his powerful drive eating up the ground.*

It turned out that one of Gambino's men, Vito Paglio, an alias for Salvatore Rizzo, was there with his Doberman, and Hemingway had picked up his scent. I ran to catch up. That's when I saw the man and his dog running pell-mell for the black truck. The dog, Smith, outdistanced Vito. Then so did Hemingway.

Vito grabbed his Ruger when Hemingway downed Smith. He waited for a clear shot as the two dogs rolled in the dirt, snarling. Then he pulled the trigger, but the dogs were lightning fast. There was a sickening yelp; then Smith went limp. Vito got in his truck and peeled away.

The next afternoon, Joe and I found Vito dead at the Scrap Heap wrecking yard. He had a bullet in his forehead, and his other Doberman, Wesson, lay dead on the ground beside him. Apparently, Vito messed up his assignment at Pines & Quill, and Gambino killed him as a message to the rest of his goons: you fail, you die.

Mick shakes the memory clear. *Gambino has Emma, our unborn child, and Carly and Brianna, so the stakes are painfully high. We can't fail, or they'll die. He plays for keeps, but so can we. And the only acceptable person dying in this scenario is Gambino.*

Well past the entrance gate, Mick pulls the Jeep next to Joe's Camaro on the side of the lane where he left it when the tire went flat.

"Under normal circumstances," Marci says, unbuckling her seatbelt, "I'd offer to drive the Jeep to the main house. But in this instance, I'm going to walk."

They all get out of the car. Marci hugs Joe and then hands him the pen and tablet.

"We'll be there as soon as we can," Joe says.

Marci kisses Joe, then says, "You better come back to me in one piece, Mr. Bingham," before turning and walking up the lane.

The pine-scented air seems electric and alive. Cool air sucks the heat from under Mick's skin. He looks up to see clouds scuttling across an elephant-gray sky. "The storm's going to be here sooner than we thought."

The guys hustle the two tires and jack out of the back of the Jeep.

As Joe squats and loosens the torque on the lug nuts of the flat, Mick and Rafferty ready the jack on the back right end. Joe nods that he's ready, and Mick starts pumping the jack. When it gets to the correct height, Joe has him stop.

Mick and Rafferty squat on either side of Joe, who writes on the tablet—

Marci had a brilliant idea.

Mick nods for him to continue.

We can't let the guests know what's happening with Emma and the girls, but we can enlist their help.

Mick and Rafferty raise their eyebrows, then Mick motions for Joe to change places with him so Mick can change the tire while Joe writes.

After we divvy up teams and hand out baseball hats, we can have them locate the tree-mounted "wildlife cameras" on the property. They don't need to know that they're surveillance cameras planted by Gambino.

Joe taps the pen on his thigh as he thinks, then writes,

Mick, do you guys have maps of the property?

Mick nods and mouths, "In the cottages."

We'll have them mark the locations of the cameras on the map and draw an arrow with the direction each one is aimed.

Mick takes the tablet and pen.

That's a great way to gather intel, but what reason do we give them for the exercise? It might seem like a "snipe hunt"—totally bogus.

He hands the tablet and pen back to Joe.

Marci thought of that. She said to call it an "icebreaker" to get to know their teammates. And a way to test their powers of observation before the game of Spy officially begins. And if we add that there's dessert afterward, they'll be all in.

Rafferty takes the pen and tablet.

Do you think he put cameras in the cottages too?

Mick writes.

It's a distinct possibility. So when the teams are out scouring the property for "wildlife cameras," I'll make an excuse to leave and check the cottages.

Rafferty and Joe nod their agreement.

As Rafferty lowers the car back down, Mick looks over the open trunk and sees a man walking toward them. *He looks like he stepped right out of a cowboy movie.*

Mick walks to the front of the Camaro. When the man reaches him, he extends his hand. "I'm Jake Porter. I was walking my wife, Sarah, to the main house when we met a woman named Marci heading the same way. She said I'd find you guys out here."

Mick wipes his right hand on his pants leg, then shakes Jake's hand. "I'm Sean McPherson, but I go by Mick." He nods toward Rafferty. "This is Sean Rafferty."

Rafferty steps forward to shake Jake's proffered hand. "Everyone just calls me Rafferty. It's a pleasure to meet you."

Mick turns to Joe, "And this is Joe Bingham, Marci's husband."

Joe hands off the tablet and pen to Mick, then shakes Jake's hand.

"It's nice to meet you guys," Jake says. "My rental car's parked outside the front gate. When I got here a few hours ago and pushed the intercom button, no one answered, so I hopped the fence and found Sarah's cottage."

Mick glances at his watch—*Three o'clock.* "That'd be about the time we were bathing the dogs. They got sprayed by a skunk. We were all outside and didn't know you were here."

"Well, I can tell you firsthand that they're good guard dogs," Jake says. "I had a close call. But now that Sarah introduced me properly, they know I'm a friend."

"Oh, man, I'm sorry about that," Mick says. "Hemingway, the Irish wolfhound, is very protective."

"And Maggie, the Standard poodle," Rafferty says, "can be protective as well. She's my girlfriend Ivy's guide dog."

"I haven't met the rest of the folks yet," Jake says.

"Now that we've got Joe's flat taken care of," Mick says, "why don't I go with you to your car so you can bring it in and park it?"

"I'd appreciate it," Jake says.

Mick hands the tablet to Jake. The note he wrote says,

We're being watched, and there's a listening device and a bomb in the Jeep. Probably in the Camaro, too. We understand that you're a US Marshal. Rafferty's a special agent with the FBI. Joe's a homicide detective. And I'm an ex-cop turned PI. We've been waiting for you. We need your help.

CHAPTER 11

*"Show up, show up, show up, and after
a while, the muse shows up, too."*
—Isabel Allende

In the cabin on Mount Baker, the metal door clangs shut behind Emma, plunging her into onyx darkness. As the men retreat down the hall, the sound of their footsteps diminishes. Emma finds the wall with a trembling hand and flat palms it to anchor herself. Hardly daring to breathe, she stands statue-still, unblinking in the darkness. *I have to get out of here!* Then, beyond the noise of her shallow breath, Emma hears the faintest sound.

"Hello?" Emma says just above a whisper. She leans her back against the wall and slides down. When her rear meets the hard floor, Emma pulls her knees up to her chest. "Hello?" she says again, this time a little louder.

"Hello," comes a soft voice.

It's a woman's voice with no discernible ethnic markers. "My name's Emma McPherson. Do you know what's going on? How long have you been here?"

"My name's Andrea. Andrea Peters. Tonight will be my third sleep in this place. I don't know how long the others have been here. I'm not sure if they speak English and are just too scared to talk or if they don't speak English. The only thing I know is from what little I heard by listening to the men through the space under the door."

"What did you hear?" Emma asks.

"We're being sold."

"Sold?!" Emma whisper-shouts. "What do you mean?"

"When they get a dozen of us—twelve—we'll be moved. Whoever took us is some kind of muscle or kingpin in the Seattle area, and he's using us to pave the way for a deal with his Russian equivalent. One of the men said he worked on an oil rig for the head guy in Alaska. He calls him 'The Bull.'"

Razor-edged fear slices Emma's heart. *Tank, one of the construction guys working on the addition over the workshop, drives a truck with Alaska plates.* Emma fists her sweaty hands. *I know what Gambino's capable of and that he'll stop at nothing to get what he wants.*

Andrea continues, "He said that the narrowest distance between mainland Russia and mainland Alaska is only fifty-five miles. And in that body of water, the Bering Strait, there are two small islands—Big Diomede and Little Diomede. Apparently, that's where all kinds of exchanges are made for drugs, weapons, and humans. They said some of us will be sold into forced labor, some as sex slaves, and some for the extraction of organs and tissues."

"I've heard about forced labor. And sex trafficking's been at the top of the news headlines," Emma says. "But I didn't know about the extraction of organs and tissues."

"It's very real," Andrea says. "And lucrative. They also use women for surrogacy and ova removal."

Emma places her hands protectively on her belly. "Drugs, weapons, and most of all, people, are hard to hide," Emma says. "How do they do it?"

"From what I gather," Andrea says, "the 'merchandise' is hidden on container ships, then transported on trade routes."

"But people can talk," Emma says. "We can shout. We can scream for help."

"Not if we're drugged," Andrea says.

Emma fingers the tender area on her neck where one of the hooded men stabbed her with a syringe in the van. *Think, Emma. You've got to figure a way out of this!*

"I didn't have a chance to see how many of us there are," Emma says.

"With *you*, we're back up to eight," Andrea says.

"What do you mean, 'back up to'?"

"There'd been another woman. She was young, maybe late teens or early twenties. When two of the men came to take her, she fought. Through the door, I heard more fighting, followed by men laughing. And then she screamed. It wasn't long after that I heard a gunshot. It seemed to come from outside, but I don't know for sure. What I *do* know is that I haven't seen her since."

Tightness grips Emma's throat when she hears footsteps. Closer. Louder. Then a man shouts, "Back away!"

Emma barely has time to move before the door flies open with a clang, and blinding light blooms before her eyes. She blinks it away as light from a kerosene lamp reveals seven people: the hooded man holding the lamp and two pairs of hooded men carrying two limp girls, who they dump on the floor.

As one man squats and cuts the bindings from their ankles and wrists, another pushes at the hair splayed across their faces, then tears the duct tape from their mouths.

Oh, my God, it's Carly and Brianna!

Emma rushes to kneel between the girls and checks for heartbeats. *They're alive.*

Tall and broad-shouldered, the largest of the men steps between the girls' bodies and squats before Emma. With the aggressive grace of a predator, he yanks the leather cord holding the turtle Mick carved for Emma over her head. "I've been eyeing that piece," he says.

"No!" Emma's scream pierces the room.

As she scrambles to stand, the man shoves her back down. "I wouldn't if I were you."

"I know who you are," Emma says. "You're Tank."

"And you're dead, or you'll wish you were," he says before tucking the pendant in a front pants pocket.

When the men leave, they take the light with them. A tiny sliver of yellow under the door is all that remains of the outside world.

In the dark, Emma's hand flutters to where the mahogany pendant—a *honu*, a Hawaiian green sea turtle—had been. Just the other night, she and Mick had talked about it in bed. He said, "When lost, turtles are excellent navigators and often find their way home—in your case, I hope it's always to me."

Emptiness swallows Emma. *Mick, I need you to help me find my way home.*

Mick stands on the patio of the main house with Hemingway and Maggie at each side. Fear claws his gut. *What if the plan doesn't work?*

Mick's confident that his trusted operatives—his mom and Emma's mom, Libby and Niall, Joe and Marci, Rafferty and Ivy, and Jake and Sarah—won't give anything away. *Three lives depend on our acting skills—Emma, Carly, and Brianna.*

Leaves in the nearby trees whisper in the pine and salt-scented breeze. *A breeze that's picking up.* Mick looks up at the whisper-thin remains of a contrail against a darkening sky. *The first clouds of the coming storm are gathering on the horizon.*

At first, I didn't agree with Jake wanting to take Sarah, his wife, into our confidence. But Jake sealed the deal with, "Not only is Sarah an exceptional ally, she's also a crack shot with a compound bow."

Mick rakes his fingers through his hair. *This weekend, we have three groups of people at Pines & Quill: my trusted operatives, the writers in residence, and outside guests coming to enjoy the Labor Day festivities.*

While waiting for the outside guests to arrive, Libby found a security camera while "dusting" in the dining area and the Ink Well—business as usual for Gambino's sake. Armed with the knowledge that they're being watched and probably listened to in that location, they know to be careful of what they say in the entire main house area.

Hemingway's and Maggie's ears perk at the *thunk* of car doors in the pull-through drive in front of the main house. They bolt to meet the new arrivals.

Mick takes another minute to gather himself before putting on his game face to greet the outside guests. The group is made up of Mick's three poker buddies and their wives—Skip, a paramedic, and his current girlfriend, Olivia; Tim, a UPS driver, his wife Mary, and their newborn daughter, Hannah; Hank, the construction crew foreman, and his wife, Gail. And their vet, Kent Sutton, and his wife, Molly.

Mick, Hemingway, and Maggie guide the new arrivals into the kitchen of the main house, where Niall and Libby welcome them.

Fond of the saying, "Many hands make light work," Niall makes everyone feel at home by assigning them a task.

Mick leads the group to the pavilion—a large, raised, open-sided building with a pagoda-style copper roof—where they set picnic tables and offload pitchers, dishes, platters, and bowls heaping with food onto sideboards.

Hemingway and Maggie stay close to the action, hoping for spillage.

"Hey, Joe, it's great to see you," Skip calls out. "Where are the girls?"

"Good to see you too," Joe says. "Marci's folks took them on a surprise vacation to Whidbey Island."

"Grandparents," Skip says. "You've got to love them." He nods toward Marci. "It'll give you and the missus some time together."

Joe beams. "Damn straight."

Never one to do things by halves, Niall has outdone himself. First, he used his grandmother's recipe for fall-off-the-bone ribs, then his recipe for prize-winning grilled chicken wings—the secret ingredient is coriander.

The two main dishes are followed by homestyle barbecued baked beans, coleslaw, potato salad; a huge casserole of his to-die-for macaroni and cheese packed with Muenster, mild and sharp cheddar, and Monterey Jack; smoky Parmesan corn on the cob; and grilled ranch potatoes.

After pushing food around on his plate, Mick places his hands on his lap, where he fists them, unseen by others. *I hate sitting here doing nothing while Emma's what—Alive? Dead? Hurt?*

In addition to the savory scent of roasted meats, groans, moans, *oohs*, and *aahs* fill the air as everyone tucks into the food.

Mick notices Skip eyeing him, so he picks up his fork and takes a bite of potato salad.

Molly Sutton, the vet's wife, sets her silverware next to her plate and looks across the table. "Mick, I just realized I haven't seen Emma. Where is she?"

Mick finishes chewing the bite in his mouth, swallows, then wipes his mouth with a napkin. This buys him time to mentally rehearse his line. "Unfortunately, her doctor put her on bed rest." He places the napkin back on his lap, then exchanges a knowing glance with Rafferty.

Molly crinkles her brows. "Oh, dear. I hope everything's okay."

Mick nods. "The doctor assured us that it's nothing a little bed rest won't fix." He glances at his watch. "In fact, I'm going to make up a plate and take it to her soon."

"Please give her my love when you do."

"I sure will, Molly. She'll appreciate that. Thank you." *I promise to find you, Emma, if it's the last thing I do.*

———

Niall glances at his watch. *It's almost five thirty. The note Mick passed me said that after he "takes Emma her meal in their cabin," he'll wait until six fifteen, when the two groups are well into Spy mode, to start checking the cottages.*

Libby approaches Niall. "How are you holding up?"

He touches curly wisps of hair that escaped from the knot she skewered with the hair stick Mick carved for her. "Your hair's always a dead giveaway when a storm's coming."

Libby reaches up. "Is it frizzing?"

"Yes. And you look wonderful."

Then Niall turns westward and gazes through the open-sided pavilion and points. "I told you a storm's coming. Now we better get this show on the road before the sky opens up."

Niall cheerfully waves away the many offers of help to clean up as he walks to the front of the pavilion and claps to get everyone's attention.

"It's time to divide into teams for the weekend-long game of Spy. First, we've paired you into two groups—the red team and the green team. Each of you will receive a corresponding-colored baseball cap that you must wear unless you're indoors. Next, we've purposely paired you with people you either don't know or don't know well."

Niall turns to Libby. "Honey, I think this is a good time to tell everyone the team designations."

Libby steps next to Niall at the front of the group and pulls a folded piece of paper from a back pocket. "Before I call out the teams, I want you to know that for tonight's icebreaker, Mick will bow out temporarily to take a plate to Emma. Then he'll catch up with his team as soon as he can. Are you ready?"

Niall watches the happy faces nod in anticipation. *I would give anything for Emma, Carly, and Brianna to be here.* He glances covertly at Mick, Joe, Rafferty, then Jake, and a shiver runs up his spine. *Whoever has them will wish they'd never been born.*

Libby clears her throat dramatically as she straightens the paper. "The red team's mascot is Hemingway, and the team members are Mick, Maureen, Niall, Marci, Sakura, Dale, Skip, Kent, and Jake. Ivy, Mary, and baby Hannah are on the red team, too, but with the storm coming, they're going to sit this one out.

"The green team's mascot is Maggie, and the team members are Maeve, Joe, Rafferty, Todd, Sarah, Olivia, Tim, Hank, Molly, Gail, and me."

Niall points to the west in the open-sided pavilion. "Red team, I'd like you to gather over there." Then he points east. "And green team, I'd like you to gather over there. That makes it easier for me to hand out your caps."

"What's the icebreaker?" Dale asks as Niall hands out the last cap.

"I'm glad you asked," Niall says. He picks up a stack of paper from one of the picnic tables and then turns to Libby. "Will you get the pens, please?

"Each of you will receive a map of the property and a pen. Your mission is to locate as many wildlife cameras as you can. When you find one, mark the spot on the map with an 'X' and draw an arrow in the direction the camera is facing."

"Are the wildlife cameras in the trees?" Olivia asks.

"That's a great question," Niall says. "Let's not assume that they're only in trees. Look both high and low."

"Is there a prize?" Todd asks.

Niall nods. "Chocolate fudge layer cake."

A whoop of excitement fills the rafters and sends black-capped chickadees scuttling from nearby trees.

Niall looks at his watch. "It's five thirty. I want everyone to use the next thirty minutes to take care of anything that needs taking care of. Then we'll meet back here at six o'clock sharp."

That way, no one should wander back to their cottage during the icebreaker and stumble upon Mick checking for surveillance equipment.

———

Mick scours his and Emma's cabin for surveillance equipment. Then, when he's sure it's clear, he goes back into their bedroom, pulls back the bedspread, and buries his face in Emma's pillow, breathing in her scent—*Fresh and citrusy, like lime, with a hint of vanilla.*

In the bathroom, he splashes cold water on his face to eliminate all traces of his tears. But short of finding Emma, there's no way to untie the knots in his gut. Thoughts race through his mind, terrorizing him—*Where's Gambino holding Emma? What's he doing to her? Is she able to protect our unborn child? I've got to find her!*

Mick checks his watch—*It's six fifteen; the teams are out scouring the property.*

His adrenaline spikes as he loads and holsters his Glock 22, the same type of service weapon he was issued when hired by the SFPD. *Once a cop, always a cop.* And though his clip holster's meant for ultimate concealment inside his waistband, Mick doesn't give a damn about concealment right now. Stashing another magazine with fifteen rounds in his back pocket, he steps out the back door of the cabin and, with practiced stealth, blends almost seamlessly into the woods.

On the south side of the property, Thoreau Cottage is surrounded by western red cedar trees. It overlooks Bellingham Bay National Park and Reserve, home to El Cañón del Diablo—Devil's Canyon. He steals soundlessly into the cottage and then stands still, listening for the slightest sound. *Clear.*

He thinks of himself as a perpetrator. *Where would I hide a camera?* Then using his eyes, hands, and a small flashlight, he checks for surveillance equipment in the most obvious places first: smoke detectors, air filter equipment, books, wall decor, electrical outlets, plants, tissue boxes, couch cushions, tabletops, shelves, wall sockets, wall clock, and coat hooks.

In the bedroom, Mick finds Sarah's compound bow and arrows. *The fletch color on the arrows is white on black carbon, with a small band of silver reflector tape between the fletch and nock. And while half of the arrows have field points for an archery range, the other half has broadheads for more serious business—hunting.* Mick touches the razor-sharp point on one. *Oh man, these are wicked. I'm sure glad Sarah's not a person I have to worry about. At least, I don't think so.*

As he makes his way from Thoreau Cottage to Austen, Mick hears team members talking and laughing in the distance. He checks the glass slider on the back of Austen Cottage and lets himself into the kitchen. Again, he stands stock-still to listen and make sure that no one's here.

Five years ago, when Mick first came to Pines & Quill to recover from the accident that took his partner's life and nearly cost him a leg, this wheelchair-friendly cottage was where he stayed. And because he knows it so well, the search goes faster than in Thoreau. Though he doesn't find any evidence of surveillance equipment, he's perplexed at the book he finds on easygoing Todd's nightstand: *Anger Management Workbook for Men: Take Control of Your Anger and Master Your Emotions.*

Mick slips back out the glass slider, closes it soundlessly behind him, and heads north.

Set in a grove of big-leaf maple trees, Dickens is one of the two cottages with a sleeping loft. After ensuring no one's home, Mick goes through his now-routine search. In the bathroom, he comes across a few prescription bottles. On one of the labels is printed ROXICODONE. Mick knows it's an opioid pain medication and a brand name for oxycodone. During his recovery, he turned it down because of its addictive properties. *I wonder what Dale needs this heavy-duty stuff for?*

He remembers that Dale sat in the back of the van just in front of the luggage when they drove this month's writers in residence from the airport to Pines & Quill. When Mick looked in the rearview mirror, Dale was draped over the back seat, and he asked him to put his seatbelt back on. Then, at the sound of his name, Dale whirled around, red-faced. Holding a small prescription bottle in one of his hands, he said, "I get motion sick."

Mick scours the other items in the bathroom but doesn't find any motion sickness medication. Unfortunately, he doesn't have time to do more with that information right now, so he files it in his mind, then takes the back way toward Brontë.

When he passes the garage and workshop, he doesn't slow down. He knows that Joe and Rafferty already checked it from top to bottom when they stowed their luggage. In doing so, they found four cameras, two on each floor. And with the knowledge there could be even more, everyone who's staying there who knows about the missing women has been cautioned not to say anything they don't want Gambino to hear.

A thorough search of Brontë doesn't turn up any surveillance equipment. But Mick, a whittler and woodcarver, who always carries his Deejo wood carving knife in his pocket, is taken aback at the short martial-arts sword he finds on the bedside table in the sleeping loft. Using the intricately leather-wrapped handle, he slips it out of the sheath. *The blade's about twenty-seven inches long. There's no way Sakura got this through airport security. It had to be in her checked luggage.* He's careful to put it back exactly the way he found it.

Mick mulls over the unexpected findings on his way to find the red team: *An anger management workbook, what amounts to be narcotics, and a Samurai sword. And while I believe that Sarah's in the clear, Todd, Dale, or Sakura could work for Gambino.*

CHAPTER 12

*"If you're using dialogue, say it aloud as you write it.
Only then will it have the sound of speech."*
—JOHN STEINBECK

Mick looks past his reflection on the Ink Well window to the dark expanse outside. *It's getting cold out. Where's Emma? Is she okay?*

A glance at his watch tells him it's just past eight o'clock. The conversation behind him catches his attention. He turns and surveys the red-cheeked people filling the overstuffed chairs. The floor-to-ceiling bookshelves with well-worn favorites make an inviting backdrop for their guests. There are twenty-one people counting baby Hannah. *Do Emma's captors know that she's pregnant? Would they hurt a pregnant woman, an unborn child?*

Turning to hide the tears brimming in his eyes, Mick sees flames from the fireplace cast dancing shadows on Hemmingway's and Maggie's coats as they stretch out on the floor in front of the fieldstone hearth.

After gathering himself, Mick turns back to the room. He sees by the expression on Marci's face that she's at the end of her emotional tether too. *I know exactly how she feels. We've got to find Emma, Carly, and Brianna.*

Mick collects the maps from the green and red teams who'd marked the "wildlife camera" locations and drew arrows in the direction each one points. "Who's ready for chocolate cake?"

"I am," comes an excited chorus.

Apron-clad, Niall enters the Ink Well and delivers the preplanned directive. "Joe, here's a tablet and pen. Will you please take drink orders and then meet me in the kitchen? Mick, Rafferty, and Jake, I'd appreciate your help making drinks and cutting and delivering the cake. And Libby, while everyone's waiting for the drinks and dessert, now would be a good time for the writers in residence to draw their cards from *The Observation Deck*."

The men gather in the kitchen where no surveillance cameras had been found, then spread the maps out on the gray-veined marble top of the center island.

As Niall cuts the cake, Mick, Rafferty, and Jake mark a new map, ensuring that both teams' notations are included.

"I've had some experience with surveillance cameras," Jake, the US Marshal, says. Then, pointing to the map, he continues. "No matter the camera, no matter the cost, there are limitations."

"Such as?" Mick asks.

"Limitations of the equipment itself, the environment, and the field of range."

Mick quirks an eyebrow. "Tell me about the field of range."

"The wider the field of view, the lower the depth and quality of the picture."

Mick swallows his apprehension. *If I mess this up, they'll kill Emma and our baby.*

Jake holds up an index finger. "And," he continues, "there's the limitation of the person who's monitoring the cameras. They're *supposed* to be watching for light activation from movement. But how engaged and invested are they? What's their motivation?

"For instance, the camera at the front gate where there's not a continuous flow of traffic probably won't get a lot of attention. And they're confident they'll be notified if the sensors detect motion and the light comes on."

Mick points to an area on the northwest corner of the map. "With the least concentration of cameras between the workshop and the big-leaf maples that surround Dickens Cottage—and with the direction the cameras are facing, to pick up foot traffic in front of the main house—this seems to be the way I should leave and return to the property."

Jake rubs the stubble on his jaw. "You said that when Libby found the camera in the pavilion eaves, she didn't see a light come on. That tells me that the cameras, at least that one, are low light."

"Is that helpful?" Mick asks.

Just then, Joe joins them in the kitchen, where they bring him up to speed.

Jake continues. "Another limitation—especially with low light cameras—is that if you're close to the ground and move slow enough, they won't detect you. You'll just be part of the ground clutter. With these types of cameras, you have to move at so-many-feet-per-second before the motion sensors detect anything."

Joe says, "If Rafferty and I take Hemingway and Maggie on a potty walk opposite from where Mick's going to leave"—he points to an area behind the back of the main house—"between two large dogs and two men, we're bound to trigger some surveillance cameras. Then whoever's monitoring them will be preoccupied with *us* while Mick belly crawls off the property."

Mick feels good about the distraction, and a flicker of hope rises in his chest.

"That's a good idea," Jake says. "And with the storm compounding flashes of light, the person standing watch will be busy trying to keep track of what's what. For instance, a flash of lightning in the lens of a camera will have bright light and nothing more until the sensor recovers. That's not to say that the plan is foolproof, but it's the best we've got."

With the plan in place, the men make and tray the drinks. Then they carry cake, forks, napkins, and glasses to the Ink Well, where they deliver everything as Niall fills the wine orders.

Mick hears the moans and groans over the mouthwatering cake. The sexual tone takes his mind to his and Emma's bedroom, to their lovemaking. *Was it just last night? It seems like she's been gone forever. And with every passing minute, the captors can be taking her, our baby, and the girls farther away.*

"Oh, brother," Niall says, rolling his eyes. "It's just cake."

To maintain the pretense that Gambino demanded— "Conduct business as usual; no one must know that your wife and Joe's kids are missing or I'll kill them"—Mick says, "Niall, I'm going to plate a piece of dessert for Emma and call it a night. I'm sorry, but I won't be able to take Hemingway on his final walk this evening."

Joe picks up the verbal baton and runs with it. "I'll be happy to do that for you, Mick." He looks down at the plate of cake on his lap. "I need to walk off these calories anyway."

"And I'll join you with Maggie," Rafferty says.

Mick turns to the rest of the guests. "You've probably heard the news media warnings. A nasty storm's on the way. The latest forecast calls for high winds, heavy rain, and lots of thunder and lightning"—he takes a cursory glance at his watch—"soon. Regardless, I hope you get a great night's sleep because the game of Spy starts in earnest tomorrow."

Mick gives the barest hint of a nod to his mom.

Maeve turns to Maureen. "If we're going to get a head start on the storm, we'd better leave now."

"Perfect timing," Mick says. "I'll walk you out."

The first fat drops of rain begin to fall as Mick opens the front door of the main house. They feel cold and clean as they land on his face. He inhales the humid air. It carries the rich scent of salt and dried seaweed. *The last time Emma and I were out on the water, we went whale watching in the San Juan Islands, and Gambino ordered a hit on Emma. He failed then, and I plan to see that he does again.*

When he hugs his mom goodbye, he whispers in her ear. "Remember, bag the phones in a plastic garbage bag and put them in the trashcan just inside your back gate. Then use the secure site and contact Emma's dad and brothers. The clock's ticking, and we need them here *fast*, in the morning if possible. The sooner they get here, the sooner Joe, Rafferty, and I will have body doubles and can leave the property to find Emma and the girls."

By the time Mick's halfway to his cabin, the wind and rain have picked up. The trees rustle with a *shush* that sounds like surf in the bay below the cliffs. He reaches the front door of his and Emma's cabin just as a gale barrels through the property. Loose pine needles speed across newly formed puddles like paddleboards rushing out to sea. Flashes of lightning illuminate the incoming storm clouds, highlighting their bulging, purple-black bellies.

As rain pelts the back of Mick's shirt, he feels a tangible excitement, like sparks firing through his veins. *Soon, I'll finally be able to do something instead of sitting here—"business as usual."* His scalp tingles as the first crack of thunder vibrates the ground. He opens the cabin door and ducks inside.

In the master bedroom, rain cascades down the outside of the large window. Mick can just make out the tree line with each flash of lightning. The clouds swirl in white, gray, and sapphire spirals like a van Gogh painting. The artist once wrote, "The fishermen know that the sea is dangerous and the storm terrible, but they have never found these dangers sufficient reason for remaining ashore." *Hold on, Emma. I'm coming.*

After changing into all black, Mick rechecks his watch. *We agreed that Joe and Rafferty would start walking the dogs at ten o'clock—my departure time. And we'll rinse and repeat at midnight when I return. That gives me enough time to make the pickup at Mom's house in Bellingham and get back to Pines & Quill.*

He walks into the living room and sits on a chair beneath the exposed beams of the cathedral ceiling. He rubs his thigh. *I hate waiting.*

Restless, he stands up. He needs to move his body, so he paces the living room. Pieces of Emma's hand-thrown pottery decorate the space and remind him of their shared times together and of her fierce and loving spirit. *She's the best thing that's ever happened in my life. And now I'm going to be a dad. I've got to stop Gambino from hurting them or die trying because I don't want to live without them.*

Mick thinks of the *honu*, the turtle pendant he carved for her. It symbolizes good fortune, endurance, and long life. When he gave it to her, he told her that turtles are excellent navigators and often find their way home when lost. *Please, Emma, find your way home to me.*

Mick reaches up to the leather cord around his neck. In the heart of his right palm, he holds the whale fluke that he carved for himself while recovering from the accident that took the life of his partner, Sam. *Whales represent emotion, inner truth, creativity, and physical and emotional healing. But the association I like most is that whales embody quiet strength.* He squeezes the whale fluke in his fist, and his heart thuds with longing. *And if you can't find your way to me, Emma, I'll find you.*

The great horned owl perched on a high limb in a big-leaf maple tree gives up all thoughts of dinner as the storm rages, ensuring that small wildlife stay burrowed for the duration.

He cocks his head to the side at unexpected movement below, then watches as two men and two large dogs exit the front door of the main house and head northwest, and another man belly crawls from the shadows behind the workshop.

A spear of lightning fractures the sky, followed by a shattering boom of thunder.

The owl presses his needle-sharp talons into the tree's flesh and hunkers down. He isn't the only one schooled in the predator-prey dynamic. He rotates his head on his flexible neck to get a better look with his large yellow eyes.

The belly-crawler blends with the ground cover as he eases over root heaves and through fern shoots. He stops periodically to survey his surroundings, then continues north toward town.

The Lhaq'temish, the local Native American tribe who lives on the Lummi reservation, believes that owls think like humans—only far better.

The owl wonders if the man is the predator or the prey, aware that the night will tell.

Hours into his watch, one of Gambino's men, bored out of his mind, sits up straight in an office chair as he's alerted to movement in one of the surveillance cameras, then two. "What the fuck?" He checks his watch. *It's a little after ten o'clock.* Then he leans forward, elbows on the desk, to get a better look.

In front of him are three large monitors, each divided into four quadrants. The twelve quadrants display the views of surveillance cameras strategically placed throughout the property at Pines & Quill writing retreat.

In what looks to be a torrential downpour, the watchman sees two men walking two dogs. He widens his eyes in disbelief as they unleash the dogs and pat their rumps.

The dogs take off like NASCAR drivers getting a green flag. At first, they run parallel to each other, then they split up, setting the surveillance camera sensors into a frenzy.

Then each man heads in a separate direction looking for his dog, setting off additional sensors.

Two of the quadrants temporarily freeze with flashes of lightning. Just as they recover, another one freezes with another blinding flash.

Then out at the Pines & Quill entrance, a sensor is triggered when a buck and two does bound over the gate with ease. The man touches the pistol in his holster. *I'd like a piece of that action.*

Just then, camera four is blocked. He leans in for a closer look and squints. "I'll be damned. Whatever it is has feathers."

He kicks over the trashcan next to the desk. "How the fucking hell am I supposed to keep track of this shit?"

———

Time lurches in fits and starts for Emma in the suffocating darkness. Her butt is sore from sitting on the hard floor between the girls. She listens to the rain pelting the roof. Now and then, there's a whistle of wind from the narrow space where the window has been covered with plywood. *I wonder if I could kick it out?*

Emma crawls to the wall with the window. She feels her way until she finds it, then stands and presses against the wood for all she's worth. *Nothing.*

"What are you doing?" Andrea asks.

"I'm trying to see if I can shove the plywood away from the window."

"I already tried," Andrea says. "But maybe if we work together, we can push it away."

Andrea joins her, and they both push with all their might.

"It doesn't even budge," Andrea says. "And if we kick it, they'll hear us."

Emma crawls back to the girls. She rests her elbows on her knees and drops her head. *Even if we could dislodge the wood, the windows also have security bars.*

When Carly and Brianna wake up, they start to sob but stop when they realize that Emma is with them. She places her arms around their shoulders and pulls them in tight. Emma thinks of her unborn child. *So, this is what it feels like to be a mother. Marci must be out of her mind with worry for her daughters.*

Emma sets her mouth in a firm line. *I've got to think of a way to get us out of here.*

Carly and Brianna explain that while walking home from school, a van pulled up, the side door opened, and hooded men yanked them inside before they could run.

Thirteen-year-old Carly remembers being jabbed with a needle.

Eleven-year-old Brianna doesn't.

"Where's Mom and Dad?" Brianna asks, her voice thick with tears.

"What are they going to do with us?" Carly whispers.

Emma keeps what little she knows to herself. She doesn't want to frighten them any more than they already are. "I'm sure that Mick, Rafferty, and your dad are out looking for us right now. What we need to do until they get here is stay strong. And girls, just so you know, we're not the only ones in this room."

Brianna leans into Emma and whispers. "Who else is here?"

The girls were unconscious when the hooded men brought them into this dark room, so they didn't get the chance to see the other people when one of them held the kerosene lamp. Emma squints her eyes, trying to pierce the darkness. *I can't see the others either. So, it's no wonder the girls can't see them.*

"Other than a woman named Andrea who speaks English, I don't know who the other women are. I don't know if they don't speak English or they're just too scared to speak."

"How many of us are there?" Carly asks.

"With the two of you, we're at ten," Emma says. She pulls the girls closer, grateful for the small human comfort. *And when they get a dozen of us—twelve—we'll be moved. Maybe that's when we can try to escape.*

"I have to pee," Brianna whines.

Carly leans in close to Emma. "So do I."

From the other side of the room, Andrea says, "There's a bucket in the corner. That's what smells so bad. They don't change it very often. If you want, I'll crawl over to you and then guide you to it."

"Okay," Brianna says. "I can't hold it much longer."

After the girls and Emma relieve themselves, they crawl back to their spot, as far away from the bucket as they can get.

"Girls, to stay strong, we need to get some sleep. Let's lie next to each other to stay warm." The three of them spoon, with Emma at the back. It doesn't take long before Emma hears their breathing change to the tranquil rhythm of sleep breathing.

Outside, the wind howls like a beast. Now and then, Emma hears a clap of thunder. She takes the opportunity to roll away from Brianna and press her ear against the crack under the door. It's not long before she hears the scrape of metal chair legs and then a crash when it hits the floor.

"Are you out of your fucking mind?" one of the men shouts. "Gambino said not to touch the merchandise. And the last time you had your jollies, you ended up killing one of them."

Another chair scrapes the floor and then falls.

"He only said not to touch the PI's wife and the detective's daughters. That other broad was just part of the cost of doing business. He expects it."

"What *he* expects," the other man says, "is for me to kill you if you don't—"

Emma's body startles at the loud report of a gunshot followed by a thud when something hits the floor.

"Follow orders," the man finishes. "Now listen up," he continues. "With no *fucking* cell reception, I'm heading down the mountain with this carcass to report to Gambino. If you so much as *think* about touching the door to the room with the merchandise, you'll get the same."

Emma hears something—*Perhaps a person?*—being dragged across the floor, followed by a door opening.

"Fuck! It's pouring outside. One of you help me carry this son of a bitch and throw him into the back of my truck."

"What if you get stopped?"

"I won't," the man answers. "Between the camper shell and a tarp, he won't be an issue."

Emma hears her heart thump and a hiss of blood race through her ears as she waits for another sound from outside the dark room.

After a few minutes, she hears the roar of an engine, followed by someone coming back into the cabin.

"You want to have some fun?" one of the men asks.

"Not on your life," a man says. "Tank put me in charge while he's gone. He meant what he said. If one of us even *thinks* about touching the merchandise, he'll kill us. I saw him gut a man. And he smiled while he did it."

Emma lets out a breath she didn't realize she was holding. *There were four men outside when I was lowered from the helicopter. And two men were sitting at a card table when they brought me inside the cabin. That makes six. One of those is either dead or seriously wounded in the back of a truck that Tank just drove away. That leaves only four. I wonder...*

The wipers make a soft *thump-thump* noise as Tank drives down the mountain on the winding, rain-slicked road. He looks at the new "accessory"—backlit by the lights on the dash—hanging from the rearview mirror. He likes how it sways back and forth on the leather cord when he rounds a bend. *That's a good-lookin' turtle.*

Shortly after he reaches the base of Mount Baker and is on the straightaway, he pulls into the parking lot of a twenty-four-hour convenience store. Other than his truck, the only vehicle is a "beater" parked in front of a large silver cooler that contains bags of ice at the end of the building.

He only sees one person through the all-glass façade: a teenage kid behind the counter. *The beater probably belongs to him.* Tank parks on the far side of the gas pumps, close to the road.

He barely hears the bell jingle over the door when he walks in because heavy metal music blares from a boombox behind the counter. The clock on the far wall indicates that it's just past midnight. *Saturday.*

The kid looks up from a hotrod magazine and hurriedly turns the music down.

Tank juts his thumb over his shoulder. "That your car outside?"

"Yeah, but not for long," the kid says. He turns the magazine and shows a glossy photo of a souped-up Ford Mustang to Tank. "I'm saving up."

Tank smiles and nods. "Well, good luck."

"What can I get ya?"

"I'm just going to get some jerky and a soda. Mind if I use the restroom?"

The kid shakes his head. "Help yourself."

After Tank relieves himself, he gets a bag of jerky and fills a large cup with ice and soda, then lids it. When he pays, he tells the kid, "Keep the change. Put it toward your new car," and walks out. Before the door shuts behind him, the music blares again.

A sheriff, wearing raingear, is looking through the back window of Tank's camper shell with a flashlight. As Tank approaches his truck, he casually shifts his gaze to the end of the convenience store and sees a single Whatcom County Sheriff vehicle, lights out, pulled on the far side of the beater — out of view from the store. He looks over his shoulder and sees the kid's nose is buried in the glossy pages of his magazine. A glance up and down the road reveals no headlights, not even distant pinpoints.

"Hey, officer. How are you doing?"

"I'm fine. And you?"

"I'm doing pretty good now that I bagged a black bear." Tank smiles. He sees the sheriff's body cam is covered by his rain slicker." *That's your third mistake, buddy. Stopping at this store was the first. And snooping inside my truck was the second.*

"Mind if I see your hunting license?" the sheriff asks.

"Not at all. Let me just set this stuff down." Tank turns the lever on the back of the camper shell and lifts it open. He reaches over the tailgate and sets his soda and jerky on the tarp-lined truck bed, then lifts the latch and lowers the tailgate. "Now that my hands are free, I'll get my hunting license out of my wallet."

The sheriff shines his light inside the truck bed. "I see you've got a protective tarp on your truck bed." He nods. "That's a good idea with all the blood. The bear rolled up in that other tarp?"

Tank nods. "Yes, sir, it sure is."

Tank takes his wallet from his back pocket and removes a valid big game hunting license, including black bear as a species option. After handing it to the sheriff, he slips his right hand into his side pants pocket. "And you'll see that I'm in season—August first through November fifteenth."

As the sheriff uses his flashlight to study the hunting license, Tank manually depresses the folding mechanism to mute the click he knows the blade will otherwise make. Then, after he feels it lock into place, he takes a deep breath and, in one swift, powerful motion, pulls the sheriff's head to his chest and holds it firmly as he slices his carotid artery. Once he's limp, Tank tips him onto the tailgate, then lifts and shoves his body inside.

"That's right, sheriff. You never know when there'll be a lot of blood."

Tank grabs his drink and jerky before closing the tailgate and the camper shell. Then he looks toward the store. The young man's head bobs in time to the music as he peruses his hotrod magazine.

As Tank starts the engine, he looks down his front. The blood on his clothes doesn't faze him, but his gut gives a little twist. *I hope to hell I don't hit any more snags before I have to deal with Gambino. He's not going to be pleased with a dead sheriff. Not because he's dead, but because he didn't order the hit. I did it without his permission. Prick.*

Tank turns on the wipers and takes a long slug of soda. *Then again, Gambino only needs to know about Rocco. I'll dispose of Officer Friendly, and no one will be the wiser.*

CHAPTER 13

*"Possibly, then, writing has to do with darkness,
and a desire or perhaps a compulsion to enter
it, and, with luck, to illuminate it, and to bring
something back out to the light."*
—MARGARET ATWOOD

Maeve sweeps her car for surveillance equipment and finds it clear. She gets in her Prius, presses the garage door opener, and backs out into the downpour as fear gnaws her gut. *I hope Mick was able to dodge the surveillance cameras. If Gambino catches him, he'll kill Emma. Just like he killed Connor.* Her grip tightens on the steering wheel as she fights back the disquiet that's trying to overtake her.

The wipers slap back and forth on the windshield as Maeve listens to the directions from her car's GPS. *I hate leaving Maureen when she's sick with worry about her daughter Emma and her unborn grandchild. I wish she could have come along, but the Prius will already be tight with four grown men and me.*

Unfortunately, there weren't any red-eye flights from San Diego to Bellingham International. So Maeve's driving to Sea-Tac International in Seattle to pick up "the boys," as Maureen refers to her husband, Phillip, and their sons, Eric, Ethan, and Ellery.

The clock on the car's dash indicates that it's almost one o'clock Saturday morning. Her gut hitches again. Having spent her entire working career as a criminal psychologist profiling serial killers for the FBI, she's painfully aware of what the passage of time means for abducted victims—sometimes torture, often death.

In the dark confines of the car, Maeve pats the cross-body bag strapped into the seat with her. *I may have had little on-the-job need for my gun, but that doesn't mean I don't know how to use it.*

Mick is exhausted from commando-crawling like GI Joe across the Pines & Quill property to avoid Gambino's surveillance cameras. And his left leg throbs with pain. Yet, as he nears his cabin on the return trip from retrieving the bag from his mom's house, he stays cautious, stopping every other elbow-crawl forward across rough wet terrain to listen and visually scan the area.

He doesn't stand until he reaches his back door, where he strips to leave the muddy clothes outside. And though neither the red nor green team found a surveillance camera behind his cabin, if one was overlooked, Gambino's getting an unexpected moon shot.

He gathers his wallet, knife, gun, and the black plastic trash bag, then steps naked into the dark dining room. Leaving the lights off, Mick pads his way to the main bathroom, where he places the items and mud-covered bag on the counter next to the sink.

He turns on the hot water, adjusts the jets, then stands beneath the pulsing spray of the shower and lets the pounding water ease a little of his tension. His heart beats a mantra— *Emma, Emma, Emma.*

Before stepping out of the shower, Mick reaches out and retrieves the plastic bag by its tie handles. Using the shower hose, he sprays off the mud. Once the water runs clear, he sets the bag on the bathmat and dries himself. Then, leaving the lights off in the master bedroom, he slips into pajama bottoms, walks into the closet with the bag, pulls the door shut behind him, and turns on the light.

His heart lurches with overwhelming love and fear when he sees Emma's clothes. He presses his face into her nightgown and breathes in her scent. Then, as his tears fall, panic mounts. *Where are you, Emma?* All the horrible possibilities of what might be happening to her fill his mind so that he's almost paralyzed by fear—fear that's followed by guilt and recrimination. *I should have kept her safe.*

The weight of guilt drags him to the closet floor. When he stretches his aching leg, his foot hits the bag. He picks it up, and for the first time, his mind registers the heft. *I expected my parents' encrypted cell phones, but Mom sent more.*

Inside the black plastic trash bag, Mick finds a soft fabric bag. When he opens it, in addition to the phones, he finds a thick, rubber-banded roll of one-hundred-dollar bills, a few pairs of zip-tie handcuffs, a pocketknife, a small box of kitchen matches, a small sewing kit with needle and thread, a spool of twisted nylon rope, a Taser, and his dad's Sig pistol and Galco ankle rig with his Walther PPS. *Mom tried to cover every contingency.*

Mick gets his go-bag, an at-the-ready duffel he's had since his police force days that's packed with essential items in the event of an emergency. He adds the items his mom sent to it before slipping into bed.

The digital display on the nightstand informs him that it's almost two o'clock in the morning. *Emma, we're coming for you, the baby, and the girls.* He turns on his side and closes his eyes. His last conscious thought before exhaustion overtakes him is of Gambino. *If you touch one hair on Emma's or the girls' heads, I'll hunt you down and kill you.*

———

Libby looks at the clock on her nightstand in the second-story master bedroom of the main house. *It's just before five thirty on Saturday morning.* Then, wide awake, she slips out of bed and heads downstairs. When she reaches the bottom, she flips on lights and walks across the dining area to the glass slider that overlooks the patio.

She places a hand on her stomach. *I'm worried sick about Emma and the girls. Just yesterday morning, Emma had breakfast in this very room before her prenatal appointment. It's been almost twenty-four hours since we last saw her—the timeframe when odds drop drastically for a person's chance of being recovered alive.*

Not wanting to release any warmth, Libby pulls her robe closer before opening the patio slider a few inches to inhale the crisp, rain-scented air. Still dark outside, she looks east. *The first touch of dawn has yet to reach our part of the sky.*

While breathing in the morning quiet, a noise catches Libby's attention. She turns to see Niall and Hemingway descend the stairs.

"Good morning, sleepyheads. I was letting you boys sleep in while I make coffee."

As Niall takes Libby in his arms, Hemingway wedges his large, wiry noggin between them, hoping to get in on the hug.

Over his head, they kiss, and then Niall gets a biscuit from the glass jar by the Dutch door and tells Hemingway, "It's time for you to go outside and potty, Mister." After giving him the treat, Niall opens the mudroom door. "And stay away from skunks."

Niall pulls three large covered casseroles from their commercial-sized refrigerator in the kitchen while Libby makes coffee. The night before, he prepped his popular go-to breakfast when they have an overflow of guests—Overnight Breakfast Casserole.

On a base layer of English muffin cubes, he'd poured a mixture of diced breakfast sausage, melted butter, shredded cheddar and mozzarella cheeses, beaten eggs, onion, red pepper, milk, homemade bacon bits, and salt and pepper.

As the oven preheats, Niall says, "We've got thirty minutes to enjoy our coffee before I put those bad boys in the oven. So, now might be an excellent time to work on a grocery list."

Libby gets a pen and tablet from the Pines & Quill office just off the kitchen. When she returns, the bitter yet invitingly warm aroma of coffee fills the atmosphere. Sitting at the dining room table, she inhales deeply and tries to relax her shoulders.

Niall joins her with two brimming, thick sangria-red coffee mugs and sits beside her.

Libby starts writing:

> We know the dining area has a surveillance camera. So, we'll pretend to make a grocery list while we figure out the wording for this morning's Spy game note. Then I'll type and print them to include in the insulated containers when we deliver breakfast.

Out loud, Libby says, "Oh, and Niall, remember that we have two deliveries this morning—furniture for the new addition and a washer and dryer for Mick and Emma's cabin. That way, when the baby comes, they won't have to lug laundry to the set in the workshop."

Libby writes:

There, now Gambino knows we're expecting delivery trucks and why—nothing more than business as usual.

"I'll make sure to be on hand for that," Niall says. "Now, about lunch this afternoon; I was planning on watermelon slices as a side, but I think it's too late in the season. What do you think about avocado corn salad with feta instead?"

"That's one of my favorites," Libby says. "If you name the ingredients, I'll write them down."

"I'll go get the recipe. While I'm in the kitchen, do you want me to top off your mug?"

"Oh, yes, that would be great. Thank you."

Niall carries their mugs to the kitchen, adds hot coffee to each, then gets a recipe. He sits next to Libby and slowly says one ingredient at a time as she writes: ". . . frozen corn, avocados, cherry tomatoes, cucumber, fresh basil, crumbled feta cheese, red onion, butter, olive oil, lime juice, Italian seasoning, salt, and honey."

Sliding the tablet to Niall, Libby says, "And when you go to the Community Food Co-op, you need to remember to get enough for twenty adult guests. You might want to add amounts next to each ingredient. Oh, and while you're out, you might as well kill two birds with one stone. Will you please stop at Seifert & Jones? I noticed that Dale Brewer's been hitting the Pegaso 'Zeta' 2016 Garnacha pretty hard."

"That's a good idea," Niall says. "And I'll pick up a few other wines while I'm there." When he takes the tablet from Libby, he reads the proposed note she wrote to launch today's game of Spy:

Mum's the word—this is a test of your ability to maintain secrecy and a poker face. The team that pulls this off best—red or green—will receive an avalanche of points. If there's a tie, both teams will receive an equal number of points.

Mission: While Mick, Joe, and Rafferty are off the property today preparing part two of our game of Spy, there will be three stand-ins—two on the green team covering for Joe and Rafferty and one on the red team covering for Mick. Because they're "undercover operatives," don't draw attention to them. And when you speak to them, use the name of the person they're standing in for.

The timer dings, and Niall goes into the kitchen to put the casseroles in the oven.

When Hemingway barks, Libby opens the mudroom door to let him in. The day has dawned bright and clear. Other than the wet ground and the mud on Hemingway's paws, all traces of the evening's storms are gone.

"Okay, Hemingway, you know the drill."

Hemingway's aware that there's a treat in his near future if he cooperates, so he lets Libby dunk each of his paws in the pan of water they keep outside the mudroom door just for this purpose.

Libby towels his paws and then sends him inside. "Niall," she calls out. "Will you please give Hemingway a biscuit?"

After pulling the door closed behind her, Libby steps out from under the overhang toward Niall's garden and stands in the pink morning light. *God, Gambino already killed my dad, Connor and my brother-in-law, Paddy. Please don't let him hurt Emma, my future niece, or the girls. You can't hold me accountable for what I'll do if you let that happen.*

Joe Bingham hasn't slept well in the camp-style sleeping arrangements in the new addition above the workshop. It's not for lack of comfort but because he and his wife, Marci, have whispered back and forth in their sleeping bags throughout the night about their kidnapped daughters, Carly and Brianna. Guilt burns in his chest. *I'm their father; it's my job to protect them.*

He checks the lighted display on his watch. *It's almost seven fifteen, and we're supposed to be at the main house for breakfast at eight. And then, right after that, the plan for Mick, Rafferty, and me to get off the property goes into effect. I hope it works because if it doesn't . . .*

A seasoned homicide detective, Joe knows full well the ramifications of a ticking clock. *Unfortunately, being married to me, Marci knows what that means too.*

"The only thing that keeps me from losing my mind," Marci whispers, "is at least the girls are with Emma. She loves them and will do what she can to protect them."

In the dark room, Joe's face burns with shame. He cups Marci's face between his hands. "We'll find the girls and Emma," he whispers. "Now, here's the plan. Once the furniture and appliance trucks arrive, Mick, Rafferty, and I will walk up the ramp into the back to help unload the large boxes. The guys with the hand trucks coming back down the ramps will be our replacements—Emma's brothers Eric, Ethan, and Ellery. With our hats pulled low over their brows and wearing essentially the same clothes—jeans and flannel shirts—it shouldn't raise any red flags to whoever's monitoring the surveillance cameras.

"Emma's dad, Phillip, will be manning the secure site at Maureen's house while she and Emma's mom, Maeve, are here at Pines & Quill playing Spy—business as usual."

"How on earth did you plan that while everything's being monitored?"

"You know Mick's poker buddy, Tim, who's here with his wife, Mary, and their baby Hannah, right?"

"Yes, but how does that figure into things?"

"Through a series of handwritten notes passed between Mick and Tim on the sly yesterday, they worked out that part of the plan. At breakfast in the main house this morning, Mary is going to ask Tim to make a quick trip home for more diapers. Once he leaves, he's going to the furniture store, and from there, he'll ride along on the delivery truck with a buddy who works there. And Tim's brother, Doug, is a delivery guy for an appliance store. He's delivering empty washer and dryer boxes."

"That's brilliant."

"That's not all." Joe scoots even closer to Marci. "One of Emma's brothers, acting as Mick, will check what's inside one of the appliances boxes and say that it's damaged and needs to be replaced. He'll take that opportunity to slip Mick's go-bag inside before closing it up."

"If Mick's go-bag is anything like yours, you guys will be prepared for just about anything."

Joe's nostrils flare at the fresh fragrance of Marci's perfume, a hint of floral and citrus with just the right dose of woodsy.

"Let's hope so." Joe squeezes Marci's soft, warm hand. "I want you to be just as prepared. Keep your gun hidden in your bellyband at *all* times. The only other armed people at Pines & Quill are US Marshal Jake Porter and probably Maeve."

"Mick's mom?" As Marci starts to sit, Joe gentles her back down and takes her in his arms.

"I'd never underestimate that woman. You wouldn't think it to look at her, but she's formidable. And in the event Gambino sends any of his goons, you, Jake, and Maeve are what stands between him and the others."

"Don't forget Jake's wife, Sarah," Marci whispers. "Emma said she's wicked good with a compound bow."

"That's true," Joe whispers, "but it would raise a lot of eyebrows for her to carry it around while playing Spy."

"Be careful, Joe. I won't survive if I lose you or our girls."

"Marci, I promise I'll find the girls and bring them back to you." *Or die trying.*

———

Rafferty has been awake for quite some time. He lies still in his sleeping bag next to Ivy and Maggie in one of the guest rooms in the addition of the workshop. Surrounded by the faint smell of new construction—lumber, fresh paint, and carpet—he thinks.

Three years ago, my son, Drew, was killed in a car accident just before his sixteenth birthday. Had I known that Gambino orchestrated that "accident," I would have found the son of a bitch—badge be damned—and killed him. Now he has my best friends' loved ones, and I'm going to do everything in my power to help them get Emma, Carly, and Brianna back.

As he clenches and unclenches his fists, Ivy stirs.

"What's the matter, Rafferty?"

"I'm just thinking about the time, that's all." Rafferty slips his glasses on. "And you know what? I bet Miss Maggie needs to go potty."

At the sound of her name, Maggie stands, yawns, does a butt-in-air, full-body stretch, then plunks herself down next to him and wags her stubby tail, waiting for the promised walk.

After they get ready, Rafferty takes Ivy's hand as Maggie leads the way toward the main house at seven fifty under a rain-washed morning sky. Rafferty knows that Niall appreciates punctuality. That and the fact that he'd never voluntarily miss one of Niall's home-cooked meals ensures their timely arrival.

Ivy put Maggie's harness on her today, aware that Rafferty's leaving and won't be by her side.

Like any self-respecting Standard poodle, Maggie leads the way with her head held high. And being the well-trained guide dog that she is, she's careful of her charge and avoids the puddles.

Rafferty squeezes Ivy's hand with reassurance as she responds to a previous remark.

"But, Rafferty, I've never fired a gun before in my life. In case it slipped past you, I'm *blind*."

"I don't think there's going to be any reason for you to use it," Rafferty assures her. "It's just for in case Gambino or one of his thugs comes to Pines & Quill and gets up close and personal. They won't expect a blind woman to have a gun. Just shove the business end in their stomach and pull the trigger like I showed you."

"I'll carry it in my purse," Ivy says, "but I can't imagine using it. And what about *you*?"

"You've got my ankle carry," Rafferty says. "I've got my Sig Sauer. And once this whole thing's over, we're going to join the monthly target practice dates with Mick, Emma, Joe, and Marci. The wife of an FBI special agent—*my* wife—needs to know how to handle a gun."

Ivy stops abruptly. "Was that a marriage proposal?"

A trickle of sweat runs down the back of Rafferty's neck. *Oh, my God, this isn't at all how I planned it. And I've only just started looking at rings because I haven't been able to determine Ivy's finger size without her getting suspicious. I wanted the proposal to be special, and I just wrecked every-thing by blurting it out. What if she says no?*

Rafferty pushes his glasses up the bridge of his nose. "It's not at all how I planned it, but yes. Yes, it is."

With her hand still in his, Rafferty lowers himself to one knee on the rain-soaked ground in front of Ivy and Maggie. "Ivy, when I look into my heart, I only see you. When you look into your heart, if you only see me, then I'd like for us to grow old together. Will you please marry me?"

Niall hears three brisk raps on the front door of the main house. Tossing a dish towel over his shoulder, he makes his way to the foyer and opens it. "Rafferty, Ivy, Maggie—you're right on time. Come in."

Niall backs out of the way to let them in. *What the heck? Rafferty looks like he's going to be sick, and Ivy looks like it's the best day of her life.*

As Maggie leads Ivy over the threshold, Ivy tips her head up and flares her nostrils. "Oh, Niall, that savory scent is like heaven, and my mouth's already watering."

"I hope you like it," Niall says. "Libby would have greeted you, too, but she's out on the grounds making breakfast deliveries to the writing cottages."

"Hemingway must be with her," Ivy says. "He's usually front and center when Miss Maggie comes calling."

When she hears her name, Maggie's exclamation-point tail wags like an up-tempo metronome.

"Yes," Niall says. "He tagged along with Libby when he realized he wasn't getting anything to eat from the kitchen."

"What can we help you with?" Rafferty asks.

The poor man doesn't look like he can help himself, let alone anyone else. Niall glances at his watch. "I expect everyone other than the writers in residence to show up any minute now. As they arrive, will you let them in?"

"You've got it," Rafferty says.

As he pulls out a chair for Ivy at the large pine table in the dining area, Niall sees Rafferty's nod of approval at the printed notes at each place setting.

Dread fills Niall's chest. *I hope no one says or does anything to spark suspicion in whoever's monitoring the surveillance camera.*

By the top of the hour, Libby and Hemingway have

returned and so have the guests: Maeve and Maureen, Joe and Marci, Skip and Olivia, Tim, Mary, and baby Hannah, Hank and Gail, Kent and Molly, and Mick brings up the rear.

As everyone seats themselves at the table, Niall notices a muddy patch on the jeans of Rafferty's right knee. "Hey, buddy," he says, pointing to the spot. "I didn't notice it before, but what happened to you?"

After a short, awkward silence, Ivy scoots back her chair and stands. "As a matter of fact," she says, smiling, "Rafferty got down on his knee and proposed to me."

The women around the table clasp their hands in front of their hearts and gasp in delight.

A dramatic beat goes by while everyone waits to hear the outcome.

Niall clears his throat. "Well, not to be nosy or anything, but am I opening champagne?"

Ivy reaches for Rafferty's hand so that he stands too. Then, she turns to him and says, "Yes, Sean Rafferty, I will marry you."

Skip's girlfriend, Olivia, asks, "What about the ring?"

Niall sees the distress return to Rafferty's face and comes to his rescue. Removing a ribbon from the floral centerpiece, he hands it to Rafferty, who ties it around the ring finger on Ivy's left hand.

"Now that the cat's out of the bag," Rafferty says, relieved, "we can go shopping for an engagement ring together." Rafferty takes Ivy in his arms as applause and hearty congratulations erupt around the table. Then, much to everyone's delight, he tips her back and kisses her soundly on the lips.

"I'll be back with the bubbly," Niall says. In the privacy of the kitchen area, his heart is torn. *I'm thrilled for Rafferty and Ivy's happy news, but I'm heartbroken for Mick, Joe, and Marci because the ones they love and hold most dear are still missing. And God only knows what's happening to them.*

The watchman's stomach rumbles as he watches the Pines & Quill monitors and listens to the conversation around the large dining table.

By contrast, the food he packed for his shift looks less appealing by the minute. He fiddles with his pen. *This can't get any more boring.* Finally, the watchman opens his duffle. He's torn between the magazine he brought—the latest issue of *Guns & Ammo*—and his job, watching the monitors.

Just then, he's alerted to activity at the entrance as a monitor reveals a white Honda Accord, with a child seat in the back, leaving the property.

The man shrugs with indifference when he sees that it's just the guy, Tim, whose wife sent him home for more diapers. *Chump—I wouldn't let anybody get me by the short hairs like that.*

The watchman's into the first pages of *Guns & Ammo* when he's alerted to the entrance gate again. *Shit!*

This time a furniture van pulls up. After the driver gets out and presses the intercom, the gate opens, and the truck pulls through.

A few different cameras monitor its drive up the winding, tree-lined lane before it pulls in front of the workshop area and stops. The driver gets out, then pulls a long, ridged metal ramp from the back and secures it as his helper lifts the roll-up door.

As one of the garage-type doors opens on the workshop, a closer monitor picks up the activity.

The watchman leans in for a closer look and notices the time—*Ten o'clock, straight up. It must be the first delivery of the day. Now, three guys from Pines & Quill join the driver and his helper.*

The watchman double-checks the photos taped to the wall for confirmation, then looks back at the monitors. *Yep, it's the PI, Mick, and his two buddies—the homicide detective Joe and Rafferty, the FBI special agent.*

He watches as they and the two delivery guys walk up the ramp.

A minute or two later, the same guys come back down the ramp. Three struggle with a bulky mattress while the other two carry a box spring.

This scenario repeats three more times. *Must be beds for the bedrooms in the new addition over the workshop that Tank worked on.*

Just when he thinks they're done, they go back up the ramp. This time, three of them carry down a full-sized couch while the other two carry a loveseat.

As that activity's underway, the entrance gate monitor alerts him to movement. He watches as the driver of an appliance truck speaks into the intercom. After the gate opens, the truck makes its way down the lane. It drives past the workshop, turns south, and doesn't stop until it gets to the PI's cabin.

Mick, Joe, and Rafferty follow the appliance truck on foot. *This must be hell on Mick's leg. His limp seems to have gotten worse.*

Once they offload the appliance boxes, Mick opens the top of one, then stops and points at something.

Oh, man. He looks angry.

Mick pulls a knife out of his pocket and squats in front of the large box. The watchman can no longer see the PI, but he sees the driver bend to look at something.

Then both men stand and seem to be arguing.

The driver gets a clipboard and pen from the truck cab and hands them to Mick.

Damn, it must be damaged.

Mick fists the clipboard on one hip and jabs the pen toward both boxes as he talks.

The driver throws up his hands, kicks the ground, then has his helper reload both boxes as he waits in the cab.

The PI must be royally pissed to send both the washer and the dryer back. The watchman shakes his head. *I'd of just shot the guy.*

Mick, Joe, and Rafferty sit on the floor in the back of the furniture delivery truck. "It seems we pulled that part off without a hitch," Mick says. "From what I saw of it, Emma's brothers— Eric, Ethan, and Ellery—did a good job posing as us."

"We're not out of the woods yet," Joe says. "They've got to keep it up for as long as it takes."

And the clock is ticking. Twenty-four hours ago, Emma left Pines & Quill for her prenatal appointment. That was the last time we saw her. And even though I can't see Joe's face in the dark, I know he's thinking the same thing about his daughters, Carly and Brianna. Every passing second counts.

"The next stop," Mick says, "is Boulevard Park on Bayview Road in Bellingham, where we'll meet up with the appliance truck to get my go-bag. That's where Tim's brother Doug will give us the keys to his wife Patty's car. She drove it there, and he'll drop her back off at their home before he finishes his deliveries."

"Then what?" Rafferty asks as the delivery truck pulls to a stop.

Before Mick can answer, Doug rolls the back door up. "I hope the ride wasn't too bad."

"It was fine," Mick says. "Thanks so much for helping us out."

"It must be a pretty elaborate game of Spy," Doug says, handing Mick a key. "Tim says it's a highlight that he looks forward to each year."

He points to a black Toyota Highlander. "Here's your ride, guys. Have fun. I hope your team wins."

"We owe you, big time," Mick says, as he, Joe, and Rafferty shake Doug's hand and then get into Patty's car.

When Mick turns the key in the ignition, the radio comes on. As he reaches to turn it off, they hear, "We interrupt this broadcast to bring you a special report. The Whatcom County Sheriff's Office is asking for the public's help to locate a missing sheriff, last heard from at the QuickTrip on Highway 542 when he spoke with the dispatcher just after midnight.

"Sheriff Christopher Sitler's duty vehicle was found parked and locked by the evening crew who called in the unattended car. When questioned, the attendant said that no sheriff had come into the store during his shift. Unfortunately, neither the inside nor outside security cameras are operational.

"If you have any information, please call our office at—" The announcer gives the number and then follows up with, "This is Ken Warren coming to you live from KGMI News-Talk 790. Now back to our regularly scheduled program."

Mick looks at Joe in the front passenger seat, then at Rafferty's reflection in the rearview mirror. He raises his eyebrows. "Coincidence?"

"In all my years in law enforcement," Joe says, "I've never known of a law enforcement officer to go missing. Killed on duty and off? Yes. But missing? No."

Rafferty shakes his head. "Ditto that," he says. "Agents get killed in and out of the field, but they don't go missing."

Mick turns in his seat. "I think it's more than coincidence. And I'm not just grasping at straws. I don't believe in coincidence; there's no such thing. It's not chance or luck, either. It's the universe's way of giving us a sense of hope." *Or of shattering it.*

CHAPTER 14

"Make people believe in your story first and foremost."
—GABRIEL GARCÍA MÁRQUEZ

Tank takes the still-damp cement steps two at a time from his downstairs waterfront apartment up to the street level. He looks at the time on his cell phone. *Eleven forty-five. Shit! I didn't mean to sleep that long.*

From the sheltered stairwell entrance, he calls the contact number for Gambino, and Carmine answers. "The boss ain't taking calls at this time. But I'll pass your message along. Whatcha got?"

"Two things," Tank says. "One—Rocco's dead. He disobeyed orders and fucked the merchandise; then he killed her. Two—I'm taking care of the evidence."

"Where?" Carmine asks.

"Out at the Scrap Heap."

"Okay, I got it. Anything else?"

"I'm heading back up to the holding spot once I take care of business. Do you have a timeframe for receipt of the final merchandise and relocation?"

"Receipt of the final headcount could be as early as today," Carmine says. "But the relocation of said merchandise is on a need-to-know basis. And you don't need to know. At least not yet." Then he disconnects the call.

The bastard hung up on me! Tank presses his palm against the folded knife in the side pocket of his pant leg. *Your time will come, Carmine.*

He glances up at the squawking seagulls that dot the morning-blue sky, then wrinkles his nose. *Even though it rained all night, the air still smells like rotten seaweed and dead fish.*

Cautious and silent, Tank peers around the stairwell's entrance.

Two seagulls screech at each other over a discarded fast-food bag, pecking, pushing, fighting to get to the bounty inside.

Tank scans left then right at the littered surroundings before stepping out of the stairwell onto the cracked sidewalk.

The seagulls fly off, leaving the pockmarked bag behind.

Before getting into his black Dodge Ram 1500, Tanks does a 360, wanding it for surveillance equipment as he goes. Then he checks for explosive devices. Being the one who usually plants them, he knows all about vehicle-borne improvised explosive devices—VBIEDs. *Clear.*

As he drives away, Tank glances in the rearview mirror. *A person could get killed in this hell hole. When Gambino's guy, Carmine, contacted me on the oil rig in Alaska and said, "The Bull wants you to join his local team in Bellingham," I thought I was moving up the ranks. He followed it up with, "You'll have a waterfront apartment," which clinched the deal.*

He failed to say that "waterfront" was code for living across the street from the Harris Avenue Shipyard cleanup site. Disgusted, Tank shakes his head. *I fucking live across the street from five acres of in-water contaminated marine sediment and five acres of upland contaminated soil and groundwater. The bastard.*

Thirty minutes later, Tank is on the other side of Bellingham, driving down a gravel road to the Scrap Heap. On the surface, to innocent passersby, it's a wrecking yard where vehicles are brought and their usable parts are salvaged and sold, while the unusable metal parts are sold to recycling companies. In reality, it's a place where people and things that have outlived their usefulness pass through.

A snarling Rottweiler greets him through an eight-foot chain link fence topped with triple concertina wire. The result is a highly effective barrier.

The dog's human counterpart, Skull, meets Tank at the gate. A scar runs the length of his face from hairline to jaw, slicing through his right eyebrow.

He pulls a rag from the back pocket of his greasy coveralls and wipes his hands. "I was told to expect you."

Yeah? I'll just bet you were. "I've got some business to take care of. Where's the crusher?"

Skull fishes in his front pocket, then hands Tank a key. "Big Bang's over there." He points toward a muddy dirt road between mountains of flattened skeletal cars. "When you get to where you have to choose, go right. You can't miss her; she'll be on your left."

Through the grapevine, Tank had heard about Skull's predecessor, Vito Paglio, an alias for Salvatore Rizzo. *I never did learn who capped him and his two dogs.*

After parking his truck, Tank scans the area and decides on a car with a rusted-open trunk. Then he opens the shell on the back of his truck, lowers the tailgate, and pulls out Rocco's taped body. After unrolling him, Tank clears Rocco's wallet of cash, then carries the lifeless body to the open trunk and drops it in.

He pulls the next body out. When he removes the raingear, he sees the name Christopher Sitler. *Sorry about that, ol' Chris. You should have kept your nose out of my business.* Next, he takes Christopher's sidearm, a Beretta M9, sets it by the left wheel well, and clears the uniform pockets. Tank removes the bills from his wallet and pockets too. Then he strips the body and dumps the clothes on top of the gun—*You never know when a sheriff's uniform and badge might come in handy.* Finally, he carries the body to the open trunk and dumps it on Rocco's. Before closing the back of his truck, he tucks his findings under the tarp.

Then Tank climbs into the rig of an old crane. Black smoke belches from an exhaust stack when he starts the engine. He moves a lever to guide the giant hooks to the open-trunked vehicle and then pushes a black-knobbed lever. The hooks descend. When they surround the car, he presses a button, and they close around the vehicle. He lifts it and then swings it over the crusher, dropping it. Finally, he presses the button on a remote.

Tank smiles at the screech of metal grinding on metal. Once the car's flat, he returns the levers to their idle position and shuts off the engine. *And that's the end of that.*

When Tank leaves the wrecking yard, he starts driving toward Chameleon Ink on State Street in Bellingham but decides to go to a different tattoo shop instead. *If word gets back to Gambino that I had two kill notches inked instead of one, he'll wonder why. And if he finds out that I killed the sheriff without his authorization, there'll be hell to pay. So instead, I'll go to X Tattoo, where they don't know me.*

Driving, he thinks about the excitement he feels when killing, especially if there's a struggle. He glances down at the seventeen black, half-inch tally marks tattooed on the inside of his left arm. Every fifth mark is inked at an angle across the previous four marks so he can readily see groups of five. *With two new ones, I'll have nineteen.*

He nods with smug satisfaction at his collection of kill notches—*One for each person I've had the distinct pleasure of removing from this world.*

———

Sarah's eyes are on her husband, Jake. She sees his grip tighten on a coil of rope as he gazes toward the tree line. *I know he'd prefer to have gone with Mick, Joe, and Rafferty, but someone has to be at Pines & Quill if Gambino's thugs show up. I'm glad he's here, even though it's not nearly as exciting as what he's used to. He told me he lives for the adrenaline rush. I'm afraid that one day, he'll die for it too.*

At almost two o'clock on Saturday afternoon, Sarah and Jake are with the red and green team members on the boulder and rock-strewn bluff overlooking Bellingham Bay. While Eric—posing as Mick—oversees target practice, Sarah shows some of them how to use a compound bow, and Jake shows others how to lasso.

Jake pulls the brim of his cap lower and squints toward the tree line.

He said that while walking through Pines & Quill this morning, the hair on the back of his neck rose. I told him it was the surveillance cameras. But Jake shook his head. "No, it was more than that. It felt like a flesh and blood person was watching me."

Jake turns to Sarah and mouths, "I'll be right back." His long legs cast shadows as he walks away. After a couple-minute walk across the bluff, he disappears into the tree line.

Just then, an all-terrain vehicle drives onto the bluff from the opposite end of the tree line. Niall is at the wheel with Libby next to him.

Sarah remembers Libby referring to it as a "buggy." Libby explained, "With its rugged stance, canopied top, and knobby tires, it's invaluable for getting around the property, regardless of the weather."

The ATV pulls next to the group. "You've worked off your lunch," Niall calls out. "It's time for dessert."

As he and Libby exit the front, Maggie helps Ivy get out the back.

Wagging his long wiry gray tail, Hemingway breaks off from the group to greet Maggie and see if his people brought a treat for him too.

"It's self-serve," Libby says, waving everyone over. "After we spread out the blankets, you'll find paper plates, cups, and napkins in the back cargo area. And don't be shy. Niall made plenty. There's lemonade, iced tea, and bombshell brownies—I think they might even still be warm."

"What are bombshell brownies?" Sakura asks.

"Brownies that have espresso powder," Libby says.

Niall chimes in. "That's right. The rich and bitter notes of chocolate and coffee are enhanced when combined, creating a delicious complexity you don't get from just one or the other alone."

"It sounds like one of the cool new craft dark beers," Skip says.

Todd rubs his hands together. "I'm game."

They head toward the back of the ATV.

Sarah gathers her bow and quiver, then joins Libby. "I'll be right back."

"Is everything okay?"

Sarah leans in and whispers a lie. "If I don't get to Thoreau *now*, I'm going to wet my pants."

Libby laughs. "Well, far be it from me to stand in your way. Go!"

Sarah makes quick time crossing the bluff. She slows to a crawl when she enters the tree line and hugs the shadows, listening. Then, under the canopy of tall pines, she makes her way through the property, careful not to snap a twig or make a sound, scanning as she goes. *Jake's never off duty. If trouble doesn't find him first, he'll find it. And with Gambino's threat, I want to help.*

She cuts behind Austen Cottage and then heads toward the pavilion. That's when she sees Jake. He's facing her direction with his arms raised to shoulder height. The coiled rope is still in one hand. She also sees a red laser sight dot over his heart on his shirt. *Oh, my God!* A sense of foreboding churns Sarah's stomach at the horror of what she sees.

She scans the direction the laser's coming from. It takes a moment before she spots the back side of a camo-covered man up in a deer stand. He's facing away from her with a rifle trained on Jake.

And though Jake doesn't acknowledge Sarah's presence, she knows that he sees her.

"If you pull the trigger," Jake says to the man sitting in the deer stand, "you'll draw everyone's attention."

Behind the guy, Sarah loads an arrow, draws it back to her cheek, and lets it fly. It whisks off the guy's camo cap and pins it to a branch above his head. "And it'll be the last thing you ever do," she says. "Now drop your weapon, or I'll drop you."

The man in the deer stand drops his rifle to the ground in front of Jake. Then he looks over his shoulder at Sarah. "What the fuck?"

"Climb down, *now*," Sarah says.

When Jake lifts the rifle, Sarah sees a Remington 700 heavy barrel. As a thriller writer who does serious research, she assumes it's chambered for the .308 Winchester.

Camo Man starts, "I'm not coming—"

Jake sets down the rifle, lassos the man, and yanks him from the tree.

Tree branches snap as the guy swishes down, landing with a thud on the ground.

Then just like he did in his rodeo days, Jake straddles and hog-ties the stocky man—wrists to ankles.

With another arrow at the ready, Sarah steps closer. Even with camo paint on his face, she sees anger in his dark, close-set eyes. *His nose is crooked—probably from a break—and his lips are pouting. And without his hat, I can see that what once was a forehead is well on its way to becoming a ninehead—the man's going bald.*

"You better start talking, or my wife will put an arrow through your heart. And you know the good thing about an arrow?"

Wide-eyed with fear, the man shakes his head.

"It doesn't make a sound. No one will ever find out."

The man's Adam's apple bobs. "What do you want to know?"

"Where are Emma, Carly, and Brianna?"

"They're on Mount Baker."

Jake kicks the man in his ribs. "You can do better than that."

"They're in a cabin. It's somewhere near Artist Point at fifty-one hundred feet."

Jake kicks the man again. "Where? Be specific."

The man curls tighter, like a pill bug, trying to protect himself from Jake's boot. "It's at the fucking top, man. I don't have a street address. But I know they'll be relocated to a container ship in Alaska once the final two women arrive."

"What do you mean, 'final two women'? How many are there?"

"There's about ten now. When they've got a dozen, they'll be moved to the container ship."

"Why a container ship? And why Alaska?" Sarah says.

"When that ship sails through the Bering Strait, they'll be sold to some guy in Russia."

Seething with anger, Sarah draws the bow taut and aims between the eyes in his camo-painted face. "Sold?"

The man gulps and nods. "There are two islands, Big Diomede and Little Diomede. That's where The Bull makes most of his exchanges."

"Exchanges for what, exactly?" Jake asks.

"Drugs, weapons, and people."

"In other words," Sarah spits out, "sex trafficking."

"For some of them, yes."

"And for others?" Sarah says.

"Forced labor, and . . ."

Jake kicks the man's ribs again. "And what?"

"They'll use the organs from others; there's a lucrative market for those."

Bile hits the back of Sarah's throat at the thought. "How are they getting from the holding place to the container ship?"

The man shakes his head. "I don't know."

Jake kicks him again. "Talk. You're as good as dead anyway." He looks at the surrounding woods. The tree canopy makes a doily of the sky beyond. "Gambino's probably watching us on a surveillance camera right now."

"No, there's no camera here because I am."

"What's your job?"

"I'm here in the event Gambino's disobeyed and he orders a hit."

"I can either kill you right now," Jake says, "or you can answer my wife and have a head start and a fighting chance to hide from Gambino. The choice is yours."

The man glowers at Sarah. "What was the question?"

"How are they getting from the holding place to the container ship?"

"They've detailed a van to mimic a prisoner transport van. They got a guard from WSP—"

"What's WSP?" Sarah asks.

"Washington State Penitentiary."

Jake presses his eyebrows together. "That's in Walla Walla, in the southern part of the state."

"That's right," the guy says. "Gambino's no fool. A non-local guard won't be recognized."

"How did they get this guard?" Sarah asks.

The man looks at her like she lost her mind. "Everyone has a price, lady. You just have to find out what it is."

Jake kicks the man again. "Not everyone."

"Now go on," Sarah prods. "They've got a guard and a prisoner transport van. Then what?"

"They're making the women dress in orange jumpsuits and transporting them."

Sarah researched prison uniform color codes for one of her thriller books and learned they can vary by state. But, not familiar with Washington, she asks the guy, "Why orange?"

"In Washington state, inmates receive color-coded uniforms: orange for violent or unruly behavior, blue for a low threat, misdemeanor, or nonviolent felony charge, and green for suicide watch and those charged with murder. No one in their right mind's going to stop a prison transport van filled with violent inmates and armed guards."

"Guards, as in plural?" Sarah asks. "I thought you said they bought off *a* guard."

The guy scowls at Sarah. "They did. If the van's stopped, *he* has genuine creds. But if it goes further than that, the other 'guards'—Gambino's men dressed as guards—will take it from there."

Jake steps behind the guy, pulls a pistol from his concealed waist holster, and cold-cocks him. Then he looks at Sarah and smiles. "Darlin', I'm sure glad you came along when you did. You missed your calling. You'd make one hell of a US Marshal."

Sarah shakes her head at the suggestion. "I take it we're going to drag his sorry ass someplace where he'll be out of the way for a while."

Jake hefts the rifle. "That we are."

"Then when it's safe, we can send him on his way."

Jake nods. "That's right."

Sarah releases the tension on her bow and rolls her shoulders to ease the stiffness. Then, quivering the arrow, she thinks about what would have happened if she'd released the arrow. *I don't want to be the one responsible for that scumbag's death.*

"Maybe we can let him use Mick's Jeep to get away. Isn't that the vehicle you said Gambino rigged with a bomb that only he can detonate?"

Mick's white-knuckled grip tightens around the steering wheel when his encrypted cell phone alerts them to an incoming call. *Oh, God, please don't let something more have happened.*

Joe lifts it from the cup holder between them in the front seat of the Toyota Highlander.

Panic seizes Mick's chest as what-ifs assault his mind. "It has to be Jake. We've got three of the encrypted cells; he has the fourth."

Joe answers the phone. "Jake, it's Joe. Mick's driving. I'm putting you on speaker so we can all hear."

Jake briefs them about Gambino's guy in the tree stand and relays everything he said.

"Thank you," Mick, Joe, and Rafferty say simultaneously.

"Great job," Mick adds. "With that information, we should be able to track them."

"Sarah and I need to get back out to the bluff before everyone begins to wonder," Jake says. "I'll keep the encrypted cell on me. Keep me posted."

Adrenaline courses through Mick's veins. He turns onto

Railroad Avenue for faster access to Highway 5, the quickest route to Mount Baker. Rather than parallel parking, this street has angled, hood-to-curb parking. Then, in his peripheral vision, something grabs Mick's attention. On the opposite side of the road sits a black Dodge Ram with Alaska plates. It's parked a few businesses down from X Tattoo.

Mick points. "That's Tank's truck. I'm turning around."

"But he might see us," Joe says.

"This car doesn't mean anything to him," Mick says. "He won't think anything of it."

He looks at the surrounding shops. *A restaurant that doesn't open until dinner, a paint store, a tattoo shop, a yarn store, and women's clothing.* "The only place that makes sense where he'd be is the tattoo shop."

Mick drives to the end of the street, turns around, then parks in an open space three cars down from Tank's truck, even farther away from the tattoo shop.

"I'll be right back." Mick opens the driver's door and gets out before Joe and Rafferty can stop him. His nerves are raw. They tingle with the hope of finding a clue about Emma.

He takes the sidewalk and stops in front of the black Dodge Ram. What Mick sees through the windshield fills his belly with dread. He stops. *Oh, my God, that's Emma's honu—the turtle pendant I carved for her—hanging from the rearview mirror.*

Mick's fingernails pierce his palms as he walks to the rear of the truck. Fear claws his gut as he closes his eyes to steel himself before looking in—*Flat tarps, no bodies.*

Relief fills his body, and he lets out a breath.

He tests the shell's T-handle. *Unlocked.* Heart pounding, he starts to open it, then stops. *Shit! I need gear from my go-bag.*

Back in the Toyota Highlander, Mick reports his findings. "It's definitely Tank's truck." He slams his fist on the dash.

"And the turtle pendant I carved for Emma is hanging from the bastard's rearview mirror!"

Mick rakes his fingers through his hair as sweat trickles from his temples. Then, fueled by panic, he reaches between the two front seats and grabs his go-bag from the seat next to Rafferty. He opens it and starts doling out items.

"What are you doing?" Joe asks.

"While Tank's away from his truck, I'm getting into the back. He can lead us straight to Emma. You guys follow."

"He'll see you," Rafferty says.

"I looked in the back," Mick says. "It's empty except for tarps. I'll hide under one. I checked to make sure the shell's unlocked."

Joe turns in his seat to look at Rafferty. He presses the muscle at the corner of his eye. "I'm going with Mick. The bastard has Carly and Brianna, too. You follow at a safe distance."

Rafferty nods. "I don't feel good about this. But damn it to hell, I'd do the same thing if it was Ivy."

After dividing the firepower, each man has two guns—a primary and an ankle carry—and spare rounds. Mick always carries his Deejo knife, and Joe always conceals a blade, so Rafferty takes the knife from the go-bag. Then they each stuff zip-tie handcuffs in their back pockets.

"Rafferty, you keep the rest of the gear in the go-bag with you," Mick says. "And let's put our phones on vibrate."

"The moment we make visual contact," Joe says, "we'll call in backup. But not a moment sooner, or they might accidentally tip our hand. Agreed?"

Mick and Rafferty nod. "Agreed."

Mick and Joe exit the Highlander and head to the back of the Dodge Ram as Rafferty slips into the driver's seat.

Dad always said, "You can go just about anywhere by acting as if you own the place." So that's what Mick does. When they reach the back of Tank's truck, he turns the T-handle, lifts the glass rear door, lowers the tailgate, and hops in.

After Joe follows suit, they close the back.

In the shadowy confines of the closed space, the metallic smell of blood hits Mick. He lifts the tarp by the wheel well and goes slack-jawed by what he sees—a bloody sheriff's uniform with a badge inscribed CHRISTOPHER SITLER and a Beretta M9.

"I don't think the sheriff's missing," Mick says. "I suspect that he's dead."

CHAPTER 15

"First, find out what your hero wants,
then just follow him!"
—RAY BRADBURY

Emma's eyes adjust to the darkness of her new world—the locked confines of a small room in a cabin with nine other people somewhere on Mount Baker. As terror thunders down her spine, she clasps her hands together to keep them from shaking. *There has to be a way to escape!*

She scrapes her lower lip with her teeth. *The girls and I have had one sleep in this prison*—her body shudders at the thought—*That means it's Saturday, Labor Day weekend. I've never been this scared in my life, not even when Jason Hughes held me captive in Devil's Canyon. But I wasn't pregnant then, and I didn't have anyone else to protect.*

Even though the dark room's chilly, sweat trickles between Emma's breasts. *Please, God. Help Mick find us.*

She breathes through her mouth to keep from gagging on the stench of the bucket-toilet in the corner.

Two men brought us stale pizza several hours ago, so it must be late afternoon. One of them carried three half-empty boxes. The other held a kerosene lamp. I abandoned the idea of jumping the lamp holder, breaking the glass chimney, and using it as a weapon when I realized the lamp oil might cause a fire and we could burn to death in this barred room.

Faint light bleeds through the narrow space around the boarded and barred window, confirming that it's still daytime outside.

Emma places a hand on her belly. *I need to protect our baby.* She tamps down the feeling of dread and clings to a nugget of hope. *I heard one of the men warn against harming Carly, Brianna, or me. He said, "Don't touch the PI's wife and the detective's daughters." For some reason, they want us alive and in good condition.*

She squints her eyes against the darkness and reaches her hands out to find Carly and Brianna. "Girls, at some point, our captors are going to bring two more women for a total of twelve. When they reach a dozen, they said they'd relocate us. With the distraction of newcomers, it might be a good time to try to escape." Emma gently squeezes their hands. "It's probably better, though, to wait until we're outside. You were unconscious when they brought you, but I wasn't. A forest surrounds this cabin. If we can break away and hide in the trees, we'll have a chance."

"I'm scared." Eleven-year-old Brianna's voice quivers.

"I am too," her thirteen-year-old sister Carly says.

From across the room, Andrea Peters says, "I'm also scared."

Emma hears shuffling across the wood floor as Andrea crawls toward them. "If you're making a plan to escape," Andrea says, "I'd like to be part of it."

Emma scoots her bottom over to make room for Andrea in their small circle. "I've been thinking of a signal," Emma says. "One I can make without being noticed even if my wrists are bound."

"But what if we're blindfolded and can't see the signal?" Andrea asks.

"They uncovered my eyes after I was lowered from the helicopter," Emma says. "What about you?"

"No," Andrea says. "I wasn't blindfolded. I guess that's why they wear those hooded face covers. So they can see us, but we can't see them. But my wrists and ankles were bound."

"They cut my ankles loose so I could walk into the cabin," Emma says. "And then they cut my wrists free once I was in this room."

"What's the signal?" Carly asks.

"Once we're outside and the time is right," Emma says, "I'll hold out two fingers."

"Like a peace sign?" Brianna asks.

"Yes," Emma says, "but with my fingers together instead of apart. It's less noticeable."

Then, to remove all doubt of what she means, Emma takes first Carly's, then Brianna's, and then Andrea's hands and has them feel the shape of her signaling hand.

"Got it," they say.

"Then what happens once you give the signal?" Andrea asks.

"Both of the girls are in traveling soccer leagues," Emma says. "So, they play at a higher level of competitiveness than recreational teams."

"In other words, they're good," Andrea says.

"They're *really* good," Emma says. "They kick hard and run fast."

"I played soccer in high school," Andrea says, "but that was a long time ago. I jog every day, though. If it means getting away, I can kick hard and run fast too."

"All right, then," Emma says, "when I give the signal,

kick whoever's guarding you between their legs as hard as you can."

"In the nuts?" Carly asks. "That's what Dad told us to do if a guy ever tries to hurt us. He said it's excruciating, and they'll double over in pain, giving us a chance to get away."

"Your dad's right," Emma says. "And then run as fast as you can into the trees."

"But what if our wrists and ankles *are* bound?" Andrea says.

"I don't think they will be," Emma says. "When I listened at the crack under the door, it sounds like once the last two people get here, they're going to move us—*fast*. Like it's time sensitive."

"Maybe they're on a deadline," Andrea offers.

"It's possible," Emma agrees. "If they don't bind our ankles, after you kick for all you're worth, crawl or drag your-self into the trees." *Please don't let them bind our ankles. The entire plan hinges on that.*

"From what I saw under the bottom of my blindfold while I was in the helicopter," Emma says, "I think we're some-where on Mount Baker. Head downhill as fast as possible, and when you get to the highway, flag down help."

One at a time, Emma feels for and gathers a hand from Carly, Brianna, and Andrea, placing them one on top of the other. "We're a team," she says. "And once we get outside, we're going to do *whatever* it takes to escape."

———————

Libby glances at the wall clock in the dining area of the main house. *It's almost six o'clock—time for dinner. Guests will arrive any minute. Half of them know what's going on with Emma and the girls. The other half is still in the dark, and we need to keep it that way. The fewer people who know, the less chance someone will slip up and Gambino learns that Mick, Joe, and Rafferty left the property.*

If I can get everyone outside on the patio, away from the surveillance equipment, then those of us who know can talk without fear of our conversation being broadcast to Gambino or his thugs. Besides that, Jake's got the fourth encrypted cell phone, and I want to know if he's heard anything from the guys.

Libby stops herself from looking up into the corner. *I'm on camera right now, so I need to act normal.* When she pauses to adjust the floral centerpiece on the large pine table, she notices her hand tremble. *I'm so scared for Emma and the girls. What's happening to them?*

When Libby enters the kitchen, Niall looks up from the pan he's stirring. She can't help but smile. *In his apron, and with a smear of tomato sauce on his chin, he looks somewhat Hobbit-like—adorable.*

"Hello, husband. Where's your sidekick, Hemingway?"

"He's with Maggie and Ivy."

"Who knew that a rough and tumble Irish wolfhound would fall for a prissy Standard poodle?" Libby asks. "But he's head over heels."

"That he is," Niall agrees. "You'd think they were attached at the hip."

"It's so lovely outside it might be nice to eat on the patio," Libby says. "And Hemingway and Maggie have a lot more fun when they're not confined."

She watches a subtle change in Niall's demeanor. She was twenty-one and Niall was twenty-three when they got married. *After thirty-two years, I know the meaning behind all of his expressions, and he just shifted into pondering mode. He's going to think about my suggestion for a few minutes before answering.*

Niall dips a wooden spoon into the sauce, then steps toward Libby, lifting it to her lips. "What do you think?" he asks.

Libby blows on the red sauce before accepting the proffered spoon. Then she rolls her eyes back and closes her lids.

"Oh, honey, this sauce is *delicious*. It tastes like it came right out of the garden."

"It's the sauce I canned from this year's bumper crop of tomatoes. But part of what you're tasting is from the meatballs. I made them with a mixture of ground beef and Italian sausage, so it also has the flavor of fennel and coriander."

Libby nods. "And garlic, too."

"Yes," Niall says. "But I think that's what you smell." He points toward the counter.

Next to a bowl of freshly grated Parmesan cheese, Libby sees a bowl of whipped butter with visible chunks of pungent garlic, red pepper flakes, and freshly torn basil leaves.

"You're brilliant," Libby says. "The basil will add a sweet, fragrant, peppery taste."

"It's for the crusty French baguettes," Niall says. "Because we have a larger than usual crowd, I used a new recipe for larger loaves. I'll pull them from the oven in just a few minutes. Then I'll slice them down the center, slather them with the butter mixture, and put them under the broiler for just a minute."

"Our guests are going to love it." Libby looks around the kitchen and furrows her eyebrows. "Niall, earlier, I prepped the ingredients for a salad. Where'd you hide it?"

"I tossed everything together and put it in the fridge along with the Italian dressing I made."

"Is it my favorite?" Libby asks. "The one with red wine, aged balsamic vinegar, and the olive oil you order from Italy?"

Niall nods. "I know you love it. That's why I made it."

Libby slips her arms around his waist and reminds him of her question. "Do you think it would be too much trouble to serve dinner on the patio? I'll set the tables."

He pulls her closer. "I think it's a great idea. And we can light the citronella torches to keep the mosquitoes at bay. They always seem to triple after a storm."

"Speaking of lighting the torches," Libby says. "Do you know where the straw-covered chianti bottles with dripped candle wax are? I could dress the tables with them."

Niall nods. "Indeed, I do. They'll make a nice festive touch."

With her arms still around his waist, she puts her lips to his ear and whispers. "I want to ask Jake if he's heard from Mick, Joe, or Rafferty. And maybe Mom has news from Emma's dad, Phillip, at the secure site that she can pass along. Between a PI, a homicide detective, and an FBI special agent, they've *got* to have made headway."

And if not, maybe there's something we can do from this end.

Mick checks his watch for what seems like the hundredth time. "It's just after six o'clock, Joe. We've been under this tarp in the back of this truck, winding and climbing for a long time. And it stinks like blood—probably Sheriff Christopher Sitler's—and our sweat. It seems like we should arrive at Artist Point soon." *I've got to find Emma. Please, God, let her and the baby be alive.*

Joe taps his phone against his thigh. "I still don't have any cell service. How about you?"

Mick squints at his encrypted cell. It's hard to see under the tarp. "No, I don't either." *The last text I sent was to Emma's cell. They probably took it away from her, even smashed it. But when she gets it back or replaces it, she'll receive my message:*

> I will go to the end of the earth to find you and our baby. But if something goes south, I want you to know that I love you with all of my heart.

The truck bed drops hard, and Mick braces himself. He feels the tires leave the smooth paved road and gain traction in what seems like off-roading conditions.

"Jeez," Joe says, rubbing his elbow. "I think you're right about almost being there. Holding captives is a risky endeavor. It's best done in a remote, low-traffic area. And we're definitely off the beaten path."

Mick covers his face with his hands just in time to stifle a sneeze. He imagines a cloud of dust trailing behind the tires. "At least it'll be good cover for Rafferty."

"I'm glad it's not dark yet," Joe says. "He'd have to follow with the lights off, and if he's trailing us far enough back, he'd probably lose us. At least with a dust trail, he's got something to follow."

Both men are quiet for a moment. Then Joe says, "Mick, we just had a storm. The ground has to be dry for tires to kick up dust."

"Not if it's under a thick canopy. Think about it, Joe. We're somewhere in the area of Snoqualmie National Forest—*the wilderness*—where the trees are thick. Sam and I came up here one year to snowshoe, and there was ground area where the snow didn't reach because it couldn't fall through the canopy."

Just then, the truck comes to a stop, and the engine shuts off. Mick's gaze locks on Joe's.

Each man holds a finger in front of his mouth, and they nod in silent agreement.

The truck door opens and then closes, followed by the thud of footsteps.

Mick holds his breath as his hand hovers over his gun.

Rafferty, in the borrowed Highlander, follows as far behind the black truck as possible to avoid arousing Tank's suspicion. *I can't lose them! They're my best friends, and they're counting on my help.*

He glances at the dash. The clock informs him it's six-fif-teen. *I wonder what Ivy's doing right now? I hope Gambino hasn't sent any of his thugs to Pines & Quill.* His knuckles turn white on the steering wheel, and his heart squeezes in his chest.

When he looks out the windshield, the truck's gone. *Oh, my God. I lost them!*

Rafferty scans left and right as he continues forward, looking for any possible place the truck might have left the main road.

Seeing dust up ahead, he pulls onto the shoulder as far as possible, gets out, and runs forward to check. He furrows his brow. *This has to be where they left the road, but that drop-off will destroy the car.*

Rafferty runs back to the Highlander, cuts the engine, and grabs Mick's go-bag. Before locking the car, he checks the cargo area. From a sturdy plastic milk crate that serves as an emergency kit, he extracts a small box of wooden matches, two flares, duct tape, a bungee cord, an emergency thermal blanket, jumper cables, a can of thirty-weight oil, and a box of granola bars. Everything fits in the go-bag except the jumper cables, which he drapes over his shoulders, and the oil can, which he carries in his other hand.

The forest floor is a carpet of fallen tree debris—branches, pine needles, and cones. Rafferty focuses on the ground, step-ping with care to avoid making noise. The air smells of pine, pitch, and damp. The terrain—dotted with moss, ferns, and other bushes—rises here and dips there with no forewarning of steep inclines. He slips, then continues to move with stealth from trunk to trunk next to the wide, rock-strewn, and rutted track the truck took. *Even though the dust has settled, it's the only way they could have come from that turnoff.*

About fifty yards in the distance, he spots a clearing and the front of a cabin—its back is to a thick line of trees. From behind a large tree trunk, he does an assessment: *Two boarded and security barred windows on the front, a stone chimney but no smoke, no visible telephone poles, wires, or cables of any kind, and three trucks parked in front and to the left side of the cabin—one silver and two black—one of the black trucks is Tank's.*

Fear claws up Rafferty's spine. *Where are Mick and Joe? Are they still in the back of Tank's truck?*

He gauges the distance from the back of Tank's truck to where he's hiding. *That's a lot of wide-open ground to cross without cover. And though the captors can't see out the windows, if one of them steps out the door, Mick and Joe will be caught. But if they head in the opposite direction, they'll be in forest cover. Then I'm sure the guys will make their way around to this side of the clearing so they can watch the front door and the trucks.*

Rafferty sits on the ground with his back against a tree. He opens the go-bag and extracts binoculars. In the distance, on the edge of the clearing, the trees are shadowed in light gray and purple with the faintest hint of yellow. He looks at his watch—*Six-thirty. The sun sets about seven forty-five with last light about eight-fifteen.*

He tries to picture the cabin's layout. *The largest boarded and barred window is to the left of the front door on the chimney side. I bet that's where the living room is. The dining area and kitchen are probably right behind that. And if that's correct, the bathroom and bedrooms are on the right-hand side. Based on the window placement, at least one bedroom is in the front of the cabin.*

A movement catches Rafferty's eye. He trains his binoculars on the back of the truck and watches as the shell window opens slowly. Then he sees Mick, with Joe next to him, unfold himself and tentatively reach a leg over the closed tailgate.

Another movement gets his attention. He moves the binoculars to the right of the truck. *Oh shit!* Rafferty watches with mounting horror as a hooded man with a shoulder holster steps out the cabin's front door.

CHAPTER 16

"Writers are always selling somebody out."
—Joan Didion

Jake glances at his watch—*Six forty-five. I need to get back and check on Camo Man and decide what to do with him. What if he's supposed to check in periodically and doesn't? Gambino would send another thug to see what's going on. Then things would go sideways, fast. What if they're already here?*

He scans the tree-lined periphery. *Clear.* Then he shifts his gaze to the faces around the picnic table on the patio of the main house—*Family, friends, guests. There's a lot at stake here.*

Kitty-corner across the food-laden table, Libby widens her eyes at him and gives a slight jerk of her head toward Niall's vegetable garden in what he interprets as a "meet me over there" look.

Too spun up to eat let alone taste anything, Jake looks at the barely touched food he moved around on his plate. *I need to get back to Camo Man. Now!*

He reaches under the table and squeezes Sarah's hand. Then he scoots his chair back, stands, and picks up his plate, silverware, and glass. *Libby might have new information.*

Next to Jake, Sarah stands and gathers her items too.

"Niall," Jake says, "I can't remember when I enjoyed a meal so much. Thank you."

"Yes, it was delicious." Sarah's hands tremble, causing the silverware on her plate to clink.

"You're welcome," Niall says. "I love to cook."

"And it shows," Jake says. "We're going to take our dishes to the kitchen, and then if you don't mind, Sarah and I are going to stroll through your garden where I suspect much of this" — he nods at the platters on the table — "comes from."

Libby stands too. "I'll be happy to give you a tour."

"That'd be great," Sarah says. "Maybe I can pick up a few ideas for our garden at home."

"Hmm." Niall rubs the stubble on his jaw. "The hardiness zones are different. Here in Bellingham, we're 8a and 8b. I think Billings, Montana, is somewhere in the 4s. But gardening techniques are similar, regardless. So, if you have any questions, I'll be happy to try and answer them later when we convene in the Ink Well."

As Jake and Sarah walk toward the glass slider on the main house, Jake pauses beside Niall. "After we tour the garden, we're going to call it an early night. I have to get back to work on Tuesday and want to spend some quality time with my beautiful wife before I leave."

Niall nods. "I understand. We'll see you two tomorrow."

Once Jake and Sarah are past the surveillance camera in the dining area and have entered the kitchen, he whispers, "I don't know if you saw, but Libby orchestrated the meeting in the garden. Maybe she has information. Whatever it is, we need to *hurry*."

They make quick work of rinsing their plates, utensils, and glassware. Then Jake takes Sarah's hand. "Let's go."

As they pass back through the patio area, Libby joins them. Once they're beyond the guests and in the garden, ensuring their backs are to the closest surveillance camera, she asks, "Have you heard from Mick, Joe, Rafferty, or even Phillip at the secure site?"

"No," Jake says. "I was hoping you had new information." First, he briefs Libby on Camo Man and his current location—". . . hog-tied and gagged in the closet in Thoreau Cottage." Then he shares the proximity of where Emma, Carly, and Brianna are being held, the fact that they'll be transferred to a cargo ship sailing through the Bering Strait, and the reason.

Libby's eyes widen with terror. "They're going to be *sold*? Some into forced labor, some as sex slaves, and some for the extraction of organs and tissues?" She presses her hands to her chest. "Oh, my God!"

"When I last spoke with the guys," Jake says, "I shared the same information I just shared with you. Gambino's not aware that Mick, Joe, and Rafferty are off the property and know the proximity of the hostage location, so the guys have the element of surprise."

"And to maintain that advantage," Libby says, "none of us will share any information where it might be overheard."

"Good," Jake says. "Now Sarah and I need to get back to *our* hostage. We'll see you tomorrow." *Unless Gambino comes calling because Camo Man failed to report in.*

Mick feels Joe's hand grip his ankle, preventing his leg from clearing the tailgate. He turns and mouths, "What?" *We've got to get out of this truck and into the cover of the trees. If they find us, we're dead.*

Joe points out the side window of the truck's shell, and Mick leans down to see. *Oh shit!* His heart clutches as if in a vice. *A guy just came out the front door.*

He exhales with relief as the hooded man walks away from them toward the tree line. Then he draws his leg back inside the truck and eases the shell's window down into place.

A glance at his watch informs him that it's seven o'clock. *Sunset is in less than an hour. It'll be safer to wait in the truck until after dark to get out of here and find Rafferty.*

Mick squats down next to Joe and looks over the ledge of the side window. The guy's taking a leak on a tree when all of a sudden, he cocks his hooded head. He finishes quickly, zips his pants, and checks his watch. His steps are quick as he walks back to the cabin, opens the door, and motions for someone to hurry up and come outside.

A moment later, three guys walk out the cabin's front door, pulling hoods over their heads as they go.

Mick hears the rhythmic buzz of approaching rotors. *The last time I was in a copter was when I was life-flighted after a sniper killed Sam. He was driving our squad car when the windshield shattered, and he slumped forward. The shoulder belt prevented his weight from hitting the steering wheel but not from gunning the accelerator. Our car surged onto the right shoulder.*

Mick's mouth fills with the copper-like taste of blood at the flashback, and he winces at a phantom sound—almost four thousand pounds of steel careening into a concrete abutment.

I don't remember being life-flighted. I do remember not being able to attend my best friend's funeral and memorial service because I was in intensive care. I feel guilty for surviving when Sam didn't. He pulled the driver's straw that morning; I didn't. Sam was a parent; I wasn't. And now I'm going to be a father, but Sam's child will never get to see his dad again.

Mick turns to Joe, circles the air with his index finger, and mouths, "Helicopter."

Joe gives a thumbs-up and nods. The muscle next to one of his eyes pulses.

I bet a hundred scenarios are running through his mind like mine—each one worse than the previous. The underarms of Mick's shirt are damp from sweat. He smells the pungent, gamey scent of fear.

The distinctive blade slap of the chopper hovering overhead interrupts his thoughts.

Easing back under the tarp, he and Joe lift it over their heads and move from the side window to peek out the back. *The hooded guys are so busy watching a rescue basket being lowered that they're not scanning the periphery.*

The prop wash from the chopper's rotor blades stirs everything on the ground, propelling dust through the shell's crevices. Mick covers his face with his hands to stifle a sneeze.

"That's the *second* time in a few hours that you've sneezed from dust clouds," Joe says. "I didn't know you have allergies."

Mick lifts his shoulders. "It's news to me, too."

Based on the height and muscular build of the hooded man releasing the restraining straps and removing the hood from a person lying in the basket, Mick surmises that it's Tank.

Unfortunately, the men's legs block Mick's view, so he can't see who is in the basket.

Mick looks up and notes the tail number—a unique registration number displayed on every aircraft—on his cell phone as the helicopter hovers. The note is a text to his father-in-law, Phillip, who's manning the secure site in his mother's condo.

The text will auto-send the moment I have service again. When Phillip traces the tail number on the Federal Aviation Administration's website, he'll learn who the owner is, their address, and details about the aircraft.

Another hooded man steps forward. Each grabs an upper arm of the person lying in the basket and yanks them to a standing position.

The tornado of wind from the helicopter blows brown hair into a wild tangle.

It's a woman, and her face is filled with terror.

Panic fuels the rhythm of Mick's heart. *Is that how Emma got here? We're so close—mere yards between us. Acting now would be rash. Can't jeopardize her and the girls. What the hell is happening to her? And our baby?*

The basket goes back up, and the process repeats.

When they pull the second woman upright, she spits on one of the men. He backhands her across the face so hard that she falls.

Son of a bitch!

When they jerk her up from the ground, the man she'd spit on brandishes a knife at her throat.

Not more than fifteen yards away, Mick sees her squeeze her eyes shut and hunch into her shoulders.

Then they march both women into the cabin and slam the door behind them.

The blade slap from the helicopter changes to a swoosh, then a roar as it gains altitude and flies away.

Mick's white knuckles protrude from his fists at what he just witnessed.

Joe moves like he's going to get out.

Mick puts a hand on his shoulder. "As much as it pains me to say this, we need to wait until it's dark to get out of this *damn* truck. If we slip out now and they see us, Gambino will prove he's as good as his word. He warned, 'Joe, if you try to save your daughters, I'll kill Mick's wife. And the child she's carrying will die as a result. Mick, if you try to save Emma, I'll kill Joe's daughters.'

"We can't risk them; we wait until dark."

———————

Once inside Thoreau Cottage, Jake and Sarah bolt to the bed-room closet. *If this guy fails to check in on time, Gambino will send someone to find out why.* Jake pulls the gag out of Camo Man's mouth. "When's your next check-in?"

"We don't check in unless there's a problem," he says. "But I think *you're* the one with the problem."

"What do you mean?" Jake says.

"What time is it?"

Jake checks his watch. "It's almost seven fifteen. Why?"

The guy laughs. "My shift's over at seven thirty. That's when my replacement shows up. Well, that's when he's *supposed* to show up. The damn asswipe's usually late," he grumbles.

Jake shoves the gag back in his mouth. "Sarah, while I get another lasso rope out of my bag, grab your bow and quiver."

Dodging surveillance cameras, they hug shadows as they make their way to the tree stand.

"What's the plan?" Sarah asks.

"I'm going to hustle up the tree," Jake says, "and put on the camo hat you nailed with the arrow. Then I'll pretend I'm Camo Man, who's fallen asleep. When the replacement tries to wake me, you'll step out from the shadows with your bow at the ready. Once he drops his gun, I'll climb down, and we'll have a repeat performance."

Minutes later, Jake and Sarah are in position.

It's not long before they hear twigs snapping and then footfalls drawing close.

"Hey, Paolo, it's Dante."

After a few attempts with no response from Paolo, Dante sets his gun on the ground and picks up a rock.

In the ambient light, Jake sees a grin on the guy's face.

When he cocks his arm to throw the rock, Sarah says, "Drop it, or you're a dead man."

Dante spins. "Jesus fucking Christ, lady. Put that thing down."

"She's not going to put it down, and I'm not going to put this down," Jake says from behind the man, his STI 2011 trained down on him.

Dante looks up over his shoulder. His eyes widen. "Who are you? Where's Paolo?"

"That's not important," Jake says. "Now kick the gun away from you."

Dante kicks the gun.

"Farther," Jake says. "And Dante, if I have to say it again, you may not recover."

Dante kicks the gun as far as he can.

"Now, lie on your stomach, spread your legs apart, and lace your fingers behind your head."

After Dante complies, Jake climbs down, shoves a gag in his mouth, and hog-ties him.

Jake stands and wipes the dirt from his hands. "And then there were two."

———

Rafferty lowers the binocular's eyecups from his sockets. As twilight descends on Mount Baker's Snoqualmie National Forest, bruising the day's last light to deep purple, shadows darken, forming a stygian atmosphere. He glances at his watch—*It's going on eight thirty.*

Rafferty checks the go-bag and trades the binoculars for Mick's night-vision goggles. *Good for over two hundred yards on a moonless, cloudy night. Mick used them to rescue Emma when Jason Hughes held her captive in Devil's Canyon.*

Movement at the rear of Tank's truck captures Rafferty's attention. Through the night-vision goggles, he watches the rear window of the shell rise to the fully open position. Mick eases out first. He checks his six, then nods at Joe. They close the window and dart twenty yards into the tree line. *Yes!*

Rafferty moves his binoculars to check the cabin. *All clear.* Then he aims a flashlight from the go-bag in the direction the guys disappeared, flicks it on and off rapidly, then waits.

Within moments, he receives a response—what looks like a flash from their cell phone.

In the night woods, it's not so much that it's hushed as that the few sounds are clear, as if the forest is enunciating them. Birds call to attract mates, defend territory, signal alarm. Some calls are distinctive grace notes, secretive whispers. Others pierce the night.

A branch snaps, then swishes down and thumps on the ground.

What was that? Rafferty begins a three-sixty scan through the green monochrome tint of the night optics, his vision piercing the darkness.

His gun clears leather in a heartbeat when his eyes intersect another pair. In the next moment, he realizes a deer just bolted away. He shakes his head. *Well, at least it wasn't a black bear who came to investigate the smell of granola bars.*

Rafferty exhales a long breath and waits for his heart to calm down. Then, inhaling through his nostrils, the sear of brisk air clears his mind of bears, making room to concentrate on the task at hand. *Gambino killed my son. The bastard doesn't get to keep Joe's daughters and Mick's wife. And if I have to kill someone to prevent it, so be it.*

While waiting for Mick and Joe, Rafferty focuses on the tree-lined periphery of the stump-pocked clearing and everything inside it. *It's at least fifty yards in diameter.* Faint light bleeds around the edges of the plywood secured over the window on the left side of the cabin.

A couple of guys came outside to take a leak, which tells me there's either no water or the plumbing's faulty. There aren't

*any visible wires or cables to support a functioning residence,
so I suspect they don't have electricity or it's been turned off.*

Rafferty spins and aims his gun toward the thump of
footfalls. When Mick and Joe emerge from the shadows, he
holsters his weapon. "Am I ever glad to see you two. You
guys must be starving." He opens the box of granola bars and
holds it out.

Mick and Joe take two each.

"And though my only encounter so far was with a curious
deer," Rafferty says, "we need to keep a lookout for black bear.
They're bold when they're hungry."

As the guys eat, Rafferty shares his suspicions about the
electrical and plumbing situation.

"Well, that explains the excrement we passed just inside
the tree line," Joe says. "It wasn't scat; it was human. It looked
like a sewage dumping ground."

Mick and Joe debrief Rafferty on the blood-covered
sheriff's uniform they found in the back of Tank's truck. "The
name badge says Christopher Sitler," Mick says. "The missing
sheriff we heard about on the radio broadcast earlier."

With the aid of the night vision goggles, Rafferty's eyes
focus on the cabin and its perimeter. *A badge doesn't exempt
any one of us from what happened to Christopher Sitler.*

"We don't know what's *behind* the cabin," Rafferty says.
"There could be a back door, or a slider, and more windows.
Let's take a recon tour. It shouldn't take long to get there,
gather intel, and get back."

The men move with stealth over uneven ground strewn
with pine needles, cones, and dead branches.

"With the arrival of those last two," Mick says, "Gambino's
reached a dozen women."

"Two of them are still *girls*," Joe says. "*My* little girls."

"Yes," Mick says. "And with Emma, he also has an
unborn child."

"Gambino doesn't have any real skin in the game," Rafferty says. "The loss of money and perhaps some power, but no *skin*—nothing personal."

"He's a psychopath," Joe says. "He had his own daughter killed."

"And he had my son killed," Rafferty says.

"Money and power *are* personal to him," Joe says. "So, what's his fail-safe?"

"What do you mean?" Rafferty asks.

"Gambino has it planned so that no matter what happens," Joe says, "it's 'safe' for him and no one else. He doesn't have anything to lose—lives don't matter to him. Everyone's expendable. But we have *everything* to lose."

"Then we'll change the endgame," Mick says. "Let's do the math. We know they have twelve captives. There are three trucks, but only one has a shell on the back. So, unless they plan on cramming twelve people in the back, a puzzle piece is missing. And there were four guys outside when the chopper came."

"Do you think that's all of them?" Joe asks. "Or do you think they left some inside to watch the hostages?"

"I bet they left at least one inside," Rafferty says. "But let's play it safe and say two. That makes six, two for each of us."

Rafferty feels the familiar slowing of time he experiences at the initiation of conflict—heightened clarity, narrowing of focus, the quickening of his pulse, and slight dissociation as if he is watching what's unfolding rather than actively participating in it.

"If things go south," Rafferty says, "will you guys please tell Ivy that I love her?" He swallows hard. "And that sometimes I just stop and smile because she's in my life."

Emma turns in her sleep as she dreams about the two newcomers. It turns out the women are volunteer couriers for a nonprofit donor-patient network. They explained that they use specially designed containers to hand-carry bone marrow and stem cell donations. Some containers have custom-fitted ice packs to keep stem cell donations cold, but ice isn't necessary to transport bone marrow.

"Those thugs took the containers," one of them said. "And time is of the essence—" Her voice broke. "If the donations aren't handled properly, they're worthless."

Turning again, Emma places a protective hand on her belly. Her dreaming mind races with the information she read Friday morning in the waiting room of her prenatal doctor's appointment: "These days, stem cells can be taken from your bone marrow, abdominal fat, or are sometimes donated by healthy mothers from healthy live-birth infants, using placenta and umbilical cord products, not from aborted fetuses. We always tell our patients, 'No fetuses were harmed in the production of your stem cells.'"

Emma stirs at the metallic squeal of a folding chair scraping across a wood floor. Heavy footsteps bring her fully awake. *It must be morning.*

On high alert now, she scrambles across the floor and presses her ear to the crack at the bottom of the door. *We've been here two sleeps now, so it's Sunday morning.*

A man's deep voice barks, "It's almost sunup, and the van'll be here soon. You two get the women ready and then bring them outside," followed by the pull and thud of the front door opening and closing.

Then the thumping of multiple feet comes down the hall. "Back away," someone shouts.

Emma rolls out of the way just in time.

The door flies open with a clang against the wall.

She squints her eyes against the unaccustomed light as three hooded men enter the room.

The first one carries a lit kerosene lamp.

The second one holds a Glock 22.

The third one grips an open cargo-type container and sets it on the floor. The lamplight reveals duct tape, zip-tie handcuffs, and knit hoods like the ones they have over their heads.

Emma's stomach curdles with dread. She repeats the mantra—*No bindings, no bindings, no bindings. If I say it enough times, maybe everything will fall into place, and our plan will still work.*

"We can do this the easy way," Container Guy says, "or the hard way." He juts his chin toward the man holding the Glock.

He raises his gun. "Just give me a reason."

Emma, Carly, Brianna, Andrea, and the two most recent arrivals nod their understanding.

The six gaunt-faced women huddled together against the far wall sit wide-eyed with incomprehension.

The gunman walks over to the non-English-speaking group and hits one of them with the butt of his weapon.

The women huddle even closer together.

"I'll take responsibility for them," Emma says.

"Well, aren't you the little saint?" Container Guy sneers. "I'll skin you alive myself if even one of them steps out of line."

Emma nods.

"I'm going to bind your feet, handcuff your wrists, and cover your heads with hoods, Container Guy says. "If you resist, my friend here will put a bullet in your brain. Have I made myself clear?"

Emma's heart lurches. *Oh, no! Our entire plan hinges on the ability to see each other, kick, and then run into the woods.*

CHAPTER 17

"Success in a fight depends on three factors: strength, strategy, skill. To win a fight, your protagonist needs at least one of them. Otherwise, a good outcome is implausible."

—RAYNE HALL

Mick opens his eyes and stands. His body's stiff from sitting in the cold tree line of the cabin's clearing. Faint light rises upward in the sky, suggesting that night is giving way to morning. His heart quickens its pace. *Today we do whatever it takes to get Emma, Carly, and Brianna back.*

Mick's neck crunches when he rotates his head. *Joe's standing watch, and Rafferty's starting to stir.* He turns his wrist—*It's just after six o'clock, twilight—the period just before sunrise and after sunset in which it's neither totally dark nor completely lit.*

His thoughts return to last night's reconnaissance when they did a three-sixty around the cabin. *The back has three windows covered with plywood and security bars. Each bar is spaced about a hand width apart.* Joe said, "They probably removed the glass so it couldn't be broken and the shards used as weapons. Or"—Mick swallows hard as he remembers—"to commit suicide." He shakes that thought away. *The cabin also has a back door sealed with two-by-fours. No entrance. No exit. The cabin has a single point of entry—the front door.*

Mick, Joe, and Rafferty take turns relieving themselves, and then, still hidden behind the trees, they move their bivouac closer to the clearing—*About five yards from the tree line.*

Unimpressed with the humans below, birds begin to chirp and call in earnest. Then the *shook-shook* call of Steller's jays tears through the morning air. Mick marvels at their lightness and joy while he's anchored with worry about everything that can go wrong. *Get ahold of yourself. Focus on what could go right—getting Emma, Carly, and Brianna out alive.* The jays fly across the clearing one at a time, in single file, then swoop up to perch in the tall periphery pines.

The cabin door opens, and two hoodless men step out. They walk to the edge of the clearing and relieve themselves. *Damnit, it's still too dark to see their faces.* When done, the shorter one goes back inside and closes the door. The giant one—*The same height and build as Tank*—stays outside. He checks his watch.

Mick hears the distinct growl of an engine. He holds a hand up toward Joe and Rafferty, then points to his ear.

They cock their heads to listen, then nod.

Tank must hear it, too. He pulls a hood over his head.

Mick, Joe, and Rafferty check their weapons. Each man has a primary gun, an ankle carry, backup ammo, and a knife.

Mick motions and mouths, "Joe, you take the right side of the cabin. I'll take the left side, by the trucks. Rafferty, you've got the front."

His tread is soft as he moves shadowlike from tree to tree. He tucks into position in the tree line near the trucks just as the source of the growling engine pulls into view—*A Washington State Penitentiary prisoner transport van.* The penny drops, and comprehension dawns. *That's the missing puzzle piece; that's how they plan to transfer a dozen women.*

As the sun climbs higher in the morning sky, Tank walks over to the van window. *The driver's not hooded. I wonder if that means he's expendable.* Mick hears their voices, but he's not close enough to make out the words.

The driver gets out of the van. *He's wearing a guard uniform.* Then he disappears into the tree line. *He probably needs to take a leak after a long drive.*

The front door of the cabin opens, and four men come out, each gripping the upper arm of a hooded woman. The women's wrists are cuffed, and they have to hobble-hop because their ankles are bound with duct tape.

While the guard's peeing and Tank's focused on the cuffed women, Mick crouches low and dashes the short distance from the tree line to the driver's side of Tank's truck, where he can peer around either end and remain unseen—ten yards from the handcuffed women.

A trickle of sweat runs down the back of Mick's neck. His heartbeat thunders in his ears. *None of them is Emma, Carly, or Brianna.*

Tank strides toward them from the van. He's close enough now for Mick to make out the words. "What the fucking hell is wrong with you, Geno?"

"Whadaya mean, what's wrong with me? You told me to hood and bind them."

"*After* they change into the jumpsuits, you imbecile. And they can't do that if they can't see or move. Now get the others, and we'll enjoy a little peek-a-boo show while they change."

Mick peers around the back end of the black Dodge Ram.

Tank angles one of the women away from him and yanks her hood off. "If you turn your head, I'll kill you."

He hands the hood to the guard. "Put this on, then cover me while I unbind them."

Tank pulls out his knife. After the sharp blade makes quick work of the zip-tie handcuffs and duct tape, he yanks the hoods from their heads.

The four men escort four more women through the cabin door. This time they're not bound.

That's not Emma, Carly, or Brianna either. Mick's nearly out of his mind. *Where are they?*

"Take their hoods off, Geno. We're covered, and they need to see what they're doing."

After Geno pulls off the first hood, he reaches out and skims the back of his hand across one of her cheeks. "This one's pretty."

"Touch her again, and you're dead," Tank says. "Now go get the last four."

Tank gets out his knife again. "If you move," he says, nodding toward the guard, "he'll shoot." He unbinds the women. "That makes eight. After the next four, and once they're all changed, we leave. Did you bring uniforms?"

The guard nods. "I brought two."

"Okay then. Two of my men will ride with you in the van. The rest of us will follow in our trucks."

Mick's heart nearly explodes when Emma, Carly, Brianna, and another woman are marched outside. *Emma. Oh, Emma!*

Tank throws an orange jumpsuit on the ground in front of each woman. "Change into these." Then the giant man steps behind Emma and draws his gun. "I especially want to see what this one looks like."

Mick's thinking clots with rage. As Emma bends over to pick up the jumpsuit, he sets his mouth in a hard line and draws his weapon. *Target acquired.*

While gathering the fabric, Emma holds out two fingers. Then all hell breaks loose.

Emma concentrates her strength into a backward donkey kick, thrusting her heel into Tank's nuts.

His gun drops first. Then he drops and rolls in agony. "You fucking bitch!"

One of the non-English-speaking women is frozen with fear.

I can't leave her behind. Emma slows long enough to take her hand.

Tank grabs Emma's ankle.

She lets go of the woman's hand. "Run!" she screams.

Like buckshot, the women spread out and bolt for the trees.

Shots ring out. Two of Gambino's thugs go down.

Tank pulls Emma down—her back to his chest—like a shield. Then he starts scooting toward his gun.

Another shot pierces the air. Another of Gambino's thugs goes down.

It all comes flooding back. *Tank. The back of the van. The syringe.* Emma throws her head back.

Tank's nose breaks in a satisfying crunch. He pulls his hood off and yells— "Fuck!"

She punctuates it with a heel slam into Tank's gonads a second time.

Bellowing, he lets go of her, grabs his crotch, and rolls over.

Emma goes for the gun Tank dropped.

Through pain-hazed eyes, Tank sees Emma reach for the gun he dropped when she kicked him in the nuts. *Oh, no, you don't.*

He clamps a mitt-sized hand around her wrist and squeezes it like a vice. "Drop it, bitch."

Emma's fingers release the gun. "You bastard!"

He yanks her on top of him again. "They'll have to go through you to kill me."

An explosion of gunfire rents the air.

Tank glances toward the noise. The guard and his fourth and final man go down. *This whole thing's turned into a cluster-fuck. Gambino put me in charge. My head will be on a platter by nightfall as a message to the Family—no one fucks up and lives to tell about it.*

Chest to chest, Tank clings to Emma as he struggles to a standing position.

"Look at all those dead guys," he says, nodding toward the clearing. "One of them's Mick, or he'd be here to protect you."

"No!" Emma screams. She yanks his hair with one hand and goes for his eyes with the other.

Tank roars, shaking his head left and right. He grabs at Emma's hands to no avail. "That's it, bitch!"

He drops to the ground on top of her. Blood from his nose splatters Emma's face.

Tank rears up, raises a fist—

A shape looms over Emma. Something arches through the air. There's a loud crack like a home-run hit.

Air whooshes from her lungs when Tank's weight crushes her.

Emma opens her eyes wide and sees Mick. She sucks in air. "I knew you weren't dead."

As Mick moves to push off his massive body, Emma sees Tank slide a knife from his pants pocket.

"Mick, look out!"

Tank presses the blade to Emma's throat. "Freeze, McPherson, or she dies."

Mick stops.

Emma lays stone still. *If I could just get that knife . . .*

Tank rolls onto his back with Emma on top. "Back away, McPherson."

Mick backs up.

Maintaining his hold on Emma, Tank stands. He has her in a chokehold—one forearm against her throat, the other hand fisting the knife at her belly.

Please don't hurt my baby!

"Drop the branch, McPherson, or I'll kill her."

Emma pleads with her eyes. "Do what he says, Mick. I don't want anything to happen to our baby."

———

Mick drops the thick branch. *Son of a bitch!*

He trains his eyes on Emma's. *I love you.* Mick drops his gun and kicks it to the side.

Moving the blade of his knife to Emma's jugular, Tank works his way to his feet. He keeps her in front of him as a shield.

A line of blood trickles down Emma's neck.

Fear coils around Mick's heart. *Please, God, no!*

"We're going into the cabin. If you move, she's dead." Tank backs them toward the open front door. Then he steps them over the threshold and slams it.

Mick turns, looking for help. In the distance, Rafferty's occupied with someone lying face up on the ground. *Is it Joe?* Two more people lie facedown.

The front door of the cabin bursts open.

Tank steps out with a crazed look and maniacal laugh.

Sweat stings Mick's eyes. His heart races. "Where's Emma?"

Tank tosses a lighter on the ground. "I just bolted her into the holding room and torched it."

Ice-cold tentacles of fear wind their way through every nerve in Mick's body.

"There's enough kerosene in there for an inferno," Tank says. "Let's just say she's part of the kindling."

Mick glances at the cabin. He doesn't see flames or smoke. Uncertain, he sniffs the air. The only thing he smells is pine and terror—his.

The giant man heads for Mick like a bull antagonized by a matador in a ring.

Eight yards to contact.

Mick draws a Sig P938 from his ankle holster. It's chambered for 9mm Luger ammunition. The clip holds six rounds. Another round fits in the chamber for a traditional 6+1 setup: seven shots and a backup clip—thirteen shots.

Aiming to disable, he takes a deep breath, puts his sight on Tank, lets his breath ease out, and pulls the trigger.

The round catches Tank in the shoulder, but he keeps his footing and continues toward Mick.

Six yards to contact.

Mick hears the sizzle and pop of hot sap in the cabin's logs. His nostrils catch the smell of smoke. *Oh, God!*

Tank's face is red. His upper lip's curled in a menacing snarl. There's a sheen of sweat on his face. A deep rumble like a growl emanates from his mouth. He's fisting a knife.

The man's unhinged. Mick adjusts his sight.

Four yards to contact.

Mick looks into Tank's deranged eyes. *This monster provided Gambino with women and girls to sell for sex, labor, and organs. He took Emma, Carly, and Brianna.*

The next shot catches Tank in the midsection. Astonishment ripples across his face. He flinches and stops momentarily. Then he straightens back up and continues, blood pouring from his shoulder and stomach.

He's close enough that Mick sees the knife clearly. *It's a spear-point, plain-edged blade, just shy of four inches in length.* It glints wickedly in the morning light.

Tank raises the knife for attack. "I'm going to kill you." *Two yards to contact.*

Mick aims at center mass. Then puts three rounds into the giant man's chest.

Tank twitches, staggers forward, does a half pirouette and falls with a thud at Mick's feet.

Mick races around the side of the house. "Emma, stand back!" He squeezes off two rounds, each at one of the four corner bolts holding the window security bars.

He aims at the third bolt and squeezes the trigger. Nothing.

Mick slams in a fresh clip, shoots the two remaining bolts, then yanks the security bars from the cabin wall and starts to pry the plywood off. "Emma!"

He hears a distant yell. "Mick, I'm over here. Hurry!"

Mick races to the back of the house. He shoves his fist between the security bars and bangs on the plywood over one of the windows.

Emma bangs back. *Thank God!*

"Move as far away from this window as you can." Four more shots annihilate the corner bolts that secure the iron grill. He pulls it free. As he works to pry the plywood from the side of the cabin, Emma kicks it from the other side.

When the board lets go, Emma, coughing in a billow of smoke, falls over the frame into Mick's arms.

Carrying her against his chest, Mick races from the cabin in his uneven gait. As he crosses the clearing, he sees the women emerge from the tree line. They form a semicircle tableau around Rafferty. He's working on Joe, one of three people lying on the ground.

No! Mick's mind rebels at the thought of Joe. Dead.

Joe's conscious, but he can't seem to open his eyes more than a sliver.

Woodsmoke and the strong, sharp, almost painful smell of blood fill his nostrils. He grits his teeth. *I was shot twice, once in my right shoulder, and a bullet grazed my forehead.*

Through slit eyelids, he sees Rafferty bent over him, trying to staunch the flow of blood from where his right shoulder connects to his chest. A fist of fear squeezes his heart. He tries to speak. "Are the girls—" His voice is nothing more than a whisper.

"They're both fine," Rafferty says.

Racked by pain, Joe lies still and concentrates on breathing. His thoughts play like a movie behind his eyelids:

Tank grabbed Emma. When she screamed "Run!" all the women, including Carly and Brianna, bolted. That's when I saw one of Gambino's thugs aim at Carly. I fired and caught the guy in the forehead. Blood erupted, and he went down.

Another one of Gambino's men sighted one of the running women.

Rafferty was shooting from behind me. He squeezed off two shots, and the guy dropped.

Brianna was barreling toward me, straight into the line of fire. As I dove to tackle her, I saw movement in my peripheral vision—one of Gambino's men had acquired her. I knocked her to the ground and rolled. Thankfully, the first bullet creased my forehead, not hers. Then my right shoulder exploded.

Covering Brianna with my body, I flash-checked my left flank. Rafferty rolled, then two-fisting his gun, he triple-tapped the thug who shot me. The next thing I knew, Rafferty was leaning over me, and Carly and Brianna were crying.

I kept my promise to Marci. The girls will be back home soon.

Rafferty clears sweat from his eyes with his forearm. *I've got to stop the bleeding from Joe's shoulder.* He glances at his friend's forehead. "You're damn lucky it's just a graze. Another quarter inch, and it would have shattered your frontal bone." He looks up from tending Joe at Emma when Mick sets her on her feet. "I'm glad to see you."

"I was never so happy to hear gunfire in my life," Emma says. Then she looks at Joe and the other two casualties lying face down. There's a red blossom of blood on each of their backs. "But not at this cost." Tears streak her soot-covered face. "How's Joe?"

"He caught a bullet." Then glancing at Carly and Brianna, he adds, "But he's going to be fine."

Emma steps between the girls, puts an arm around each one, and pulls them into her sides.

"Are you okay, Emma?" Brianna asks. "Your face is bloody."

"It's not my blood. I'm okay," Emma says.

Mick steps next to the two bodies. "Emma, do you know who these women were?"

"The one closest to you, she didn't speak English. In fact," — Emma nods to the group of standing women — "six of them didn't. But the one closest to me said her name was Andrea Peters."

Rafferty snaps his head up. "Andrea Peters? Here, Emma, hold this." He places one of Emma's hands on the sleeve he tore off and wadded to staunch the flow of Joe's blood. Then he crawls over to the closest woman and gently rolls her onto her back. "Oh, my God. It's Special Agent Peters. She was on a task force checking into the disappearance of refugees. The refugee resettlement in Washington State has experienced an influx of refugees, many of them Iraqi and Afghan women." Rafferty looks up at the women. "These women probably speak Arabic or Dari."

"Why a special task force?" Emma asks.

"Because many refugee women have gone missing. They don't speak the language, they're trusting, and they're taken. The suspicion is that they're captured for the sale of their tissue and organs."

Rafferty glances at the women's faces. *These are mothers, daughters, and sisters like Ivy, Emma, and Marci. They're human beings, not a commodity to be bought and sold.* His gaze takes in the bloody bodies strewn across the clearing—*Tank, four other thugs, and the guard.* Fueled by rage, he clenches his fists. *We've got to shut Gambino's operation down!*

"Rafferty, those two women," Emma says, pointing to the group, "arrived last night. They're volunteer couriers for a donor-patient network. They hand-carry bone marrow and stem cell donations."

An explosion erupts from the cabin—black smoke billows from the chimney. The acrid smell of burning fills the air. Flames lick up, heavenward, leaping and grabbing for oxygen, tinder—whatever it can take.

Rafferty jumps up from the ground. "Mick, we've got to move those trucks, or they'll blow too."

"I've got Joe," Emma says. "Hurry!"

Rafferty and Mick run for the trucks.

Mick has to fish keys out of Tank's pants pocket before he can move his black truck.

Rafferty finds keys over one of the visors and moves the truck away. Then he moves the prisoner transport van.

After Mick moves Tank's truck as close to Joe as possible, he moves the second one near the transport van and two other trucks.

When Rafferty and Mick get back to the now-semiconscious Joe and the group hovering around him, Rafferty says, "We've got to get Joe to the hospital. If Mick and I take him in Tank's truck, he can lay on the backseat. Emma, will you follow in the transport van with the rest?"

"Yes, let's hurry."

"Mick, if you drive," Rafferty says, "I'll sit in the back with Joe and call in this shitstorm once we have reception, including the fire." He nods toward the flaming cabin. "I bet the smoke will be seen long before that, and the Department of Natural Resources will be on it with engines and air tankers."

Rafferty's functioning on pure adrenaline. "Here's what scares me," he says as they gingerly transfer Joe into Tank's truck. "Gambino's thugs are like cockroaches. They've infiltrated even the most inaccessible places to do his bidding. If he gets wind of this failure—his men are dead, his captives are gone, and he has nothing to sell—before we have reinforcements in place, he'll reciprocate at Pincs & Quill, and our friends and family will be at the absence of his mercy—dead."

CHAPTER 18

"Every character should want something,
even if it's only a glass of water."
—KURT VONNEGUT

Mick white knuckles the steering wheel in Tank's truck as he careens down the winding road that takes them to the base of Mount Baker. He checks the rearview mirror. *Emma's staying close behind in the white prisoner transport van. Joe's unconscious in the backseat. And Rafferty's doing his best to staunch the flow of blood from Joe's shoulder.*

"Rafferty, any cell reception yet?"

"No, dammit, and Joe's still bleeding."

"We can't trust anyone," Mick says, "so you go with him on the bird. Gambino's killed people at St. Joe's, so you need to stand watch while Joe's in surgery, and then we'll take turns while he's in recovery."

"We're on the same page," Rafferty says.

"Once you guys are on the chopper, I'll get in the van with Emma and the other women, and we'll go to the hospital too. They need to be checked to make sure they're all right."

Please, please, please let the baby be okay.

Rafferty nods. "You know the moment Gambino hears that his men are dead and the hostages are gone, he's going to send foot soldiers to Pines & Quill for revenge. We need an FBI team there to intercept them. And when they learn that Amanda Peters is dead, shit's *really* going to hit the fan. When an agent gets killed, all hands are on deck."

That's why my partner, Sam, was killed. His death was a diversion tactic to create an "officer down" situation. As a result, the precinct dwindled to a skeleton crew, making it easier for Toni Bianco, a dirty cop, to steal over ten million dollars of heroin from the lockup for Gambino.

"Call Chief Simms too," Mick says. "Even though it's Labor Day weekend, when he hears that Joe's been shot, he'll add uniforms to the FBI's team at Pines & Quill."

The men's cell phones start pinging with outgoing and incoming texts.

"Finally, we've got reception," Mick says. "Now, we've got to beat Gambino to the punch."

———

Rafferty puts his cell on speaker so he can apply pressure to Joe's shoulder while he talks. *Please, God, don't let Joe die.*

His first call is to Life Flight. When he identifies himself as a special agent with the FBI, they agree to meet the truck at the nearest open space large enough to accommodate a helicopter. It's located next to a twenty-four-hour convenience store at the base of Mount Baker, where the straightaway begins.

His second call is to Stewart Crenshaw, his commander in the FBI Seattle office. Rafferty informs him about Gambino's hostage cabin on Mount Baker, the ensuing fire, and eight deaths—five of Gambino's thugs, one corrections officer, a female refugee, and FBI agent Andrea Peters. "And McPherson found the bloody uniform and badge of the missing sheriff, Christopher Sitler."

When Crenshaw says he'll coordinate with Bellingham's police chief, Bruce Simms, Rafferty informs him that US Marshal Jake Porter is at Pines & Quill and gives him the number for Jake's encrypted cell. Crenshaw agrees to loop him in as well.

Before Rafferty disconnects, he adds, "And sir, you might want to send a bomb squad. Gambino planted an explosive device in Mick's Jeep, and it's possible that there's one in Bingham's Camaro too."

"Good Lord, Rafferty, you've been busy. It's not even nine o'clock in the morning!"

His third call is to Phillip Benton at the secure site in Maeve's condo. After Philip confirms receiving the helicopter's tail number—"I'm working on it now"—Rafferty informs him of the FBI and Bellingham police coordination at Pines & Quill.

His final call is to St. Joseph Hospital to inform them about the Life Flight patient—Bellingham homicide detective Joseph Bingham—and the female hostages. "One of them, Emma McPherson, is pregnant. Dr. Freeman is her OB/GYN."

I wish I could call Ivy, but Gambino might hear our conversation, and I don't want him to have any warning. I want to nail that bastard's ass to the wall.

Emma follows behind the black Dodge Ram carrying Mick, Rafferty, and Joe. *Ever since Tank slammed me to the ground, I keep waiting for cramping or blood.* She checks her pants for spotting or bleeding. *Thank God, nothing.*

She looks in the rearview mirror. *Carly, Brianna, and the rest of the women look exhausted. I can't believe that two of the twelve women are dead.* The two volunteer couriers for a donor-patient network sit shoulder to shoulder, their faces bent close, talking.

Joe's daughter, eleven-year-old Brianna, looks at Emma's eyes in the rearview mirror. "It's my fault that Dad got shot," she says amid tears. "If I hadn't run to him, he'd be okay."

Carly, her thirteen-year-old sister, puts an arm around Brianna's shoulders. "You did what Dad wanted you to do."

"Is he going to be okay?" Brianna asks. "There was so much blood."

Emma nods. "A lot of that blood was from the graze on his forehead. I'm sure it hurts like the dickens, but it's not fatal."

"Yea, but what about his shoulder?" Brianna asks.

"Rafferty's riding with him in the backseat of the truck. He's applying constant pressure to keep it from bleeding."

I wish I had a cell phone. She follows the truck with the men as it pulls off to the right and into the parking lot of a convenience store. A Life Flight helicopter sits in the center of an empty field to the side of the store.

As she makes to open the van door, Mick signals for them to stay.

A triage unit, hair flattened by the prop wash, runs under the moving blades to the truck, places Joe on a stretcher, and then carries him to the waiting helicopter.

Rafferty climbs in.

The doors close, the rotation blades blur against a vivid blue sky, and the helicopter lifts off.

Emma rolls her window down as Mick trots up.

"We're heading to St. Joe's so each of you can be checked to make sure you're okay. Dr. Freeman's going to be there to check the baby." Mick leans in and lavishes kisses on her cheeks, eyelids, and the freckles that march across her nose. Then he moves to her mouth.

Emma feels the movement of his tongue against her lower lip. *I wish the van door wasn't between us.* She deepens the kiss and moans into his mouth.

Then, hearing a giggle, she pulls back, remembering the filled seats behind her. Emma glances in the rearview mirror. Understanding smiles grace the women's faces while Carly and Brianna wear toothy grins.

Relief floods through Emma now that she's firmly back in the safety of Mick's presence. She's exhausted from the ordeal on the mountain and the subsequent fear of losing the baby. She feels the need to collapse. Her eyes well with tears. "Thank you, Mick. So far, there's been no cramping or spotting."

Mick furrows his brows as he cups Emma's face with his hands. "Do you want to drive, or do you want me to?"

Emma's hands shake as she unbuckles her seatbelt and pushes herself from the driver's seat into the empty front passenger seat.

Mick gets in, buckles, and then leans over and presses something into her hands.

Emma gasps when she sees what it is. She holds the *honu* pendant—a Hawaiian green sea turtle—that Mick carved for her. "I thought this was gone forever when Tank took it from me," she says with more tears spilling down her cheeks.

"I remember what you said when you gave it to me. 'When lost, turtles are excellent navigators and often find their way home—in your case, I hope it's always to me.'"

Emma slips the leather cord over her head. One hand presses the turtle against her sternum; the other hand rests on her belly. "Mick, *you're* my home, and we're back where we belong."

In the living room of Thoreau Cottage, Jake disconnects a call on the encrypted cell phone and turns to Sarah. "Well, I'll be damned."

"Who was it?"

Jake puts his arms around Sarah's waist and pulls her body against his. Then he whispers against the hair covering one of her ears. "That was Stewart Crenshaw. Rafferty's boss in the Seattle FBI office. He just finished speaking with Murphy."

Sarah whispers back. "As in Daniel Murphy, your boss in Missoula?"

"Yep, that's the one."

"Why?"

"To get permission for me to coordinate with the local police and an FBI unit who are heading to Pines & Quill. They're concerned that Gambino's sending a team of foot soldiers here to get revenge."

Jake walks into the bedroom, opens the closet, and checks Gambino's two thugs. *They're still bound and gagged.* When he returns to the living room, he pulls Sarah back into his arms, bringing her up to speed on this morning's events on Mount Baker. Then he says, "It's time to gather the others for a little target practice out on the bluff."

Jake checks his weapons and backup ammo.

Sarah gets her compound bow and quiver.

Together, they walk toward the main house using the path by the tai chi pavilion. The parts of its pagoda-style copper roof that haven't yet patinated with age glint in the morning light. The sun dapples the ground where it pierces the thick, dark-green pine canopy.

Jake squeezes Sarah's hand with affection when their footfalls startle black-capped chickadees into silence.

When I packed for this trip, I learned that September temperatures in Bellingham fluctuate between fifty and sixty-five degrees. He inhales the crisp air as they pass Niall's garden. In addition to pine and freshly turned earth, Jake would swear he smells basil. The garden's alternating rows of vegetables and flowers are military straight in their precision. The captivating floral hues include rich deep burgundies, reds, coppery oranges, and golden yellows. And though Jake doesn't know their names, he appreciates their beauty.

"It's a little after nine o'clock," Jake says. "I'm sure the other guests just finished breakfast like us. Gambino's used to seeing everyone head to the bluff for target practice, so on the outside chance he's not yet aware that his men are dead, the women are gone, and his plans have gone south, if he sees weapons, it's 'business as usual.'"

By nine thirty, everyone's gathered on the bluff wearing their Spy team baseball caps.

The red team consists of Eric standing in for Mick, Maureen, Niall, Marci, Ivy, Sakura, Dale, Jake, Skip, Mary and baby Hannah, Kent, and Hemingway as their four-legged Irish wolfhound mascot.

The green team consists of Maeve, Libby, Ethan standing in for Joe, Ellery standing in for Rafferty, Todd, Sarah, Olivia, Tim, Hank, Gail, Molly, and Maggie as their four-legged Standard poodle mascot.

Out on the bluff, with the wind blowing and the crash of surf below the cliff, there's no chance that Gambino will overhear. Jake, with Sarah by his side, explains the grim truth about everything that's happened since Friday morning when Emma was abducted after leaving her eleven-week prenatal appointment.

"You mean Emma's not really on bed rest?" Gail asks.

"No, she's not," Jake says.

Marci, Joe's wife, steps forward. "And you're *certain* that Carly and Brianna are okay?"

Jake nods. "I'm positive."

"And Joe?" "And Rafferty?" Marci and Ivy ask simultaneously.

Oh, shit. "A bullet grazed Joe's forehead, and he was also shot in the shoulder," Jake says. "Rafferty, who's unharmed, is with him, and they're flying to St. Joseph Hospital. In fact, they're probably already there. And the others—Emma,

Carly, Brianna, and the other women—are with Mick heading there, too, to make sure everyone's okay.

"This morning's activity is *not* a game," Jake says. "I have every reason to believe that crime boss Georgio 'The Bull' Gambino will send foot soldiers to Pines & Quill to exact revenge—to *kill* us. The local police and the FBI are coordinating teams to intercept them, but they may not get here before Gambino's thugs do.

"In the meantime, most of us—those who can climb trees—are going to spread out on the property and hide. It's *imperative* that you keep your team cap on. That's how the police and FBI will distinguish us from them."

Most of the faces staring back at Jake are aghast with horror.

Mary gasps, pulling her swaddled baby tight against her chest.

Molly, the vet's wife, and Gail, the foreman's wife, have tears streaming down theirs.

Olivia's pissed. She steps forward in a huff, pretends to drop a mic, and says, "*Boom.* I'm outta here!" Then she marches across the bluff toward the main grounds at Pines & Quill.

Skip, her boyfriend, calls after her, but Olivia holds up a hand and shakes it back and forth in a "talk to the hand 'cuz the face ain't listening" manner and keeps moving—the distance between them growing larger.

Skip stays put. "I'm in."

"I'm in, too," Libby and Niall say in unison.

Hemingway stands between them. No longer the friendly mascot of Pines & Quill, his feet are planted in a fighting stance—one hundred and fifty pounds of menace, a terrorizing sight of strength and savagery waiting to protect his family and friends.

Damn, Hemingway seems to understand the gravity of the situation, Jake thinks.

Eric, Ethan, and Ellery, Emma's brothers who stood in for Mick, Joe, and Rafferty, walk over to Jake. Kent, Tim, Hank, Dale, Sakura, and Marci follow. "We're in, too."

Maeve speaks up. "If it's okay with Jake, those of you who can't or don't want to climb a tree can stay here with me on the bluff."

Jake eyes the group. "That's a good idea." Then he turns to Maeve. "Are you armed?"

She nods. "And before you ask, yes, I know how to use it."

Jake represses a smile. "I had no doubts."

Maureen, Emma's mother, walks over to Maeve and stands next to her. "I'm with you."

Molly joins them. "I am too."

Todd rolls his wheelchair near Maeve. "Clearly, I'm not climbing any trees." He turns to Jake. "I don't have a gun, but I also know how to use one."

Jake slips a gun from his boot and hands it to Todd. Then he turns to the remaining people. "Ivy's blind. Maggie's her guide dog, and Mary's the mother of a newborn. There's a good chance that none of you are climbing a tree. And newborns cry."

Then he turns to Gail.

Eyes wide with fear, she shakes her head and holds up her hands. "I can't do this," she screams before tearing after Olivia. "Wait up!"

Jake exhales audibly. "For the team members staying out here, those will offer some cover." He points to a cluster of large boulders; some are shoulder height. "Stay low, and keep your eyes open."

I've got two loose cannons to worry about. If Gambino's thugs catch Olivia and Gail, they can be used as hostages for leverage or killed. And I'll be damned if anyone dies on my watch.

Mick tenses, then relaxes the muscles in his hands as he paces the hospital waiting room. *What's taking so long? Is everything okay with the baby?* Periodically he sits to massage the pain in his left thigh. He's just outside the swinging doors that Emma, Carly, Brianna, and the other women were ushered through earlier by a team of female nurses. Dr. Freeman, Emma's OB/GYN, passed through the same doors shortly after. That's when she informed him, "Mick, I'm sure you understand that after the trauma these women experienced at the hands of men, no males are permitted past these doors."

The waiting area that Mick was relegated to is warm and comfortable. There are only a few other people. Most of them are leafing through magazines from the wall rack. The round wall clock, its black numbers in stark contrast with the white background, indicates it's not quite noon. *And while the second hand on the clock pulses forward sixty times per minute, the only thing I can do is sit still or pace. My hands are tied.*

Mick's stomach rumbles, reminding him that the last thing he ate was two granola bars the previous evening while hiding with Joe and Rafferty in the tree line surrounding the cabin where the women were captive. *I wonder how Joe's doing? Just one floor up, he's still in surgery—Rafferty's with him.*

He furrows his eyebrows as he scans the space. Mick isn't sure what period or effect the decorators were going for, but the combination of pale ochre walls, woven yarn hangings, and sage corduroy chairs does nothing to soothe his nerves.

He stands when a nurse in blue scrubs enters the waiting area from the main corridor. She's with another woman, whom she guides toward the swinging doors. From the snippet of conversation Mick overhears, the woman is an Arabic translator they've brought to help the Iraqi refugees in Emma's group communicate with the medical team. The nurse's crocs squeak with every step as they cross the polished black-and-white tile.

Then it's back to the hum and whir of the air conditioner as the doors hush close behind them.

Mick's silenced cell phone vibrates. He slips it from his pocket and reads a text from Phillip, who's manning the secure site at his mom's condo:

> Tail number belongs to a helo reported stolen from Landmark Aviation in Richmond, British Columbia. When the pilot put down to refuel, he was ambushed in the restroom. He's in the hospital but expected to recover. I gave the info to Crenshaw and Simms. They're on it.

Gambino's menace has spread from New Orleans to San Francisco to the greater Seattle area. He stole a helicopter in Canada and was going to sell this group of captive women, including Emma and our baby, from a container ship in the Bering Strait to a Russian crime boss. He has an army of expendable people to do his bidding. When we eliminate one, it seems like two more take their place.

No one's safe until Gambino's out of commission. And I aim to do just that.

The bored watchman, discreetly tucked away in a nondescript office complex in Bellingham, leans back in his chair and surveys three large monitors, each divided into four quadrants. The twelve quadrants display the views of surveillance cameras strategically placed throughout the property at the Pines & Quill writing retreat.

He looks at his watch—*Noon straight up, time for lunch. Carmine, Gambino's right-hand man, called to say something was going down at Pines & Quill today and not to be alarmed when I see unusual activity. Well, I ain't seen nothin' yet.*

As he pushes his chair back from the desk, it groans. He views his pregnant-looking belly. *I've got to lose some weight.* Then he leans over and pulls a to-go bag from his duffel. He smiles when he removes the lid on his leftover lasagna from D'Anna's Café Italiano. *Tomorrow. I'll start my diet tomorrow.*

When surveillance camera number three flicks with movement, the watchman sits up straight. One of Gambino's guys crouches as he makes his way through the forested area. Then other monitors ping. Cameras one, nine, and eleven reveal more of Gambino's guys crouch-walking between tree trunks. *Damn, Carmine wasn't kidding.* He shovels another fork of lasagna into his mouth, then leans forward, elbows on the desk, to get a better look as he chews.

He nearly chokes when people drop from the trees behind each of Gambino's guys. Arms outstretched, the baseball-capped newcomers each holds a gun clasped with both hands. "Drop your guns!"

Gambino's men follow orders. First, they drop their weapons, kick them away, and lie facedown on the ground. Then they lace their fingers behind their heads and spread their feet wide apart.

More cap-wearing people step into view. *Fuck! One of them's wielding what looks like a small samurai sword!* They zip-tie the thugs' wrists and duct-tape their ankles and mouths.

As one of Gambino's men sneaks from the shadows with his gun drawn, a massive gray dog leaps from behind him. The man's gun drops from his hand when he tries to break his fall, and the dog pins him to the ground.

The watchman leans in closer. The canine's ears are tucked to the sides of his head, his hackles raised, and lips pulled back, revealing teeth that can tear the flesh of formidable prey.

The watchman tears his gaze away as cameras five and seven ping. *What the fucking hell?* He widens his eyes in disbelief as two large vans—SWAT and FBI—pull to a stop, and an army wearing tactical gear and carrying assault weapons swarm over the entrance gate spreading out into the woods.

Gambino's going to be royally pissed. And when he's pissed, heads roll. The watchman knocks over the trashcan in his hurry to vacate the premises.

Jake's boots clunk as he walks between Gambino's thugs lined up facedown on the raised wood floor of the tai chi pavilion. Nitrile-gloved hands have bagged and tagged weapons and the contents of their pockets—guns, knives, and ammunition.

When a SWAT team member yanks the duct tape from their faces, one of Gambino's foot soldiers says, "You assholes mighta caught us, but ya didn't get Lorenzo."

"Where is he?" Jake asks.

When the man remains silent, Jake kicks him in the ribs with a boot. "Where is he?"

"He's probably long gone now, but he was coming in from the bluff."

Tim steps forward and asks, "Where's Mary and Hannah?"

"Yeah," Kent says. "And where's Molly?"

Jake scans the faces of the red and green team members. Terror races down his spine. *Oh, shit!* He leaps over the pavilion steps and races toward the bluff.

CHAPTER 19

"If you don't have time to read, you don't have the time—or the tools—to write. Simple as that."
—STEPHEN KING

Rafferty paces back and forth by a narrow bed in a recovery room at St. Joseph Hospital. Its silver rails are raised on each side. He looks at its occupant, Joe Bingham, who, post-surgery, is still unconscious. His skin bears a grayish cast that has nothing to do with the lighting.

Rafferty matches his steps to the rhythm of the steady, unrelenting beep emitted by the machines monitoring Joe. There's a distinct click and whir after every fourth beep— that's when he pivots and turns. Regardless, he can't outwalk the aseptic smell he remembers so well.

Just two months ago, while watching the Fourth of July fireworks display from the bluff at Pines & Quill, Toni Bianco shot me. She hit my left shoulder, so it didn't affect my right arm or gun hand. But Joe got nailed in his right shoulder. He's right-handed. I'm worried it'll affect his ability to shoot. If it does, his career as a homicide detective could be over.

Joe's hands rest on a white sheet pulled up to his chest. A thin green blanket covers his legs. A clear bag of fluid hangs from an IV pole with a tube running to the inside of Joe's right arm. Gauze wraps his head like a mummy from his eyebrows up.

Rafferty shakes his head. *He'd be dead if he'd been a quarter-inch farther into the body dive he made to save his daughter Brianna.*

Afraid the thump of his shoes on the tile will wake Joe, Rafferty pulls a vinyl chair to the bedside and settles in for the long haul. Lacing his fingers behind his head, he appraises the surroundings. The overhead fluorescents are off. Instead, soft light illuminates the sterile room. Chalky blue walls and pockmarked ceiling panels envelop the hospital bed and side table. A laminated sign reads: Since the Coronavirus lockdown, the National Health Service has approved the use of cell phones to keep in contact with friends and family.

Rafferty concludes that the monotonous environs of a hospital room can drain even the thickest-skinned fighters and their visitors of strength. He pushes his lenses up the bridge of his nose and then glances at the wall clock. *It's just after one o'clock on Sunday afternoon. Will Ivy be okay if Gambino sends his foot soldiers to Pines & Quill? She'll be safe if the FBI and SWAT team get there before Gambino's thugs do. But if they arrive late, Ivy could be taken hostage or caught in the crossfire. I need to get there as soon as possible, but I can't leave Joe until Mick relieves me.*

Rafferty stretches his arms back behind his head, closes his weary eyes, and replays Joe's surgical procedure. St. Joseph is a teaching hospital, so the surgeon agreed to let him have a bird's-eye view from the surgical theater alongside the medical students there wasn't room for in the operating room. The vantage point allowed Rafferty to see and hear everything.

He mulls over the answer Dr. David Kloss gave one of the attending interns during Joe's surgery, who'd asked, "Was this patient lucky to get shot in the shoulder?"

"I don't consider getting shot lucky," Kloss said.

The intern's blue surgical mask did little to hide the rosy tint that suffused his face. "I meant as opposed to somewhere else on his body."

Kloss said, "The shoulder contains the subclavian artery, which feeds the brachial artery—the main artery of the arm—as well as the brachial plexus, the large nerve bundle that controls arm function."

The surgeon bent close to his patient, mumbled something, then lifted a pair of bloody forceps with a bullet between the tips. He peered over his glasses at the intern and said, "Mr. Bingham is *lucky* that the shooter used a .22-caliber piece, a relatively low-powered weapon. The outcome would likely have been different had the assailant used a Bushmaster assault rifle. But in this case, the bullet narrowly missed the artery and the nerve bundle. As a result, our patient isn't going to lose his life or limb."

Rafferty opens his eyes when he senses movement.

A male doctor starts to step into the room, then stops when he sees Rafferty. He's wearing a surgical cap, mask, blue scrubs covered by an open white lab coat, disposable shoe covers, and has a syringe in one of his surgical glove-covered hands.

Rafferty's eyes meet his.

"Excuse me," the doctor says. "It appears I have the wrong room." He backs out, and the door closes behind him.

The name embroidered on the lab coat was David Kloss, MD. Not only was the voice wrong, but Dr. Kloss has red hair. That guy's hair is almost black.

Rafferty bolts for the door and yanks it open. Two men and a woman in pink scrubs gather at the nurse's station at the far end of the corridor—other than that, the hallway's empty.

He grabs his cell phone from his pocket and speed-dials Mick. "One of Gambino's thugs posing as a doctor just paid a visit. When he saw me, he disappeared. Gambino probably has a backup plan. I can't leave Joe. He may be heading for Emma next."

"I'm on it," Mick says, then disconnects.

Rafferty tries Jake's cell phone next, but it just rings and rings and rings.

———————

Jake runs full tilt across Pines & Quill, ducking and weaving to miss low branches and dodging moss-covered surface roots and jagged edges of lichen-covered stone that jut from the earth.

Finally, he breaks through the tree line and onto the rock-strewn bluff—his gun at the ready—as he thunders toward the group he left by the boulders so that Gambino's thugs wouldn't hurt them only to realize one of the foot soldiers had taken this route to Pines & Quill. *I've got to get there before someone gets hurt!*

Hemingway, the epitome of power and swiftness, charges past him across ten windswept acres of rugged land reminiscent of the Scottish Highlands. His stride is long and smooth with great reach and a strong, powerful drive that eats up the ground. When he reaches the group at the cluster of boulders, he continues running past them.

As Jake reaches the group on the bluff, they part.

One of Gambino's foot soldiers stands behind Ivy. He has one arm around her throat in a chokehold. The other is pressing a gun to her temple.

Maggie bares her teeth and growls. She looks like she's going to lunge.

"Someone control that goddam dog now, or I'll shoot it!"

Molly, the vet's wife, takes the handle on Maggie's harness and pulls her away. "It's going to be okay," she soothes the Standard poodle.

Ivy's eyes are hidden behind her shaded lenses, but Jake imagines that they're wide with terror. Her knuckles are white as she clutches the purse in front of her.

"Take another step, and I'll blow her head off," the thug says.

Hemingway approaches the foot soldier from behind.

The man waves his gun toward the group. "Drop your weapons."

The moment he moves the weapon from her temple, Ivy pulls Rafferty's gun from her purse, presses the barrel into the man's right thigh, and pulls the trigger.

The man howls with pain, drops his gun, and falls facedown on the ground; blood blossoms on the fabric of his thigh.

Hemingway lunges forward and stands over the guy, teeth bared. A deep growl emanates from his throat.

Jake picks up the guy's gun, hands it to Todd for safekeeping, then toes the guy over. *He's actively losing blood.* He kneels on the ground beside him and uses the thug's belt as a makeshift tourniquet.

The guy opens his eyes and looks at Jake. "You've got to help me," he manages through gritted teeth. "These people are *insane,* especially that one." He points at Ivy with a bloody hand.

Jake shakes his head. "*Never,* under *any* circumstances, underestimate a woman."

"I think he assumed that a blind person wouldn't have a weapon," Ivy says. "To him, I was the weak link."

"Fuck, yeah," the guy growls. "What person in their right mind would give a *blind* person a gun?"

Jake smiles bigger than a Montana sky. "Her fiancé, FBI Special Agent Rafferty. That's who."

Jake extracts his cell phone and calls police chief Bruce Simms, who's with a lead FBI agent at the Pines & Quill tai chi pavilion—their temporary command center. Between them, the two men oversee several teams: the SWAT team that's on stand-down; the bomb squad, whose members are actively checking all of the vehicles on the property, not just Mick's Jeep and Joe's Camaro; the team responsible for transporting Gambino's foot soldiers, including the two from the closet at Thoreau Cottage; the team removing the surveillance equipment in the forest and also scouring the rest of the property and buildings for any equipment capable of capturing or recording data; and the forensics team, which is doing its own thing.

"The group on the bluff caught another one of Gambino's thugs," Jake tells Simms. "He has a through-and-through in his right thigh. I've got a makeshift tourniquet on it. An ambulance can't make it out here. But if you send Niall or Libby with the ATV, we'll get him back to the main property. From there, he can get an ambulance to the hospital if you have one ready."

"I'll order one now before I head to the main house," Chief Simms says. "And good work, Porter."

"I can't take the credit," Jake says.

"Who got him?"

"Ivy Gladstone."

"Rafferty's girlfriend?" the chief asks, his voice laced with surprise.

"Yes, but she's his fiancée now, sir."

"When did he—? Oh, never mind. But how on earth—"

"I'll leave that for this group to explain," Jake says.

It's not long before the ATV makes quick work of the distance between the tree line and the outcropping of boulders on the bluff.

Libby pulls up next to the man on the ground. "Niall wanted to come, but he's feeding the troops."

With help from the others, Jake loads the wounded man onto the backseat, where he sits next to him, though it's doubtful he could escape.

Ivy doesn't need any encouragement to get into the front passenger seat. She has her collapsible cane with her, so she unharnesses Maggie.

Two streaks, one gray, the other black-and-white, race toward the main property. Clouds of dust billow in their wake.

As the remaining people start to make their way across the bluff, there's an audible consensus: "I'm starving." "I need a hot shower." "I need a drink."

"Come to the main house when you're ready," Libby says. "There's plenty to eat. And after a day like today, the bar in the Ink Well's wide open."

Jake looks at the thug in the seat next to him. "*Where* is your boss?"

"First off, I don't know. Second, he'd kill me if I told you."

"I've got news for you," Jake says. "Gambino's going to kill you either way. He sent you here to do a job, and you failed. Now he has to make an example out of you so the rest of his foot soldiers understand: you fail, you die."

CHAPTER 20

"Writing's a lot like cooking. Sometimes the cake won't rise, no matter what you do, and every now and again the cake tastes better than you ever could have dreamed it would."
—NEIL GAIMAN

Niall's blood feels thick as it squeezes through his heart. Surrounded by commercial-sized stainless-steel appliances, he stands numbly in the center of his sanctuary, the kitchen in the main house. Bacon sizzles in a pan, and the aroma of freshly ground coffee beans wafts through the air.

Cooking and baking—usually a therapeutic balm—do nothing to ease the weight of worry pressing down on him as police, FBI, and SWAT teams converge on his beloved Pines & Quill.

Gambino has tipped our world on its side. Again. Isn't it enough that he had my brother, Paddy, shot and killed as he sat unknowingly on the other side of a thin partition in a confessional in St. Barnabas? Niall's eyes glisten, and a lump forms in his throat. *A part of me went with him when he died.* Pressing a hand to the counter to steady himself, he also grieves for Connor McPherson, his father-in-law. *We had an excellent relationship because of our common denominator, Libby. Gambino robbed us of him too.*

Police chief Bruce Simm's voice breaks into Niall's thoughts.

"We sure appreciate all this," he says, pointing at the dining table loaded with platters of sandwiches ready to take to the pavilion. "But you certainly didn't have to go through all this trouble."

Niall pastes a pleasant smile on his face as he resumes the familiar task of fueling people with urns of coffee and endless food. But his heart's not in it today. "It's no trouble," he says. "And it's the least we can do for all you've done for us, and on a holiday, to boot."

Niall cocks his head as the rhythmic thrum of a helicopter reverberates overhead. *It's probably the local news station. I wonder how many camera crews are clustered outside the entrance gate this time? Gambino's trying to destroy us by taking, tainting, or killing everything we hold dear—family, friends, and Pines & Quill. The more negative news that happens here, the fewer writers in residence we'll have until he shuts us down and extinguishes our dreams.*

A smile creases the sides of Chief Simm's eyes. "Are you always prepared to feed an army?"

"We usually host extra guests over the Labor Day weekend." Niall points to the radio on the chief's belt and then to several platters of sandwiches covered with clear plastic. "If you call for help to carry the food, I'll stay here and keep at it." *Everyone has a coping mechanism—mine's cooking, baking, and keeping my hands and mind busy in the kitchen.*

Simms clicks on his radio and requests two people who aren't currently busy to come to the main house's kitchen.

"Before they get here," Niall says, "let me label them." He pulls masking tape and a marker from a drawer and begins to write:

BLT. Turkey Bruschetta Panini. Grilled Tuna Melt. Chicken Salad.

"I'll have a platter of vegetarian sandwiches ready shortly. Most everyone loves pita sandwiches stuffed with veggies, chickpeas, fresh herbs, tabbouleh, and homemade tzatziki sauce."

Chief Simms pats his flat stomach. "That even sounds good to a meat eater like me."

A buzzer goes off, indicating the arrival of a vehicle at the entrance gate. When no one activates the intercom, Niall says, "It has to be someone who knows the code. Maybe it's Mick or Rafferty."

Just then, Hemingway and Maggie come barreling through the open patio slider. With a chin that clears the height of countertops, Hemingway starts sniffing the food. His nostrils open and close fast like a rabbit, taking in the delicious scents.

"Mind your manners, young man," Niall says.

Hemingway drops his bottom onto the floor.

Next to him, Maggie follows suit.

Both of their tails dust the floor with enthusiasm.

Niall gives a hand signal for "stay," then crosses the room to the biscuit jar by the mudroom door and extracts four biscuits—two for each dog.

As Hemingway and Maggie finish their treats and lick imaginary crumbs from the floor, the foreman Hank and his wife, Gail, enter through the open patio slider. "I'm sorry to interrupt," Hank says, "but Gail's pretty worried."

Niall rinses his hands and dries them on the bib of his striped bistro apron. "How can I help?"

"Olivia and I were too scared to stay on the bluff with the others," Gail says, "so we came back to the main property. Olivia headed for her guest room over the workshop, and I hid on the floor behind the driver's seat in our truck. When the bomb squad came to check our vehicle and told me it was safe, I started looking for Olivia. I've searched *everywhere* and can't find her."

Niall's belly cramps. *Oh, no.* He turns off burners, puts a few items in the refrigerator, lifts the apron's neck strap over his head, and sets it on the gray-veined marble counter. "I'll help you look."

Fighting a rising panic, he leads the way through the glass slider.

Hemingway and Maggie bolt past him.

"We'll find her," Niall says to Gail over his shoulder, as much to reassure himself as her.

CHAPTER 21

"Don't expect the puppets of your mind to become the people of your story. If they are not realities in your own mind, there is no mysterious alchemy in ink and paper that will turn wooden figures into flesh and blood."
—LESLIE GORDON BARNARD

Mick rushes through the swinging hospital doors that Emma, Carly, Brianna, and the other women were ushered through what now seems like hours ago.

Walking toward him is Dr. Freeman, leading Emma, who's crying. And the girls.

His heart twists, and it feels like a hot anvil is in his gut. *Oh God, the baby!*

Mick enfolds Emma against his chest and places a cheek on the top of her head.

She sobs silently into his shirt, her warm body vibrating with pent-up emotion.

Tears run down Mick's cheeks. They're rough and bitter from waiting so long to come out. *We must have lost the baby.*

He looks at the doctor and, in a voice thick with tears, asks, "What happened?"

Dr. Freeman smiles. "Those are *happy* tears, Mick. The baby's fine, and so is Emma. The only thing that she and the girls are suffering from is exhaustion and the residual effects of prolonged fear."

Overcome with happiness, Mick lifts Emma off her feet and twirls her in a circle. When he sets her down, he kisses her eyelids and nose. Then he plants a resounding kiss on her smiling mouth.

Carly and Brianna laugh at his enthusiastic display of pure joy.

After assuring and reassuring both of them that the baby's fine, Dr. Freeman adds, "Emma, I want to see you again in two weeks. The office is closed tomorrow because of Labor Day. So please call on Tuesday and set up an appointment."

Emma turns to the doctor. "Thank you for everything. I'll see you in two weeks."

"We'll *both* be there," Mick says.

As Dr. Freeman walks away, the girls ask, "Where's Dad? Can we see him? Is he okay?"

"He's doing well," Mick says. "Rafferty's with him in recovery right now."

"Can we see him, *please?*" Brianna asks.

Mick guides Emma and the girls to the bank of elevators. When the doors slide open, they step in, and he presses a button that takes them up one floor. As they step out, Mick says, "Wait here just a minute. Your dad's still in recovery, so this may take a little persuasion."

Mick walks to the nurses' station and explains the situation. More sympathetic than the others, the nurse shift supervisor agrees to a short visit. She waves Emma and the girls over. "I'm breaking all kinds of rules here," she says. "But I'll give you *five* minutes. Not a *second* longer. Do you understand?"

Both girls smile and nod.

Once they're in Joe's room, Emma and Mick move to the back.

Carly and Brianna each take a side of Joe's bed and one of their dad's hands.

Rafferty steps to the foot of the bed and explains why their father's not responding to their attention. "Your dad's still unconscious from the anesthesia. It'll be a while yet before he wakes up."

Tears slip down their cheeks.

Mick draws Emma against his side and whispers. "More than anything, I don't want to be apart from you, but it's my turn to stay with Joe. That, and Rafferty hasn't had a chance to see Ivy yet. And you can bet that Marci's anxious to see her girls."

Emma squeezes his hand in understanding. "If I were Ivy or Marci, I'd want Rafferty and the girls back at Pines & Quill."

Mick hands the keys for the prisoner transport van to Rafferty. "Emma knows where it's parked."

Then he checks his watch. "Okay, girls, time's up. I'll tell your dad that you were here. I promise it'll do more than any medicine can to make him feel better."

Mick takes Emma in his arms and whispers. "I love you more than you'll ever know. Please stay in the guest room at the main house. I don't want you to be in our cabin by yourself." *Not until we remove Gambino from the equation, and he's no longer a threat.*

———

Rafferty walks with Emma and the girls to the prisoner transport van. From a distance, they can tell there's a person in the driver's seat.

Rafferty presses the index finger of one hand against his lips—*shhh*—and flattens the air with the palm of the other—*stay here*.

Emma and the girls stop. She places an arm around each of their shoulders.

Rafferty scans the area, then squat-walks to the van, arms extended with his Sig in both hands.

The person in the van is wearing a scrub cap and face mask. Their head, tilted down, is leaning against the door window.

Rafferty raps his left hand on the glass, his gun at the ready in his right. *No movement.*

When he opens the door, a man falls out facedown onto the ground. He's wearing blue scrubs and a lab coat. A gaping hole in the back of his scrub cap and skull reveals blood and gray matter.

Rafferty hears one of the girls stifle a scream.

He toes the man over. There's a small hole in his forehead. His eyes are open, ghostly gray, as they stare at nothing. *He was shot from the front. Entrance holes are neater and clean-cut; they tend to be smaller. Exit holes are large and messy.*

A note is pinned above an embroidered name on the lab coat, DAVID KLOSS, MD. He squats to read it.

This is what happens to people who make mistakes. You crossed me. That was a mistake. It may be sooner, or it may be later, but you'll pay.

It was signed

The Bull.

Rafferty calls in the homicide, then calls Mick. After briefing him, he says, "We're not going to take the prison transport van to Pines & Quill. I wouldn't put it past Gambino to rig it with a bomb. And I don't trust that he doesn't have other thugs in wait posing as Lyft, Uber, or taxi drivers. We're going in a way he won't expect."

A few minutes later, they're in the back of an ambulance. With siren blaring and lights flashing, it doesn't take long for them to get to Pines & Quill from St. Joseph Hospital. When they pull to a stop, Rafferty helps Emma and the girls out the back doors.

Two paramedics follow them with a gurney. "We got a call about a person with a gunshot wound."

Surprised expressions meet Rafferty's gaze. Then everyone converges on him, Emma, Carly, and Brianna.

One of the FBI agents says to Rafferty, "You came in an *ambulance?*"

"I don't trust Gambino," Rafferty says, "so I went to hijack an ambulance. The paramedics said they'd just received a call to come to Pines & Quill anyway to pick up a gunshot wound, and we came along. Who got hit?"

The FBI agent points to the ATV that Libby pulls up in. "Another one of Gambino's thugs."

The paramedics relocate the patient, who delivers a feral monologue during his transfer into the ambulance.

Chief Simms assigns two uniforms to accompany the thug to the hospital and stay with him.

"Yes, sir." They snag sandwiches before hopping in the back of the ambulance.

Marci gathers Carly and Brianna into her arms. Tears stream down her face. Then, over their heads, she asks Rafferty about Joe.

"He's on the mend," Rafferty assures her. "Mick's with him right now. I'll take you to see Joe when I relieve Mick."

Emma's mother, Maureen, tries to hug Emma, but Hemingway beats her, wedging between them in full-body-wag mode.

Emma's brothers Eric, Ethan, and Ellery surround the women and giant dog, each wearing a face-splitting grin.

"Where's Dad?" Emma asks.

"He's been manning the secure site at Maeve's condo. But he's on his way now," Maureen says. She palms Emma's belly. "Is the baby all right?"

Emma smiles through tears. "Yes. Dr. Freeman assured me that everything's fine. I go back again in two weeks."

With his charges accounted for, Rafferty scans the crowd until he sees Ivy and Maggie. He consumes his fiancée with his gaze as he closes the distance between them and then gathers Ivy into his arms.

Maggie repeatedly rubs his thigh with the length of her body, her exclamation-point tail in propeller mode the entire time.

Then Rafferty hears Ivy say his name. *I'm home.*

When they reach the tai chi pavilion, which is teeming with law enforcement personnel, writers in residence, and friends, Niall's heart buoys at the sight of Emma, the girls, and Rafferty. Niall, who is a sensitive man, swallows back tears as his world begins to right itself.

He shares the concern for Olivia with the others. "We'll cover more space faster if we divide up," he suggests.

Chief Simms looks at his watch. "Agreed. It's two-thirty now. Let's meet back here at three o'clock."

Much like a stone dropped in a pond generates ripples that radiate outward from the center, civilians and law enforcement personnel ripple out in every direction from the pavilion.

Niall heads north. A soothing combination of pine and brine permeates the air. He inhales deeply, filling his nostrils with the heady scent. He steps off the pathway to look behind tree trunks and foliage, calling, "Olivia!"

Black-capped chickadees scuttle from nearby trees.

Niall's just past Austen Cottage when a long primal scream pierces the air.

His heart plummets. *Oh, my God. Libby!*

CHAPTER 22

*"[As a writer] you have to have the three D's:
drive, discipline, and desire. If you're missing
any one of those three, you can have all the
talent in the world, but it's going to be really
hard to get anything done."*
—NORA ROBERTS

Powered by adrenaline, Bellingham's Police Chief Bruce
Simms is the first person to respond to Libby's scream.

Libby stands statue-still in front of an open chest freezer
in the workshop. One of her hands is over her heart. The
other covers her mouth. Her eyes, filled with terror, release
unchecked tears that stream down her face, over her hand,
and onto her shirt.

Simms steps forward and looks in the freezer. His heart
drops as he gazes into brown eyes staring sightlessly back at
him. He closes his own momentarily. *Good God!* No matter
how many times he encounters death, it's unsettling and can
make even the most stoic person wary of their mortality.

The victim's head is tilted at an awkward angle. Her legs are bent backward like a cheerleader in a midair jump to fit into the cramped space.

"Libby, do you know this woman?" Simms asks.

Before she can answer, Skip, Mick's poker buddy and seasoned paramedic, rushes in. When he glances into the still-open freezer, he cries out, "Oh, God. Olivia!" He starts forward, but Simms stops him. "I'm sorry, but this is a crime scene now. We can't touch anything. You knew the victim?"

"Yes," Skip cries. "She's my girlfriend. I brought her to Pines & Quill for the weekend because I thought she'd enjoy the holiday here. And now she's dead." He covers his face with his hands. A deep moan bubbles up from his chest and ends with a blistering wail. "If I'd left the bluff with her, she'd still be alive."

Not for the first time today, Simms is wistful, wishing that Mick, Joe, and Rafferty—the "Three Musketeers" as he thinks of them—were here. *Together, the ex-cop turned PI, homicide detective, and FBI special agent make quick work of things. And as a PI, Mick has the added benefit of fewer restrictions, protocols, and no red tape—freedoms that Joe and Rafferty don't have.*

Breathless, Niall arrives and rushes to Libby. He takes her in his arms, rocks her back and forth, and murmurs something into her hair.

As Niall starts to lead Libby and Skip away, Simms says, "Niall, I need to get their statements. Are you heading to the main house?"

"Yes. Unfortunately, we know the drill. They'll be there waiting."

Simms radios for crime scene tape to cordon off the area and two uniforms to stand watch and ensure it remains undisturbed. While waiting, he uses the camera on his cell phone to photograph the petechial hemorrhage on Olivia's face—tiny pinpoint red marks that often indicate death by manual strangulation, hanging, or smothering.

After about a dozen photos, Simms calls Dr. Jill Graham, the medical examiner.

She says she'll alert the crime scene unit and that he can expect them soon. "You know how much this is going to cost over a holiday weekend?"

"Yes," Simms says. "With all of the other teams I have here, I'm burning through the budget like kindling."

———

Phillip Benton, Emma's father, closes the secure site at Maeve's condo in Bellingham. Then, after calling for an Uber, he locks himself out of her unit and waits. *I'm not going to rest easy until I see for myself that my wife, daughter, and sons are okay.*

Minutes later, he's in the front passenger seat of a white Volkswagen Jetta on his way to Pines & Quill.

The entrance gate is a beehive of activity with new crews. Like circling vultures, they're ready to dive on anything that moves. And they would have if it hadn't been for two uniformed officers standing guard.

Phillip pushes microphones away from his face as he makes his way to the officers, explains who he is, and shows his ID. After one of them makes a call, he's cleared to enter.

Just then, the marked vehicles of the medical examiner and crime scene investigators arrive. Phillip's heart accelerates at the thought that something may have happened to one of his family members.

The ME lowers the window on her car and shows her ID to one of the uniforms.

Phillip takes the opportunity to speak with her, and then, after pressing the code on the keypad, he gets a ride with Dr. Graham. He motions to the CSI van behind her car. "Someone died?" He feels his Adam's apple bob up and down as he swallows his fear.

She keeps her eyes on the tree-lined lane in front of her. "Yes, I'm afraid so."

"Do you know who it was?"

"No, I don't. And I'm sure you can understand that I wouldn't be able to share any details even if I did."

Phillip respects her professionalism. He nods his understanding, careful not to let the tears in his eyes spill.

By three o'clock, Emma arrives back at the tai chi pavilion. The other people who hadn't heard Libby scream arrive too. Emma feels lightheaded and sick when she learns that Olivia Frey, Skip's girlfriend, has been killed by one of Gambino's foot soldiers. *Oh, my God, another death at Pines & Quill. I need to call Mick and tell him what's happened.*

Was it by one of the thugs who's already been apprehended? Or a different one, someone who got away? If it's the latter, are they still at Pines & Quill hiding somewhere?

Emma's father strides across the pavilion toward Emma with Hemingway at his side. She's thrilled to see him. In addition to Mick, her father and brothers are the most important men in her life.

Phillip pulls her into a bear hug. "I've been so worried about you."

"I'm okay, Dad. And so's the baby."

Hemingway dances around them, barking and wagging his excitement.

When her dad finally releases her, Emma cups Hemingway's huge head in her hands, then bends and rubs her forehead against his. "I'm happy to see you, too, you big lug."

Hemingway's tail waves figure eights at Emma's undivided attention until Maggie joins them. Then they bolt off into the trees on their next adventure.

Emma watches her father navigate to the other side of the

pavilion, gather her mother into his arms, and lead her away from the assembled group. She blinks back happy tears. *I'm so lucky to have them. I learned everything I know about a good marriage relationship from my parents.*

Exhausted, she tells Rafferty and Ivy that she's getting fresh clothes from the cabin and then heading to the main house for a hot shower and a long nap in the guest room.

Overwhelming relief floods Emma when she opens the door to the cabin she shares with Mick. The rustic interior wraps her in a welcoming hug of indigo, cream, and splashes of soft yellow. *I'm so glad to be home. There were a few times over the last two days I wasn't sure I'd live to see it again.*

Gambino's thugs got Emma's cell phone when they took her purse, so she uses the landline to call Mick.

He picks up on the first ring. "Emma. Are you okay?"

"I am," she says. "But, Mick, there's been another murder."

"Oh, God. *Who?* A moment before you called, I got a text from Rafferty. I haven't opened it yet."

Emma hears the strain in Mick's voice. "It's Olivia Frey, Skip's girlfriend. Libby found her in the chest freezer in the workshop. Pines & Quill is teaming with law enforcement personnel. They're taking statements right now."

"I'm worried about you and the baby. I'll be there as soon—"

"I'm okay, Mick. *Really.* I'm just getting a change of clothes from our cabin and then heading to the main house for a hot shower and a long nap. Rafferty said that he's bringing Marci to see Joe soon. How is he?"

"I think he's starting to come around. He's moaning a lot, and there's activity behind his eyelids."

"I'm glad to hear that," Emma says. "While you're watching over Joe, please take care of yourself. I love you, and our baby needs their father."

After speaking with Emma, Mick leans forward in the chair next to Joe's hospital bed. He rests his forearms on his thighs. *That son-of-a-bitch Gambino!* His hatred for Gambino grows like a cancer that can't be cut out unless Gambino's cut down.

Then he reads the text from Rafferty.

One of Gambino's foot soldiers killed Olivia Frey.
I'm with CSI on the premises.

A seasoned paramedic, Skip is used to seeing death. But this is different; it's up close and personal. I'm sure this loss has broken his heart.

Mick leans back in the uncomfortable chair and thinks about his blessings. *Since I met Emma in May, I have a new lease on life—I'm a private investigator, a husband, and I'm going to be a dad.*

Then he thinks of the carnage, of all the death in the same window of time. *I'd need more than two hands to count them all, but the two losses that hurt the most are Niall's brother Paddy, and Connor—my father, my role model, the man I idolized. The man I want to be for my child.*

Joe moans, turns his head toward Mick, and opens his eyes.

"It's about time," Mick says.

"Carly and Brianna?" Joe asks, his voice a raspy whisper.

"They came to see you, but you were still out cold. They're with Marci at Pines & Quill now. Rafferty and Emma are there too."

Joe tilts his head back and looks at the ceiling. Then, with a face painted in resignation, he reaches his left hand across his chest to touch his right arm.

He closes his eyes and exhales audibly in relief. "In my dreams, they amputated it."

"No," Mick says. "But if the bullet had been a fraction more in either direction, you might have lost it." He nods toward the bandage around Joe's head and smiles. "A bullet grazed your forehead, though. So you're going to be even uglier than you already are."

Joe's laugh turns into a wince. "Stop it, or I'll beat the crap out of you when they release me."

"Which won't be for a while, my friend. In the meantime, I heard a rumor that Rafferty's bringing Marci to see you a little later. And then he's going to sneak the girls in after that." Mick hands Joe a lidded cup with a bendable straw. "The doctor told me to have you drink water. Don't worry," he says, "I already took a sip to make sure it's not poisoned. There's only my spit in it."

Again, Joe's laugh turns into a grimace. Finally, he takes a long pull, hands the cup back to Mick, then closes his eyes. Moments later, he's sound asleep.

Glad that one of his best friends will be okay, Mick tilts the chair back on two legs. He lets his mind return to the recent carnage at the hands of Gambino. *The fact that he took Emma, Carly, and Brianna to sell them. The fact that he actively traffics humans, guns, and drugs.*

And the fact that I'm going to stop him.

In the kitchen of the main house, surrounded by the bittersweet aroma of coffee mingled with the sharp scent of freshly cut onion, Niall uses an eight-inch chef's knife to dice sweet onions for the evening meal—caramelized onion and roasted garlic pasta. As tears stream down his cheeks, he insists that Libby does what Emma's doing—take a long hot shower and then a nap.

"But what about our guests?" she asks, petting the top of Hemingway's head as he tries to shove his wet nose between them.

"After giving their statements to the police and having had enough excitement for the weekend, all of our non-writing guests have gone home."

"But—"

Niall sets the sharp knife on the cutting board, washes his hands in the sink, and then places them on his hips. "No buts. I've packed sandwiches and salads in our insulated totes. Hemingway and I will deliver them to the writer's cottages for dinner. I'll make up for it in the morning by hosting them in the main house for breakfast."

"What about Raf—"

"Rafferty took Marci to the hospital to see Joe. And before you ask, Carly and Brianna are with Ivy and Maggie in the guest rooms over the workshop."

Hemingway whips his tail back and forth at Maggie's name.

Niall chucks Hemingway under his chin. *I wish I felt as happy-go-lucky as this big lug. After something happens— good or bad—he continues merrily along with his business.* "And before you ask, so are Emma's parents and brothers." He crosses the room to get a biscuit from the jar by the mudroom door, makes Hemingway sit, and then gives it to him. "Now, stay put."

He walks back to Libby. "Your mom and Maureen carried dinner over to the workshop for all of the guests staying in the new addition. I've invited Jake, Sarah, and everyone else who's not a writer in residence to join us in the Ink Well tonight after we've all had a chance to catch our breath. That way, we can debrief and catch each other up."

"What if—"

"Police Chief Simms has two uniforms at the entrance gate and six others monitoring the property and bluff overnight. They're going to take turns eating dinner downstairs in the workshop. They know there's a bathroom in there too."

"But, Hem—"

Niall adjusts the ever-present dish towel on his shoulder. "I've already introduced Hemingway to the officers on watch."

At the sound of his name, Hemingway leaves his spot and rejoins Niall and Libby, sticking his wet nose in Niall's hand, looking for more.

Niall pats his head. "Hemingway knows they're friends and won't try to chase them off. *Or worse.*"

They both look down at Hemingway. Niall scratches the giant dog under his chin. "With your tongue lolling out the side of your mouth, no one would ever know you're a fierce warrior."

Libby puts her arms around Niall, sandwiching Hemingway between them. "You've thought of everything, haven't you?"

"Damn straight," Niall says. "I'm not just another pretty face."

That evening in the Ink Well, US Marshal Jake Porter sits on an overstuffed loveseat next to his wife, Sarah, nursing a scotch and soda. *I wouldn't usually have a drink at almost ten o'clock in the evening, but I'll be damned if the last few days haven't made me grateful for this exception. I want to hear the details of what happened on that mountain.*

Jake scans the faces of the others in the large, cozy after-dinner gathering place with its small well-stocked bar: Niall and Libby MacCullough; Emma McPherson, her parents, and three brothers; Rafferty, Ivy, and her guide dog, Maggie, with Hemingway snuggled next to her; and Joe's wife, Marci, who had the opportunity for a long visit with her husband earlier.

Mick's with Carly and Brianna at the hospital after Rafferty snuck them in for a second visit with their dad, Joe. Rafferty will go back to pick them up shortly.

In the telling, retelling, hashing, and rehashing, Jake listens to the events of the last few days as they unfold from different perspectives: Emma's from inside the cabin on Mount Baker; Rafferty's from outside the cabin; Ivy, Maeve, and Maureen's from out on the bluff by the boulders.

"It's a wonder that only one person lost their life at Pines & Quill, and a damn shame at that," Jake says, taking another sip of his scotch and soda. "Everything has a price, even justice. And sometimes, that price tag is hefty—human lives."

Maeve nods. "Unfortunately, Olivia thought she'd be safer from Gambino's thugs in the workshop than out on the bluff."

"It seems that Gambino's got a long reach," Jake says. "That there's *no* place safe to hide."

"Rumor has it you got a job offer," Rafferty says to Jake. "You'd be an asset to *any* team."

Sarah turns to her husband, a look of surprise on her face. "You didn't tell me that."

"I didn't tell you because I'm not considering the offer I received from Stewart Crenshaw, Rafferty's commanding officer. I love being a US Marshal." *Although it felt good to receive the offer.* He glances at Rafferty. *I may not be as young as that buck and his buddies, but I'm not out to pasture yet.* "And if this past weekend is anything to go by, it's a hell of a lot safer." Jake winks at Rafferty.

"Seriously though, *why* does Gambino have his sights set on you guys?"

Rafferty leans back in his chair. "It was initially just Mick. Five years ago, Gambino shot Mick's partner, Sam, to create an 'officer down' diversion and steal over ten million dollars' worth of heroin from the SFPD lockup. The heroin went missing, and Gambino thinks Mick knows where it's at."

"Does he?" Jake asks.

"Mick doesn't have a clue," Rafferty says. "But Gambino doesn't believe him and is killing his family as payback." He nods toward Niall. "First, it was Niall's brother, Paddy, followed by Mick's father, Connor. That's when Joe and I got involved."

Rafferty leans forward, bracing his arms on his thighs. "Here's where it gets really interesting. Joe's ex-partner, Toni Bianco, was a dirty cop. It turns out she was Gambino's daughter. He had her killed so she couldn't turn state's evidence against him to save her own hide."

"Damn, that's brutal," Jake says, shaking his head. "Well, if you guys ever need a hand—nothing formal, mind you—call me. I'd like to help. Or if you need a vacation, you and yours are welcome at our ranch in Big Sky Country."

CHAPTER 23

"In the planning stage of a book, don't plan the ending. It has to be earned by all that will go before it."
— ROSE TREMAIN

wo weeks later, on September twenty-first, the kitchen in the main house is alive with a mingling of sweet and savory aromas from Niall's handiwork as he puts the finishing touches on the farewell breakfast. To him, this meal is of equal importance to their guests as their first meal at Pines & Quill. *It has to be grand.*

Niall glances at one of two kitchen timers, careful to make sure everything will be ready at the same time: baked berry French toast stuffed with blueberries, blackberries, and cream cheese; maple candied bacon; beignets—New Orleans style fried dough—from a recipe Emma brought him when she and Mick returned from their honeymoon. And "toad in the hole"—a fantastically frugal egg dish for those who are watching their weight.

The twenty-first day of every month is always bittersweet for me. Over the past three weeks, we've made new friends with the writers in residence, so it's hard to see them go. But I also relish the last week of every month when it's just us putting everything back to rights and getting ready for the next batch of writers. And from what Libby told me, October's guests are fascinating. Then comes November and December, and the holidays are upon us. And though they're guest-free months, I cherish the time at Pines & Quill with family and friends.

Carrying a carafe and pitcher, Mick joins Niall in the kitchen. "Mind if I get refills? We're going through coffee and orange juice like there are holes in the bottom." He smiles, lifting the containers.

"Help yourself. But once you deposit those back on the table, will you please tag someone and come back to help me carry these platters?"

"You've got it," Mick says.

As Niall tongs sizzling bacon onto a platter and the delicious scent fills his nostrils, in his mind's eye, he replays years of writers in residence who've come through their door. *I've changed a lot since Libby and I opened Pines & Quill. I lacked experience and maturity when we started, and I was fresh out of cooking school.* He looks at the scars on his left thumb and grins. *It took me a while to learn how to use the various knives. Now we're a garden-to-table establishment and have a waiting list. Libby says that food is my love language.*

Niall balls his free hand into a fist, and the grin on his face disappears. *From the cottages to the food and everything in between, every person who comes here deserves the best experience we can offer. And Gambino's doing his damnedest to ruin it.*

Rafferty and Libby follow Mick back into the kitchen. Between them and Niall, they quickly convey the morning's feast to the table amid an eruption of *oohs* and *aahs*.

As Rafferty sits down next to Ivy, Niall hears a distinct thumping. "Did Hemingway make it from the mudroom into the dining room?"

The telltale thumping gets faster and louder.

"It's Maggie's fault," Ivy says. "It's her last day at Pines & Quill, and she doesn't want to be separated from her best friend."

Two furry heads peek over the tabletop—one, a black-and-white curly topknot; the other, a wiry-haired face with awnings for eyebrows and a beard.

"Lie back down," Niall says, pointing at Hemingway.

Both heads disappear under the table.

Still standing, Niall kisses his fingers and lets them bloom. "Bon appétit."

Family, friends, and guests lift their glasses in unison. "Bon appétit."

"What are those things with powdered sugar on top?" Sakura asks.

"Those are beignets," Niall says. "A type of fritter, or deep-fried pastry, usually made from pâte à choux—a very light dough. When done"—he lifts his hand and stirs the air—"they're soft, pillowy, fluffy, and airy."

"Not to mention totally scrumptious," Libby says. "Just wait until you take a bite. They have a sweet yeasty flavor."

Niall places a beignet on Ivy's plate. "I'm so glad you were able to extend your stay. It's great that your school was able to find a substitute teacher for your class."

"It's a great place to work," Ivy says.

"Speaking of school," Marci says, "as long as they keep up with their studies, Carly's and Brianna's schools gave them a grace period before they have to return. Thank you for letting us stay here while Joe was in the hospital. We felt a lot safer than being back at home by ourselves."

Eleven-year-old Brianna says, "This is the thickest French toast I've ever had, and it's yummy."

Pointing at her sister, thirteen-year-old Carly laughs. "Your teeth are purple from the berries."

"People who live in glass houses shouldn't throw stones," Marci says. "Yours are too."

Then Marci pats the top of her husband's hand. "I'm glad they finally released Joe." She turns in her chair and moves her hand to the scalding-pink scar that a bullet seared across Joe's forehead. It interrupts his right eyebrow, giving him a slightly disreputable appearance. "And he's even more rakish now than he ever was." She leans in and kisses his cheek.

Joe laughs and pats his flat stomach. "Man, oh man, is it ever good to eat real food again. That hospital stuff pales in comparison." He reaches for more bacon with his left hand because his right arm is still immobilized. "And before you know it, I'll be out of this thing." He nods down at his right arm.

"Speaking from experience," Rafferty says, "that's when the *real* pain begins—physical therapy."

When Joe groans, his daughters laugh.

Sakura Nishiwaka says, "There's a Buddhist proverb that goes, 'Pain is inevitable. Suffering is optional.'" Then she laughs. "It's probably bullsh—" She stops, looks at the girls, and begins again. "It's probably a *bunch of malarkey.*"

Joe says, "All I expect from people is human decency." He takes a bite of bacon and washes it down with coffee. "By the way, I heard you're quite the martial artist with a samurai sword. I bet Gambino's foot soldiers were surprised." He takes another bite. "I'm curious, though. How did you get a sword past TSA? The Transportation Security Administration's pretty tough."

"Oh, that's easy," Sakura says. "I didn't buy it until I got here. I purchased it at the souvenir shop of an intern-ment camp. I should say, a *memorial* to an internment camp that I visited while I was here. Did you know that there were nine Japanese POW camps and three enemy alien internment camps in Washington State alone during World War II?"

Everyone stops eating, including Niall. *We should be ashamed of what our forefathers did.*

"Don't worry," Sakura says. "I took the sword to the post office in town yesterday and shipped it to myself because I didn't want any trouble getting on my flight today."

"Speaking of trouble," Niall says, turning to Sarah. "We sure would have been in a world of it if you and your husband, Jake, hadn't been here to help the rest of us while Mick, Joe, and Rafferty were on Mount Baker rescuing Emma, Carly, and Brianna."

Sarah looks at the faces around the table. "Jake wished he didn't have to leave, but he had another assignment." She takes a sip of coffee. "But I think we all did a bang-up job of it—every one of us." She lifts her cup. "Hear, hear."

The others raise their cups, affirming Sarah's assessment.

After many sleepless nights over yet another death at Pines & Quill, Niall's determined to stop worrying about the future and start enjoying the gift of now. *Life's a risk with no guarantees of happiness—there's always the possibility of loss and pain.* He glances at the smiling faces around the table. *And love is life's biggest risk, but I'm willing to take it.*

Niall stands and taps his spoon against his cup. "May all that is unlived in us blossom into futures graced with the love of family and friends."

———

Emma can't contain her excitement as she fastens her seatbelt in the front seat of the Pines & Quill van. *I know the ultrasound that Dr. Freeman ordered is primarily to confirm nothing happened to the baby when I was held hostage on Mount Baker. But I'm thrilled about the possibility of finding out the gender!* Steered by pregnancy hormones, her mind takes a different tack. *Oh, my gosh, will I be a good mother?*

Having stowed the luggage in the cargo area, Mick slips

next to her in the driver's seat and fastens his seatbelt. "Buckle up, everyone."

Emma looks over her left shoulder. Todd Jones sits in the bucket seat immediately behind her. *He seems way more relaxed than when he arrived.*

On the bench seat behind them sits Sarah Porter and Dale Brewer.

After we drop everyone off at Bellingham International, we're going to see Dr. Freeman. Most OB/GYNs schedule an ultrasound at around eighteen to twenty-one weeks, but the baby's gender may be determined by ultrasound as early as fourteen weeks. And though it's not always one hundred percent accurate this early, because of the extenuating circumstances on Mount Baker, Dr. Freeman ordered one. I wonder if we're having a boy or a girl? We'll be excited either way.

Emma turns forward to look out the windshield and think about her friends and family who've been making gender guesses based on old wives' tales. Two days ago, when she video-called her best friend, Sally, in San Diego, Sally asked her to step back from the phone and lift her shirt.

"You're carrying high and wide, so it's got to be a girl."

"That's wishful thinking on your part," Emma said, laughing. "I barely have a bump."

Then, yesterday, her mother said, "Gender prediction myths persist because they can appear to be right. However, when you're looking at fifty-fifty odds, predictions are bound to come true half the time. And surprisingly, at least a couple of these methods do have some evidence to back them up." Once Maureen delivered that caveat, she insisted on Emma doing the Drano test.

"What on earth?" Mick asks, wide-eyed.

Phillip, Mick's father-in-law, pats Mick on the back. "It's better if we don't get involved."

The women—Maureen, Maeve, Marci and her daughters, Ivy, and Libby—had all filed into the guest room of the main house and sent Emma into the en suite bathroom with a canning jar and spoon. Once the door was closed, Emma's mother, Maureen, called out, "Pee in the jar and then stir some Drano into your urine. Then come out here. If the mixture turns green, it's a boy. Any other color, and it's a girl."

A few minutes later, Emma came out with the jar. The contents were yellow.

Between the women, there was a squeal of excitement.

"Now, dear," Maeve—Emma's mother-in-law—said. "Let's confirm the results." And with that, she opened the bedroom door. "Mick, will you come here for a minute, honey?"

When Mick arrived, Maeve reached up to the top of his head, where his hair was the longest, and pulled out a strand.

"Ouch! What did you do that for?" Mick asked, rubbing his head.

"You'll know soon enough," she said, closing the door.

It took Maeve and Maureen a few minutes to secure the hair to Emma's wedding band. "Now, Emma, lie on your back on the bed," her mother said.

Caught up in the excitement, Emma did precisely that.

Then her mother-in-law Maeve explained. "We're going to hold your wedding ring from a strand of Mick's hair over your belly. If the ring swings around in circles, it's a girl. If it sways back and forth, it's a boy."

When Emma lifted her head to watch, her mother gently pressed it back down. "Be still. We'll describe what's happening."

"I sure hope so," Ivy says. "I'm blind, remember? So I can't see what's going on either."

"And don't worry, Emma," Libby says. "It doesn't hurt, and it'll be over in a minute."

"Did they do this to you when you were pregnant with Ian?" Emma asks.

"Yes. And it was dead-on accurate."

Moments later, there is another squeal of excitement. "It's swinging in a circle," Carly says.

"Both tests say it's a girl," Brianna says.

"Does that mean for *certain* Emma's having a girl?" Carly asks.

"We have to remember that these 'tests'"—Marci makes air quotes with her fingers—"are myths. But I'd say it looks like there's a pretty good chance that it's a girl."

"What are you going to name her?" Brianna says.

Emma shakes her head. "I don't know yet, but you'll be among the first to know."

Now, she glances at Mick and smiles as he drives through the Pines & Quill gate. *I know exactly what we'll name the baby, and Mick will be over the moon.*

———

Mick pulls the silver van curbside in the Departures area of the Bellingham International Airport. His heart pounds with excitement. *Today's ultrasound will confirm the baby's progress, health, and possibly gender. I never knew it was possible to love someone so much who I've never even met. Oh, God, please help me to be a good father. Please help me to keep our baby safe in this world.*

Then his guts twist in a knot. *But there's no way Gambino's grudge with me is over. And now my two best friends and their families are involved.* A wave of guilt washes over Mick.

Gambino wants us to pay for killing his goons and rescuing the women he was selling. I suspect he lost some of his credibility in that failed transaction. So we've got to stay alert and proactive. Rafferty and I will keep our heads low and put out feelers until Joe is healed and returns to active duty.

Mick checks his watch. *Hurry, hurry, hurry! We're going to be late.* He pushes a button on the dash that opens the side panels and cargo area. As he offloads the baggage, Emma hugs each person as they get out. "I'm so sorry for everything that happened with Gambino. When you get home and check your accounts, you'll see that Libby and Niall refunded your fees in full. We want you to return to Pines & Quill. But next time, under much better circumstances."

"Are you kidding me?" Sarah asks. "I wouldn't trade it for the world. I have enough writing fodder to last me the next four novels."

"And I learned that whether I'm in my chair or using my prosthetic legs," Todd says, "I can still contribute."

"I agree," Sakura pipes in. "I don't know when I had so much fun. Well, *fun* may not be the right word exactly. But I came here looking for a fight for what had been done to my ancestors. And while the fight I got into wasn't about that, at least some justice was served."

"I arrived using prescription meds to numb the reality of my life," Dale says. "I'm a widower and miss my wife terribly. But when the Gambino shit hit the fan, I realized that if I was in a haze, I could get killed—or worse, someone could die because I wasn't on the ball. I haven't touched that crap for almost three weeks, and I feel better than I have in ages. I'm never touching it again."

Mick shakes each writer's hand to a chorus of baby and parenting well wishes.

As the glass doors leading to the departure area close behind Sarah, Sakura, Todd, and Dale, they turn for a final wave.

Mick lowers his arm, puts it around Emma's shoulders, and pulls her into his side. "Are you ready to go see Dr. Freeman?"

Emma kisses Mick soundly on the lips. "You bet I am."

Once they arrive and check in, Dr. Freeman greets them and explains that a sonographer—a trained technician of ultrasound procedure—will do the ultrasound. "But I'll see you two afterward."

When the receptionist calls Emma's name, Emma requests that Mick stays with her during the entire visit.

After ushering them into an examination room, Emma removes her jewelry, changes into a gown—with the opening in front—and lies on the examination table as instructed.

They don't have to wait long before a sonographer arrives. She explains, "Because you're having an ultrasound a little earlier than usual—they're usually done between eighteen and twenty-one weeks—instead of an abdominal scan, I'm going to do it transvaginally."

She lifts an instrument for them to see. "This is a transducer. We usually call it a wand. It's attached to a probe. The wand emits pings that safely bounce off your baby's tissues, fluids, and bones, and the echoes help create an image, called a sonogram, of your baby on the screen." She points to a machine on Emma's right.

"It's important for you to know that during early development, the male and female genitalia look almost identical. After fifteen weeks, it is much easier to determine gender. I understand that you're beginning your fourteenth week. Is that correct?"

Emma squeezes Mick's hand and nods. "Yes, that's correct."

Mick leans forward. "How long does an ultrasound take?"

"Generally, an ultrasound takes between twenty and sixty minutes and causes no pain. That said, mild discomfort may be experienced as I move the wand."

"When the picture comes up on the screen," Emma asks, "what is it specifically that we're looking for?"

"Another good question," the sonographer says. "There is a nub at the end of the spine called the caudal notch. If the nub is angled upward, the sex is likely male. If the nub points straight out or down, it's more likely female.

"However, most people with an untrained eye can't identify the nub. But since you indicated that you *want* to know the baby's gender, I'll point to it on the screen and show you the angle.

"But I need to warn you that sometimes the nub isn't visible, even to me. That doesn't mean that anything's wrong. It just means that you'll need to wait until your next ultrasound and hope it's visible then."

Mick's heart gallops in his chest at the thought of seeing their unborn child. He takes Emma's warm hand in his as they focus on the screen. His tears overflow when an image appears on the screen. "That's the head, right?" he says, pointing to the screen.

"Yes, that's correct."

He leans closer. "How big is the baby?" The awe in his voice is unmistakable.

"At fourteen weeks, roughly the size of a nectarine and can measure up to three and a half inches long, crown to rump."

Emma turns to Mick. There are tears on her cheeks, too.

He thinks, *This incredible woman is the most beautiful person I've ever met. I'm so grateful that she's my wife—the mother of our child.*

Mick leans forward and kisses the tip of her nose before they both focus on the screen again. Now and then, Emma squeezes Mick's hand. "Are you uncomfortable?" he asks.

"A little, but it's not bad," Emma says.

After a short while, the sonographer rolls her stool closer to the monitor. "I'm about to point to the nub, but before I do, I want to confirm that you both want to know the baby's gender?"

"We do," they say in unison.

She touches the screen with her index finger and says, "Now that I've pointed it out, can you see the angle?"

Mick and Emma squeeze each other's hands and nod.

"On that note, I'll step out and let you two enjoy this special moment alone."

Mick buries his face in Emma's chest and sobs.

"If it was a boy, I wanted to name him Connor after your father. But now that we know we're having a girl, I want to name her Constance, *also* after your father."

Mick's heart explodes with joy as Emma wraps him in her arms, and they press this memory into each other's hearts.

Turn the page to read an excerpt from
Illusionist: A Sean McPherson Novel, Book Five

PROLOGUE

"Being a writer all boils down to this: It's you, in a chair, staring at a page. And you're either going to stay in that chair until words are written, or you're going to give up and walk away."
— ALESSANDRA TORRE

The sunshine on the lake's surface glistens, just like the tears that had pooled in the eyes of Gambino's most recent conquest before he extinguished her life. *My favorite part is when I see the realization that it's not a sex game dawn on their faces.*

He's aware of the statistics: women subjected to nonfatal strangulation are eight times more likely to be murdered. He scoffs at the idea. *If they're with me, it's one hundred percent guaranteed.*

Georgio "The Bull" Gambino is a man who thrives on research, precision, and covering his tracks. He knows many women of his most recent victim's generation—those aged forty and under—have grown accustomed to the idea that plain, vanilla sex is for prudes. Women have been trained to believe it's empowering to ask a man to choke them. Some women's magazines even normalize it as "breath play." To suggest there might be anything wrong with this potentially lethal practice is dismissed as kink-shaming.

Gambino glides the tips of his manicured fingers over his white mustache as he stares out the massive plate glass window in his opulent home. It overlooks Lake Whatcom—from the Lummi word for "loud water"—and is the drinking water source for the county's residents.

He picks up his cell phone from the antique table next to his leather wingback chair and initiates a video call.

Carmine, his right-hand man, comes into view.

"Are you in position?"

"Yes."

"Show me."

Carmine reverses the camera on his cell phone, then scans the student-filled room from his seat in the upper left quadrant of a university lecture hall. Unlike a traditional classroom that accommodates between one and fifty pupils, the enormous room's pitched floor and tiered seating allow for a capacity in the hundreds. After zooming in on a single student to Gambino's satisfaction, the men consider the difference in their time zones and synchronize their watches.

"Make the call on time, Carmine. Not a moment sooner or later." Gambino disconnects and returns his gaze out the window.

Not nearly as massive as his high-rise in Seattle, this well-hidden luxury residence is nestled in the woods. He bought it through a shell corporation a few years back when he realized that Bellingham Bay is part of a much larger waterway system, thus ideal for his purposes—trafficking guns, drugs, and humans. Optimal for rapid movement and concealment, Bellingham Bay is a bay of the Salish Sea—the encompassing term for the nearshore Pacific Ocean, Strait of Georgia and Johnstone Strait in Canada, Strait of Juan de Fuca, and Puget Sound.

My hate for Sean McPherson is no longer just about the missing ten million dollars of heroin I had stolen from the SFPD lockup. That's a pittance. Because of him, a half dozen of my foot soldiers are dead, and he rescued twelve women I'd contracted to sell, making me look foolish.

He bristles at the embarrassment he felt when facing a kingpin in the Russian mafia to tell him that their deal was off. They were on one of his container ships in the Bering Strait. He'd had to make it up to him, which included everything on the bill of lading. *It cost me dearly, and McPherson's going to pay.*

Gambino picks up his cell phone and makes another call. His heart races with anticipation. When the recipient answers, he says, "If you hang up, I'll kill your child. Do you understand?"

"Is this some kind of sick joke?"

"I assure you this is no joke. When I disconnect, you'll receive a video call from my associate. He's visiting your child's class—Market Power in the New Economy. If you don't do what I say, it will cost the life of the person you love most."

"Who is this? What do you want from me?"

"I'm the person who's going to kill your child if you don't do what I say. In two days, you're heading to Pines & Quill writing retreat. While there, you will frame Sean McPherson for murder."

"Frame someone for murder? What do you mean?"

"No, not just someone. You're going to frame Sean McPherson. You're going to kill one of the other writers in residence. I don't care which one, nor do I care how you do it. You're a crime writer. Figure it out. You arrive at Pines & Quill on October first and leave on the twenty-first. You have three weeks to accomplish the task."

"But—"

"Do *not* interrupt me again. The murder will be real. You're the one who's going to do it. But you'll act as an illusionist, making it *appear* as if Sean McPherson did it—framing him for the death. It's your job to ensure that he has a motive, opportunity, and means. And that there's enough of his DNA at the scene to arrest and convict him. Everyone, especially the police, must believe that he's guilty. If you fail, your child dies."

"Wait! I have money. I can pay you."

"It's not a matter of money. It's a matter of service. You do this service for me, and I'll do you the service of not killing your child." Gambino glances at his watch. "When I hang up, you'll receive a video call proving that my associate is within arm's reach of your child and ready to do my bidding."

"But how do I contact you?"

"You don't. And understand this. You're under surveillance, and all of your technology is being monitored. If you so much as even *think* about contacting the police, your child will die."

Gambino disconnects the call and sets the phone down. *With McPherson convicted of murder, it's a trifecta win: he goes to prison, won't see his child grow up, and it'll destroy the reputation of Pines & Quill.*

Picking up a pair of binoculars, he continues to track a bald eagle he'd been admiring through the massive window while on the phone. Gambino uses the center focus knob to bring clarity to the bird of prey.

The raptor swoops down, catches its mark, then soars skyward.

Gambino's face breaks into a reptilian smile.

Book reviews from awesome readers like you help others feel confident about deciding if a book is for them.

So if you enjoyed *Iniquity,* please consider leaving a review on Amazon, Goodreads, or BookBub.

ACKNOWLEDGMENTS

A heartfelt thank you to:

You, the reader, for choosing *Iniquity,* posting reviews, and emailing me to let me know you enjoy my books. I appreciate your ongoing support and encouragement.

Brooke Warner and *Lauren Wise,* publisher and associate publisher at She Writes Press and SparkPress. Between nonfiction and fiction, this is our sixth book together. I'm glad to be part of the sisterhood and one of the sparks.

Mimi Bark and *Tabitha Lahr,* talented cover and interior designers at She Writes Press and SparkPress. Thank you for the visual panache you bring to the end product.

Lisa Grau, book publicist at Grau PR. Thank you for generating media coverage and securing influential placements for this author and her work.

Professional sources—a crime fiction book is only as good as it is accurate. Thank you to *Vickie Gooch,* detective in the Major Crimes Unit of the Idaho State Police; *Rylene Nowlin,* DNA specialist at the Idaho State Police Crime Lab; *Dr. Glen Groben,* forensic pathologist; *Danny R. Smith,* private investigator and author of the Dickie Floyd Detective novels; *Camille LaCroix*, forensic psychiatrist; *Chuck Ambrose*, psychologist; *Anthony Geddes*, chief public defender and lead counsel in death penalty cases in Idaho; and *Brent Bunn*, US Marshal. Your individual and collective insights are invaluable to the storylines in the Sean McPherson novels. Despite my best efforts, I may still have made mistakes. Any inaccuracies in law enforcement or medical processes and procedures are my own.

Blackbird Writers, a collective of mystery and thriller writers. I'm grateful to be part of a flock that fosters and supports each other's work. Thank you.

Christine DeSmet, writing coach. For almost a decade, you've made me an infinitely better writer. When I'm at the keyboard, I hear your voice in my head: "What's the POV character's scene goal, conflict, cliffhanger, or disaster?" I can't imagine writing a book without your mentorship.

Andrea Kerr, beta reader. The first person to "test drive" my unreleased work and take it for a spin. Thank you for your vital feedback. It makes the end product so much richer.

Candace Johnson, copyeditor. And though you work behind the scenes, your work is highly visible: industrial-strength cleanup of grammar, punctuation, sentence structure, and anything else gone awry. Thank you for helping me deliver the most polished manuscripts possible.

The Sean McPherson Street Team—a group of advance readers who help spread the word. Your cumulative efforts have a seismic effect. Thank you for the visibility you bring to the Sean McPherson novels.

Len, my husband. The real-life inspiration for Niall MacCullough—the chef and wine connoisseur in the Sean McPherson novels. Thank you for preparing delicious meals, putting fresh flowers in the writing studio every Monday, and being the all-purpose glue that holds our home together.

ABOUT THE AUTHOR

photo © Len Buchanan

L aurie Buchanan writes the Sean McPherson novels—
fast-paced thrillers set in the Pacific Northwest that
feature a trifecta of malice and the pursuit and cost of justice.

A cross between Dr. Dolittle, Nanny McPhee, and a
type-A Buddhist, Buchanan is an active listener, observer of
details, payer of attention, reader and writer of books, kind-
ness enthusiast, and red licorice aficionado. Laurie's goal is
simple: to leave you wanting more.

Her books have won multiple awards, including the
Foreword INDIES Book of the Year Gold Winner, the
International Book Award Gold Winner, the National Indie
Excellence Awards Winner, the Crime Fiction/Suspense Eric
Hoffer Awards Finalist, the PenCraft Award for Literary
Excellence, and CIBA Clue Book Awards Finalist.

Laurie and her husband live in the Pacific Northwest,
where she enjoys long walks, bicycling, camping, and
photography—because sometimes the best word choice is
a picture.

To learn more, please visit Laurie's website at
www.lauriebuchanan.com.

SELECTED TITLES FROM SPARKPRESS

SparkPress is an independent boutique publisher delivering high-quality, entertaining, and engaging content that enhances readers' lives, with a special focus on female-driven work. www.gosparkpress.com

Indelible: A Sean McPherson Novel, Book One, Laurie Buchanan, $16.95, 978-1-68463-071-4. Murder at a writing retreat in the Pacific Northwest, but this one isn't imaginary. Authors only kill with words. Or do they?

Iconoclast: A Sean McPherson Novel, Book Two, Laurie Buchanan, $16.95, 978-1-68463-125-4. In this second installment of the Sean McPherson series, a whale-watching cruise goes terribly wrong: two lovers on deck, one sniper on shore, and no way out.

Impervious: A Sean McPherson Novel, Book Three, Laurie Buchanan, $17.95, 978-1-68463-194-0. The bride, the groom, the toast, the explosion . . . What should be a joyous occasion for Sean and Emma turns lethal in this third installment of the Sean McPherson series.

Enemy Queen: A Novel, Robert Steven Goldstein, $16.95, 978-1-68463-026-4. A woman initiates passionate sexual encounters with two articulate but bumbling and crass middle-aged men, but what she demands in return soon becomes untenable. A short time later she goes missing, prompting the county sheriff to open a murder investigation.

Firewall: A Novel, Eugenia Lovett West. $16.95, 978-1-68463-010-3. When Emma Streat's rich, socialite godmother is threatened with blackmail, Emma becomes immersed in the dark world of cybercrime—and mounting dangers take her to exclusive places in Europe and contacts with the elite in financial and art collecting circles. Through passion and heartbreak, Emma must fight to save herself and bring a vicious criminal to justice.

Peccadillo at the Palace: An Annie Oakley Mystery, Kari Bovée. $16.95, 978-1-943006-90-8. In this second book in the Annie Oakley Mystery series, Annie and Buffalo Bill's Wild West Show are invited to Queen Victoria's Jubilee celebration in England, but when a murder and a suspicious illness lead Annie to suspect an assassination attempt on the queen, she sets out to discover the truth.

Printed in the USA
CPSIA information can be obtained
at www.ICGtesting.com
JSHW022246110324
58926JS00002B/3